AUTHOR	CLASS No.
PHILLPOTTS. E.	F
TITLE	BOOK No.
HIDDEN. HAND.	2014230

THE HIDDEN HAND

Charity Crymes, whether a witch or not, can certainly bind a spell. These short stories, narrated by the octogenarian mistress of Owl Pen, will work their own enchantment on the reader. Set in the Dartmoor district of Devon, they concern the problems of those who have come to Charity for help—problems which could only be resolved by her astute, not to say cunning, wit. But Charity's is white magic; if her tactics are unconventional, or even illegal, they are invariably just, for, as she points out, justice and the law are not always on the same side. The tales, to quote the author's words, are told from Charity's 'own animated angle of vision, her own life's values, and with her own gusto, self-confidence and vain-glory'. Of Mr. Phillpotts himself—a veteran story-teller beloved by readers of many ages—one need say only that here he is as witty, as vigorous, and as entertaining as ever.

BY THE SAME AUTHOR

THE
HIDDEN HAND

By

EDEN PHILLPOTTS

HUTCHINSON
Stratford Place
London

Hutchinson & Co. (Publishers) Ltd.
London, New York, Melbourne, Sydney, Cape Town

1801

First published 1952

*Printed in Great Britain
by The Anchor Press, Ltd.,
Tiptree, Essex*

FOREWORD

As in the case of similar collections, these tales reveal their cardinal figure in the teller and it is well that she should record them from her own animated angle of vision, her own life's values, and with her own gusto, self-confidence and vainglory. Though the substance of Charity Crymes is now long sped, her shadow remains from a vanished age when such dubious spirits haunted odd corners, to win credit for their wisdom, or hatred and distrust for their malevolence. But if a witch, then this lady may fairly claim to be a white one. She resembles a waning moon, whose daylight ghost still hangs upon the blue, morning sky long after dawn has swept another night away.

E. P.

FOREWORD

I

IF A woman knows nothing about her own character, and her weakness and her strength, by the time she's over eighty years old, then I'd go so far as to say she has got no character at all; and for my part, as I survey the past and the things that have challenged me, and all I've played in the lives of other people, I can take a bird's-eye view of myself and feel well content. Eighty years is a long run for your body and a tidy good test for your brains; but, though I say it myself, you'd need to look a tidy long way before you found another ancient woman who has made better use of her time and won to such well-earned fame as I have. It would be false modesty to pretend different, and if I didn't know myself to be outstanding, I should not have taken the trouble to set down a parcel of my deeds; for when I came to burrow back into vanished years and consider all I have accomplished in them, then it looks to be only common sense to feel such doings well worth the pen and ink and paper demanded to set them down, so as they shouldn't all be lost. And writing them out has done two things: it has shown me to have a memory a good bit out of the common, and it has also served to convince me that the general opinion of me, as a remarkable person with a great power of resource in times of trouble, is well justified.

I never had any education to name, but talking with clever and learned folk has served to show me that education and wisdom are not the same thing by a long shot. And, looking back, I feel tolerable sure that it's better to be wise by a trick of Nature than clever or bursting with learning. My neighbours round about call me a wise woman, but you don't earn such an honourable name as that for nothing, and these pages I ordain to set down are chiefly about fellow creatures, man and woman, old and young, who, if they were still here, would bear witness to my efforts on their behalf. Yet, before I launch out to give instances and examples of my craftsmanship in the

7

art of living and helping lesser people to live and overget the hardships and snags of everyday life, while helping myself to earn a living at the same time (because if there's anything on earth worth good money, it's wisdom)—before setting out upon my task, you might like to know a little as to my havage and breeding, and what, by God's will, made me the unusual fashion of female I hap to be. I need to dive a long way back into the past for that, because a lot of valuable material was handed down to me by my great-grandmother. For there were qualities in that fine woman that skipped her own family and were only bestowed upon me long after she was gone. But, though her descendants were numerous, none ever rose to be the like of her, or left any memories behind them of much consequence. It wasn't until I was born that you might say her rare gifts of character flashed out once again.

There came a call to display what was in her when she was quite young, and though, until that fearful event overtook her, she went her way like any other lucky girl, married a prosperous farmer and carried on calm and self-respecting, she gave no evidence of her strength of purpose, her nerve and quickness of mind, in the ugly and fearful perils suddenly sprung upon her. Women of her generation who lived on Dartmoor were tough and brave, and needed to be in those days; but Charity Budge—to give her her married name—reached to greater heights than that and rose to be a proper heroine and a nine-days' wonder before she was twenty.

So I'll set down her one and only high adventure and challenge, for she never had another to call out her valiance; but the way she escaped from that dreadful quandary can be told yet again because of its details, which were fearsome and wild.

My great-grandfather owned Hartland—a little farm ringed round by Dartmoor and set in the midst of that great waste. The nearest point of civilised life was at Packhorse Bridge, a nest of humans at the foot of Merripit Hill, where East Dart river flows down to join with West Dart at Watersmeet. And in Packhorse Bridge I live to this day, at Owl Pen on a spur of land under Bellever Tor, where my parents dwelt before me—a habitable house builded of granite stone with an acre of cultivated land to it, two hundred years old and more, and my own freehold property. It's a perch from which I can look down over the village and take my usual open view of life in general.

Hartland lies three miles distant to the north, and there lived George Budge and Charity, who married him for love and nought else, because he had not much else to offer her worth having except himself. He'd followed his father at Hartland and laid down a 'new-take' or two and bettered his grazing farm by a few acres; but it was a poor and lonely spot at best, though well adapted for sport, with fishing and shooting and fox-hunting, which pastimes George Budge favoured more than all else. A hunter he kept—a very fine horse indeed—though above his pocket to sustain; but he rode to hounds and Charity herself rode the horse also once a week into the village for their weekly shopping. There wasn't many wheeled vehicles on Dartmoor in their day and few roads for them to run on if there had been. 'Truck-a-mucks', the folk used—little sledges pulled by a pony where they happed to be needed; for these things fell out a mighty long time ago—in the reign of King George the Second by all accounts—and it was then that my great-grandmother, Charity Shortland, took Budge. There had been a lot after her and she was well known to be worth her weight in gold, though poor as a coot; but when Budge came along, he cut out the pack of her suitors and did the cleverest stroke of his life. He was a little man, not above five foot and a half, and she is said to have been uncommon tall for a girl, with black hair and grey eyes and a hard mouth but a good temper and cheerful disposition. Her countenance was said to be in keeping with her fine nature and gift for good willing, and friendship. Like me she was one who never knew the meaning of the word 'despair', which is a hateful word too often on the lips of this distraught generation.

My great-grandmother knew she was going to a lonely home when she wed Budge and that there was plenty of hard work offering and mighty small promise of fun and games; but she loved him well and weren't afraid of the Moor, being born and bred on it. She liked the thought of freedom, just as

9

she had always been fancy free herself, and was no stranger to the wild things or their ways, so happily enough she went to Hartland and started on the common experience of being married and living in a home of her own with a man thrown in. She was very fond of telling what overtook her in the first six months, and, after her day, her children, who treasured the story, told it again to her grandchildren and great-grandchildren, so I can relate the facts correctly, though to modern ears they may sound unlikely. But they were true enough to the life led in those days, and no doubt many curious and dangerous things that happen now will, in their turn, be counted unlikely, when those as yet unborn come to hear tell about them.

When my great-grandmother lived at Hartland, it was a very different order of human existence from what we live now and, among other extinct orders of creation, was the highway robbers that haunted the country and did deeds of violence against honest people and gave rise to all manner of inconvenient things, including even murder now and again. Gentlemen of the Road they called themselves and, at the time of which I tell, there was a pair of these dashing rascals a good deal in the public mind by reason of their successes and audacious adventures and continued escapes from capture. They had become a byword of disgrace, and their doings filled the bettermost people with indignation and the humble folk with delight; because, if you have money and riches, then the malefactors are your enemies and to be feared, while if you have nothing at all, then no cause for fear arises, so the poor get a good deal of harmless amusement when they hear of the rich being fleeced and swizzled.

Blackadder and Lamb were the names of those two land-sharks, and a host of tales sprang up about them, many true enough. Their best weapon was surprise, because none ever knew where they would strike next, or what roads they might be expected upon at any given time. Today you might hear they had stopped a coach in Kent, tomorrow come the news of a robbery a hundred miles away in Surrey. There is no doubt they got a lot of secret aid and comfort from friends who served them and their horses unbeknownst to the law.

Now to turn to Charity and George Budge and a great event that overtook them six months after their marriage; for then George's only near relation, his Aunt Milly Budge, died and left him a very fine bequest, much to his amazement. She was a widow and her husband had collected valuable property in the shape of silver plate and candlesticks and 'apostle' spoons and snuff-boxes with real, proper, precious stones set in them, and other suchlike treasures. So, under her will, the lot had duly come to George and been conveyed to the Moor and reached Hartland safe enough. You see, the late lady well liked George, because he was a good nephew to her, oft sent her gamebirds and fish off the Moor and rode to see her now and again, where she dwelt in Exeter city. She had seen George's wife once also and taken a great fancy to her. Of course this glittering bequest was of no use to George nor yet Charity, for they would have graced the dwellings of the better-most; but, for the time being, he kept 'em stowed away snug in two big wood coffers locked up in his cellar; but presently his wife made him write a letter to a business friend at Plymouth, to come up one day and decide what the lot was worth and say if there happed to be anybody in Plymouth who would buy everything and pay cash down and carry the treasures away. She held out to keep one thing and one only: a gold snuff-box which she wanted for her father. So a valuer came to Hartland and told George his stuff was worth somewhere round two thousand pounds of money and he might count upon fifteen hundred at the least. Which, noised around the Moor, made Farmer Budge a famous man for the minute. Never one to hurry, he set about getting a bargain for his goods in a leisurely fashion just when there came the news that Blackadder and Lamb were thought to be in the West Country, because a properly shameful hold-up, which sounded much like their work, had happened nigh Tavistock, a township on the Tavy river. A coach had been stopped nigh there and it contained the Bishop of Exeter and other men of God. But even so everything they carried save their clothes and their sermons was taken from them, including quite a lot of money, and all they could tell was that two masked and mounted men had robbed them in a very brisk and business-like fashion, and

11

then rode off without any waste of words. The last that had been heard of Blackadder and Lamb two weeks earlier was from Salisbury Plain; but now it looked as if they'd pushed on into Devonshire; and a week after the Tavistock affair, a stage-coach was stopped outside Plymouth and a good haul taken off the passengers. Then a week passed and they didn't strike again, so Devon was glad to be rid of them and soon forgot their flying visit. There was a queer theft at the same time in a little shop at Tavistock, but that didn't look to mean high-waymen, because they never commit housebreaking, and leave such roguery to lesser thieves.

So now I come to Hartland and tell about Charity Budge as near as possible in the words she was used to tell herself. The time was November and there fell a grey, cold morning when the hounds met at Wistman's Wood nigh Longaford Tor, and George Budge went hunting. But evening was down before he came back and his wife stood at the farmyard gate under a fierce, red sunset with her eyes lifted to the ridge of moorland where he was most likely to show up. At last he came and she saw a black spot atop of the hill and marked a man and knew it was her man though still far distant. He came along presently and he'd got a mask at his saddle-bow and was very pleased with himself.

"We found under Crow Tor," said my great-grandfather, "and he took us a long, screwy run up over into some of the beastliest going on the Moor. Very few dared to follow and there was only the whip—Walter Perry—and me in at the death under Fur Tor. Perry doubted if it was the first fox, but for my part I think it was—a tough, dog fox who had been hunted before. Anyway here's the old boy's mask to hang up along with t'others."

She made much of George of course and, before he dis-mounted, ran in to fetch him a pint, for he was terrible thirsty; but when she came back with the beer he still sat on his horse, for now it was his turn to look up at the ridge and mark yet another horseman coming over.

"Who the deuce might that be?" he asked his wife, staring upwards. "If I wasn't sober I should think I was seeing double, Cherry."

For 'Cherry' was the name she always went by, same as I do myself now. 'Charity' sounded hard and cold, as it often is, and was never a name suited to that woman's nature.

Certainly a queer-looking object had hoved up against the fading sky above them; but George's wife soon cleared the mystery as to what it might be.

" 'Tis two men on one horse," she said. "There's a big chap holding the reins and a smaller man behind him, and they look to be heading for us."

They watched in silence for a while, then she spoke again.

"The little one ain't a man, George: she's a woman! And there's something in front of the man. It might be a child, or a dog, or a bundle of some sort."

"We shall know soon enough," answered Budge. "They're bound for Hartland anyhow."

The pair made poor progress and presently the big man alighted and led the horse till they fetched up, dead-beat and in a pretty sad pickle. Then the traveller fetched a parcel down to the ground and next he did the like for the woman and handled her very tenderly.

He was a big, hard-bitten fellow clad in fustian, and the woman small and a lot younger than him, but pale and terrible shaky and her face racked with pain. In plain words she was far gone with child and near her time. They'd started from Okehampton early, to cross the Moor and get to Cornwood, and been catched in the mist and bog-foundered and suffered a very nasty experience and got way-lost. But they had struggled on and were heading for Packhorse Bridge when they caught sight of Hartland and just managed to get there. Mr. Harry the man was called, and he had a small grocer's business at Oke-hampton. George knew the name and Charity set about to serve his wife and do all that might be done till a doctor could be fetched to her. It was natural the young woman should be down on her luck; but my great-grandfather hadn't any patience with the man, for tough and strong though he looked, Mr. Harry showed himself a poor-spirited, craven creature and good for nought when faced with trouble. He whined and very near wept and presently carried his wife into the house and, when Charity had made a bed ready for her upstairs, he bore

13

her up and helped her to get in. Then he left her for George's wife to minister to. The girl reckoned she must bear her babe before morning. She'd got another at home and knew all about the business.

Then the cry was for a doctor and George ordained to bring out his market-cart and farm horse.

"The nearest leech to be counted upon works down to Widecombe," he said to Mr. Harry, "and if by good chance he's home, we'll bring him back with us."

"Good," agreed the visitor; but my great-grandfather had more to say. He was a man of the world and not minded to take risks with a stranger.

"And I'll ask you to come along with me," he added. "I'd go alone, but to speak the truth, you ain't known to me except by your name, and I'd rather not leave you here, because my men live down to the village and there will only be my wife and her handmaiden and your sick partner in the house when I set off. No offence, but I must ask you to come with me."

Mr. Harry hadn't bargained for that, but saw the point of it. He went upstairs while George was harnessing his horse and had a tell with Mrs. Harry and explained he was going for the doctor and that Mrs. Budge would watch over her till he came back. But before he went, he arranged for his box to be stowed careful and carried it down to the cellar, so it should be locked up with my great-grandfather's own boxes of treasure. Mr. Harry was a very selfish person; he only thought for himself and his wife, and took all the good offices poured upon him for granted. He had a look at his horse before he went off and drank a glass of Hollands and ate a big meal and then got in the market-cart with George and they drove away into a dark and foggy night.

Charity did what she could for her unwanted guest when the men were gone and the suffering woman grew a thought easier and took down some hot drink and murmured that she felt hopeful and counted to come through it, God willing. Then she grew quiet and drowsy and thought she might sleep. Her golden hair was tumbled about her face and my great-grandmother always said afterwards that she felt jealous of it. Then Charity blew out the candle and stole away and went down

14

house to clear up and make all tidy before the doctor came. She had one slip of a girl for maid and sent her off to bed. After that she did chores round about and was just going to get a hot brick and wrap it in flannel for Mrs. Harry's feet when suddenly, through the stillness of the night, she heard a man's footfall close at hand. That looked to be mighty queer because she'd locked and double-locked the house after her husband was gone and she shook a bit when the sound of a man's tread came close to her. No dog had barked, and that wasn't strange because no dog had heard. It wasn't out-of-doors the footsteps went, but in the midst of the house over her head! Then the stairs creaked as the unknown came down, and Charity got herself well in hand, picked up the poker from the fireplace and rushed out to face him.

There—coming down the flight—was the sick woman, or rather no woman, but a trim-built, sturdy male. He grinned all over his good-looking, wicked face at her astonishment and kissed his hand to her.

"Your humble servant, mistress," he said. "Fear nothing at all. You see before you an industrious, well-mannered lad— Jimmy Lamb by name and Lamb by nature. Famous for his activities and never known to serve the female sex with aught but devotion. The big gentleman, who has gone along with your better half for the doctor, is my partner, Billy Blackadder, and your good man will find him a pleasant companion for a dark night. You keep that poker to stir the fire, my dear, because no woman ever found occasion to treat me with a rod of iron. We're men of peace, Billy and me—just like any other night-hawks—but if you hap to be a night-hawk, because your Maker built you that way, then you must behave like a night-hawk and get a bad name for no better reason than——"

Charity had been thinking quickly and measuring the scoundrel up in her mind, so she cut in now and interrupted him.

"What are you playing your tricks here for?" she asked. "There's nothing for you in this house and well you know it."

"We shouldn't have taken all this trouble for nothing, my dear," he said. "We've heard about your famous silver candle-sticks and snuff-boxes and such-like and, being rather smart in

15

that line, want to see if they're so wonderful and beautiful as we have heard. So we thought of this little game. All my own invention, because I was a play-actor once, and I'd love to tell you my story, but time lacks for that. So to work, mistress!"

My great-grandmother hedged a bit and changed the subject for the moment. Her thoughts were pretty dark no doubt and far away with her George and what he might be up against; but she kept her nerve and looked thoughtfully at Lamb, bowing and scraping like a Frenchman.

"I never saw such honest-looking, blue eyes in a bad man's head before," she said. "And all that beautiful golden hair thrown out over your pillow so natural!"

"Taken from a little shop at Tavistock, Mrs. Budge; but I'd sooner have your black hair than that yellow wig. Give me the dark girls—they've got more fire in their blood than the blondes and are mostly cleverer too."

She laughed at that, as if she'd never met with a better joke, and the man laughed too.

"Drat your impertinence," she said. "But, if you was a play-actor, I'd say you must have been a good one. To think you tell me you was the poor soul I saw shivering and whimpering at death's door just now!"

"You're in the right: it was a fine performance and I'm glad you had the wit to admire it. I should like to stop and have a chat with you, for a prettier woman I never saw—never! What's your name? It ought to be something worthy of you."

"Charity's my name, but I don't wish to do no charity to the like of you," she said.

"You can't deny me faith and hope, however. And now for the cellar!"

Then she lighted two candles and gave him one to hold while she took the other.

"My master left the key in the lock of the door when your friend took his box down for safety," she told him. "Now I'll get the key of our chests. What was in your box, I wonder?"

By that time Lamb had caught sight of the bottle of Hollands on the dresser.

"Never was a cordial more welcome," he declared, and then

16

helped himself. "Good health and long life, and may you soon be a woman with child your beautiful self!" Which pleased her no little for it was just what she wanted to happen. She got the key and led the way to the top of the cellar stairs. It was a massive key suited to the big coffers down below, and there was an instinct in her, as she always told afterwards, to hold on to it and mark time before they went down, so she asked another question.

"Where did you come by that farm horse that brought you and t'other knave with you?" she inquired.

"A secret," he answered. "Our own horses are waiting for us not very far away. You'll hear about the cart-horse to-morrow, I shouldn't wonder."

"I guess he'd be a proud horse if he knew he'd carried both Lamb and Blackadder," she suggested; and then he quickened the proceedings.

"Push on, Charity, and hurry up," he ordered. "My time is not my own tonight."

So she flung open the cellar door and bade him go down before her and he professed to feel a wound.

"Now you've hurt my feelings, by Gad!" he swore. "But some woman has always commanded me. I've danced to their bidding and always shall no doubt till I dance my last dance—alone."

"Sooner than you think for, I hope," replied Charity.

He descended before her, and there were the big, brass-bound chests, and Charity knew that a lot of money was locked up in one of them with the candlesticks and trinkets, which he was bound to see when the time came.

"As for our fal-lals, I don't care so much for them," she said to Lamb. "There's all sorts of odds and ends there which my husband ordains to sell presently. And I wish he'd done so before you got to hear tell of them. But our bit of cash is locked up too. All we've gotten for the minute, or shall get for many a long day, so I ask you, for honour and fairness, to leave that. If you've got any pride in you I pray you not to take poor people's money."

"How much might there be, mistress?"

"Fifty pounds and a bit over."

He spoke while she opened a chest.

"I'd double it if I could—for your sake. Yet what would you have? We must live. Alas! It hurts me to take it worse than you to lose it; but Blackadder is a hard devil. I must be true to him for, if he found I'd been false, he'd have my blood. He hates all women and says that some woman will be the death of me some day, but shall never be of him."

She threw open the coffer and he looked down while she drew away an old sheepskin that covered the glittering heap beneath.

Lamb must have forgot all else for a moment and his blue eyes shone. He knelt down, set his candle on the edge of the box and began to finger and weigh.

"Pretty stuff—very pretty stuff—and easy to handle," he said. "And where's the money-bag, my dear?"

It was that last question, she always said, that decided my great-grandmother, quickened her resolves and hardened her heart. No words she spoke, but did a deed and then followed it up with another. He'd forgotten her for a moment, kneeling with his eyes fixed on the treasure as if he was saying his prayers to it, and in that second, gripping the heavy key in her hand, Charity took her luck and brought the metal down on his head as hard as she could lay it on. He started to get up, but before he had time to do so, she struck again with all her strength, for she knew now it was going to be his life or hers. The second blow stopped Lamb and he dropped forward, sprawling over the open chest; and such was her nerve power that Charity hit him over the head yet again, and then he rolled over with his consciousness gone. After that she blew out both candles and fled up the cellar stairs with all her speed. Only when she had gained the top of them did she feel a thought dizzy and inclined to cry for help; but her troubles weren't over by a lot for, after she had locked the cellar door and mastered her panting heart, all her thoughts returned to George, and for a terrible moment she saw him dead and done for under Blackadder's hands.

She waked her girl and told the child to don her clothes.

"We must get down to the village," she said, "there's trouble and I've killed somebody and the master's in danger.

18

Don't ask questions—just be quick and we'll call a man or two to help us."

But things fell out differently, and just before they started there came a double knock on the outer door and she heard a horse whinny and knew that sound for her husband's market horse. So she flung ope the door with joy, all ready to put her arms round him when George came down out of the cart. But there was no cart and no George: only the horse and Billy Blackadder. In another moment she would have had her arms round his neck, but stopped in time. He was wearing a black mask but now took it off, came in smartly and slammed the door after him. Then Charity's handmaiden fled screaming, hasted upstairs to her cubby-hole and deserted Charity, while Blackadder said the fog was lifting and asked for news of Jimmy Lamb.

"You'll know all there is to know by now," he said, "and I counted to meet him before this, but when I got to the appointed spot he didn't turn up. Where is he?"

He put a brace of pistols on the table when he came into the house-place, and Charity saw him set George's bunch of seals and his watch down beside it. Then he put her at ease.

"No need to fear for your good man," he said, "though the little chap was a thought high-handed when he heard my name. He's all right. I took his watch and borrowed his horse, but he'll be back on foot presently, no doubt. Maybe you found Jimmy a bit of a shock too. Where is the fool?"

Any other than Charity Budge would have lied then and told him his friend was gone with his booty; but my great-grandmother was no ordinary woman. She knew that George lived and would not be much the worse for his adventure; and then her mind worked as it never worked before and never did again. She was long past any further feelings of fear and reckoned that if she played her hand right now she might win the game yet. So she took a deep line with the man and based her plan of action on what she had already done to Lamb. If he was dead, as she reckoned he must be, then she had but one enemy to fight and, instead of setting Blackadder off on a fool's errand, ordained to hold him at Hartland if she could. She saw what Providence was aiming at and did her part and

19

didn't wait for George to lend a hand, but got on with it all alone. She spoke, and always said after that the words were put in her mouth by the watching Lord, though they might have sounded mad to any other listener than Billy Blackadder. She looked up at him and laughed and took a leaf out of the highwaymen's book and tried play-acting herself for once.

"Your Jimmy's no fool," she said in answer to his question. "He's down in the cellar along with our treasures deciding which to take and sorry he can't take the lot. He said he'd have to wait for you to come back and help him, which you would do when you found he wasn't where you ordained to meet."

Blackadder looked at her doubtfully and picked up his pistols again.

"Lead me to him, then," he said, and she whipped on in front of him to the cellar door and threw it open before he had time to mark that it had been shut and locked.

"Get down to him," she begged, "and for God's sake take the trash and be gone both of you before my husband gets home, else there'll be murder done!"

It was neck or nothing now and when her companion peered down into the darkness and bawled to Lamb, she reckoned he would get no reply. And none he did; but when Blackadder showed doubt and shouted yet again, then, out of the depths below, to Charity's horror, an answer came.

"Yes, I'm here in the dark with a broken head," came the muffled voice. "Put a bullet into that cursed woman, and——"

Blackadder heard no more, because, in his split second of distraction, my great-grandmother acted. Lamb's voice was like the light to the Apostle Paul for her and, after the first shock of hearing it, made everything clear, and steeled her arm. There was the big highwayman perched on the top of the cellar stairs, with his mind on t'other scoundrel below, and in that fraction of time she put both her hands on his shoulders, shoved with all her might and got him off his balance. He clawed at her but missed by a hand's-breadth, and went heels over head backwards with nothing to break his fall but the granite floor beneath. It was all the work of half a second, and long before he could right himself, or climb back to her, she'd slammed the cellar door and locked it in a twinkling, though not before she'd heard Jimmy Lamb's voice bawling out again from the darkness to his friend.

Then she called her maid to come down house and they were soon upon their way to the village; but it was not until she had left the girl at the 'Hearty Welcome', to tell the tale and summon men together, that Charity hastened along the Widecombe road and cried out the name of George every hundred yards as she went. At last a mournful howl answered her and she came upon her husband crawling home slow as a shell-snail with a sprained ankle and a broken collar-bone.

The farmer heard Charity's tale while she helped him along back to Packhorse Bridge, and then she heard his.

"He kept up his pretences as we drove to Widecombe," said Budge, "and whined about his wife and how dead certain he was the child would die before he got back to her. And then he grew impatient and said I was going too slow and he could walk quicker than I drove. So I got angered with the creature and told him to shut his mouth and thank his Maker things were no worse. After that, when we were well on our way, he suddenly stopped the horse, turned upon me and dragged me out of the cart! Never have I been handled by such a powerful brute in my life. I'm tolerable tough for a light weight, but I was a child under his hands and too mazed with astonishment to put up a fight in any case. He threw me very hard, stole my watch and seal off me, and next took the horse out of the cart and rode away upon it without any more words."

"They had planned for their own horses to meet them, so Lamb told me," explained Charity, "and then, finding Lamb wasn't there, Blackadder came back to Hartland on your horse to find him."

The village was moving by the time they got back and a party already starting for Hartland. My great-grandfather took the lead and returned to his outraged home in hopes that all was well and they would find the famous pair still under lock and key and his wife the heroine of the hour. In truth she proved to be a greater masterpiece than they knew, for some among them doubted whether such men as Blackadder and Lamb might nc have broken their bondage and escaped after all with their booty and none to stop them.

21

But the cellar door was still locked fast enough when they got to it and George went down first and a dozen men, with lanterns and pistols and ropes to bind the malefactors, followed after. Neither sign nor sound greeted them for it was dark and still and everything over and done with long ago. Blackadder was dead. He had broken his neck-bones on the cellar floor when he fell backwards. And six yards away, propped against a treasure chest, sat his friend, Jimmy Lamb. He lived but was half unconscious and easy enough to handle. So they fetched him up and, with morning light, a doctor saw him, and when he recovered his senses he found himself in the gaol-house at Moretonhampstead—a raree show for the countryside. He made a good recovery and was well enough to be tried and hanged at Exeter six weeks later; but long before then their blood-horses—a grand pair, one roan and one grey—were found hid at Tavistock. Those who had been aiding the high-waymen confessed to it and got punished for their deeds but escaped with their lives.

The story goes that Charity Budge was a trifle shaken when she found her hand had slain two men and sent them to hell fire for evermore; but the minister who served the parish in those days made all plain to her understanding, for she was lightning quick in the uptake and saw the force of his arguments.

"You were appointed by God Almighty to rid mankind of a triumphant evil," said his Reverence, "and you rose to the horrible occasion, accomplished your task and wiped out two scourges of human society with a great courage and wondrous presence of mind. And you have the right to be proud of yourself, because your fellow creatures, and your Maker likewise, are all proud of you."

But her fame went farther afield than Packhorse Bridge for she was a wonder all over England and folk travelled from far to have a look at her. An artist is said to have painted a picture of her also—the which I'd dearly like to have for my parlour at Owl Pen if I knew where it might be and how to come by it.

II

ONE might have counted, with such a mother as Charity Budge, that some among her offspring would cut a figure out of the common herd and carry on her quality into another generation; but that did not happen. Her second son, Daniel Budge, called after his father's favourite Bible character, took his own line in life and showed craft and courage, but none of his brothers or his sisters ever did anything to mention and one of the maids died too young to leave more than the name on her little gravestone. That was Ethelinda, who got playing in the heather one summer day and was stung by a viper, and perished before they could fetch the doctor to her.

Peter Budge was George's eldest son and he stuck to the farm and followed his father at Hartland in due course, while Norman, the youngest boy, had a feeling for business and went apprentice to a shopman at Plymouth. Which leaves the two living girls, Mary, the eldest, wed when she was seventeen, and I never heard anything of her family, though some may be still living. And there remains my own grandmother, Charity's youngest daughter, who was called after her mother and, I am glad to say, left her name to my mother, who handed it down to me. My grandmother took Aaron Caunter, who owned Little Cator—a tenement farm—and my mother was their only child, and when my mother married Robert Crymes I was their only child. My father owned Owl Pen and worked at Vitifer Mine, a mile or two from Packhorse Bridge. He died young, of a grievous accident at the mine, and I grew up with mother at Owl Pen, which became my own property when mother died in her seventies. By that time all the old ones were sped and Hartland passed into other hands, because Peter Budge never married after the only girl he wanted refused to marry him. Now he lies hard by his parents in our church-yard; while his brother Daniel's grave was the deep sea. His story is a short one, like that of many thousands of young men who have given up their precious lives for their country without properly knowing what they had been called to fight and die for.

From the day his mother took him to Plymouth as a little boy and he had stood upon Plymouth Hoe and looked out upon the ocean, he always longed with all his might to be a sailor man, and the passion never deserted him though George, his father, wouldn't hear of any such a doubtful career for any son of his. He wanted Daniel to carry on with his elder brother and share Hartland with him after he and their mother were gone; but Daniel never took to the land and once he'd seen Plymouth Sound, and the big three-deckers lying at anchor there, his mind was made up and nothing could shake him from it. Charity had no objection herself. Indeed she approved, and would have well liked to see a son of hers in the King's Navy and engaged upon the noble task of serving the sea and preserving its freedom for the welfare of Britain against all lesser nations; but George was dead against and, being a strong-willed man and generally right in his wife's opinion, she made no fuss and didn't back up Daniel against his father. The will to do so was there all the same, as the story of Daniel goes to show. George never knew her methods and most likely nobody but herself ever did, but she had her own way when determined to do so and succeeded and launched the boy on the sea without anybody knowing she'd had a hand in it, or a cloud rising between her and George. Daniel himself had to know her plan of action and, no doubt, thanked God when Charity showed him the way, for he was an orderly young fellow and would never have thought of it himself; but, after she had made his course clear, he took it. He was nineteen years old at the time—a strong, well-made lad, taller and heavier than his father and dark like his mother. Among his tasks was to drive about and do market business, in connection with which he would sometimes visit Dartmouth, where there were relations of his family; and now and again he would stop there for a bit of a holiday and shooting, and sailing in a boat, because George's brother kept an inn at the port and his two sons, the cousins of Daniel, were fond of him and liked to have his company. So there went Daniel one summer for a bit of fun after hay harvest was over at Hartland. He meant to stop for a week, but near the end of that time there came a startler for his father and ugly news touching the young man. A messenger from Dartmouth brought it, for there was no post service to Dartmoor then.

Dear George [wrote the farmer's brother], *I'm cruel sorry to tell you of a great misfortune that has overtook Daniel, and there's nothing in mortal power us can do about it. The coast towns, as you well know, are properly infested by the damned press-gangs and they raid ports and hunt down the likely men like weasels hunt down rabbits. Dartmouth has long been a hunting-ground for 'em, and they are held to be in their rights, so all the lads can do is to make themselves scarce and get inland before they are catched. When a battleship came in last evening, I warned Dan he had best get home, and he intended to start the instant moment it was light tomorrow, which he would have done without a doubt ; but the battleship stole a march upon us. They sent two press-gangs ashore after dark and they came here just before closing time and netted five men, and Daniel was one of them. No less than seven other men they took, and the moment the frigate* Waterwitch *had 'em aboard, she sailed again with twelve pressed men. Daniel's cousins, under my orders, had cleared out and gone to friends where there was no peril ; but your foolhardy chap would stop and took the risk, and was nabbed accordingly.*

In truth, as Charity confessed long after George Budge was dead, she had been responsible, for she knew all about the press-gangs, and in dead secret long before had told Daniel what he must do if he wanted to go to sea. It was an idea that had never entered his simple mind ; but he jumped at it when she put it there and he'd tried half a dozen times to get in the path of a press-gang and be took without doing a sin against his father. And now he had accomplished his ambition. In course of half a year they got a letter from Daniel saying he was well and well thought upon aboard the *Waterwitch* and making good. But the next thing they heard was that his ship had been blown out of the sea by an enemy with far heavier metal and only a dozen men saved alive. But Daniel wasn't one of them. So that ended the young fellow's short career; but if Charity felt any misgivings as to her part in the matter she hid them.

Now I return to her daughter, my grandmother, who wed Aaron Caunter, and their only child, my mother, wife to Robert Crymes. When father was gone, she and I lived at Owl Pen and my mother, who always had a taste that way, bettered her knowledge of the herbs of the field and became very skilful in their uses and a past mistress of simples. She was a wise woman and there rose up a mysterious side to her fame for, though none could speak a hard word against her, because all she did was for betterment of man or beast, yet it was whispered how she knew more than is lawful for humans to know, and stories grew after her widowhood that there was a dark side to her craft. The opinion waxed that she must be a witch, and for all her record of wondrous cures and good advice to them who might consult her and pay her fees, the people feared her rather than loved her and there were stories told by ignorant folk of queer things that happened to her.

In a manner of speaking I missed her when she went, but found, as time passed, that I took her place in the parish and grew to be a trustable and respected character. I was a lot cleverer and more far-sighted than my dear mother, with gifts that didn't come through the Crymes family nor yet the Caunter race, but through my great-grandmother Budge and her alone. Yet my mother's secrets weren't lost because, before she went, she confided them into my keeping and I was already a bit of a scholar and could write them down. She couldn't write, but had her charms and cautcheries all stored in her head with the way to use every eatable herb of the field and the ingredients for making up her recipes. Needless to say I have employed many of these things to good purpose and continue so to do, but I've lived to see a number of them fall into neglect and be forgotten. Now the rising generation would sooner run to a physician for themselves, or a veterinary surgeon for their beasts, than come to me, and often enough they live to lament their mistake because my physics belong to the old paths and their virtue still remains in louse-wort and nipple-wort and moon-wort and liver-wort and a hundred others.

But the new follows upon the old and our silly minds must always be clamouring after change, though often only change for the worse.

However, I carried on my mother's good work and, thanks to my own qualities, built up a reputation for understanding and good willing that enabled me to live in comfort and keep up Owl Pen on its proper knoll under Belever Tor, overlooking the village like a steadfast lighthouse above all the stormy changes and chances of those that dwell within it. Folk look to my physics and charms as of old : they still seek for advice and counsel in times of stress and before problems beyond their humble wits to solve. And they are willing, according to their means, to pay me the money I earn for throwing light when in my power to do so. I was always jealous to portion the load to the shoulders that have got to bear it and have sometimes worked hard for nought but gratitude, which I welcome, though it butters no parsnips and is rare in any case. But there's nothing that advertises you like success and now, in my ripe old age, I am come to be so famous that when difficulties are cleared away, or shaky causes happily defended, my neighbours are apt to give me the credit. "Ah," they'll say, "we can guess the hidden hand that done that !"

It has been needful to side-step the laws of the land sometimes before I gained an object, or mended an evil. Freedom of action was often demanded, because you'll sometimes find a law, though just in itself, very unjust in the circumstances. Of course the laws of man and the statutes of Almighty God are two different things and don't always run in double harness by any manner of means. In fact less and less do they, if the truth must be told, and the shameful fact looks to be nowadays that the laws of man are often actually aimed against the Divine ones and even go so far as to break the Ten Commandments now and again ! You may break them, no doubt ; but there's one thing not the highest and mightiest can do, and that is alter them.

Sometimes my tasks have been easy and sometimes parlous difficult, but even when I find myself to be challenged by blank

27

ignorance I take mighty good care not to run into danger. You can convince the fools, but once you lose the credit of sensible people, then your power is lost. I have always planned to be taken seriously, for if the parish got a whisper that my craft was all humbug, then my stock would drop to nought and my livelihood be a thing of the past.

There was a case, one of the first, when I stood alone with my way yet to make after my mother died. People always felt favourable to me, for they knew I took after her and had my gifts and could read and write and handle figures; but if I'd done anything foolish then and lost favour, I might have made a mess of things and even been called to marry somebody for a living—a horrible thought to me. So, to give an example of a problem both easy yet offering its own difficulties, I cannot do better than relate my dealing with a pair of lovers, who came to me when their affairs had gotten out of hand and they looked to be heading for disaster. They were both very young and ignorant, for more than half a century ago education still tarried upon the Dartmoors.

I was at work digging in my garden plot, banking up my potatoes, and had just knocked off to rest my back for a minute, when the latch of the gate clicked and my old English sheep-dog and protector galloped off to meet the incomer. A girl appeared—a big-boned, wide-shouldered, strapping young woman with a sun-tanned, brown face, flaxen hair and blue eyes. Nelly Blake was her name and she spoke in a deep voice worthy of her big bosom. Her countenance was usually cheerful and her big mouth prone to smile at the world in general, but on this evening in high summer, with the sun turning west, I marked that she looked to be cast down and her eyes were cloudy and short of their usual brightness. I knew everybody in Packhorse Bridge and the history behind them as a rule so, though not on terms of personal friendship with Nelly, was acquaint with her circumstances and her good character. She lived with a widowed mother and, thanks to her great bodily strength and love of the open air, earned her living by doing work mostly in the hands of menfolk. She toiled with the males and best enjoyed helping to build the dry-built, granite walls that thread over the moors, or breaking

28

stones, or digging the foundation of any new house that might be planned to rise round about, or labouring with the peat cutters for next winter's fuel, when the time for that heavy job came round again.

"And what might you want, my dear?" I asked her. "We know each other's faces and each other's fame likewise, but you wouldn't come up to see me without a reason. Nought wrong with your mother, I hope?"

"She's all right, Miss Crymes; but I've got something fretting me on my own account—a very vexatious thing, and if you'll be so gracious as to give heed, I'll pay for your opinions according as you may charge."

"No call to worry on that score, child," I answered. " 'Tis well known I never touch money before I've earned it."

"Even yourself is little like to see a way out of this coil," she said. "It's got to do with him I'm tokened to."

She was going to marry a young man who enjoyed a good character and worked at Vitifer Mine nigh Packhorse Bridge. He belonged to the common herd of the village labouring men and looked to be a very good partner for his intended. Six foot three inches tall was Samuel White—Church of England from his youth up, dull-witted and without any sense of humour, but well principled and taught in the Sunday School. A red-headed giant of a chap, and friendly people hoped he would soon be able to make a home for Nelly, because he was a saver and steady as time. But it was known his conscience would never allow him to marry until at least another half-crown a week went on his money.

"Come in the house then and unfold, my dear," I said to the girl. "Sit down and muster your thoughts and tell your tale."

We went in my house-place and I loaded my pipe, being a smoker same as my mother before me, and settled into my armchair and let her run on. I was an ugly woman, but the folk, when they willed to please me, would always praise my eyes, which were very bright and black as sloes, yet full of assurance to create confidence in simple minds.

Nelly took a deep breath and started with an odd question.

"To begin with, Miss Crymes, have you ever heard tell of an inkybus?" she asked.

"You can call me 'Miss Cherry'," I said, because that was the familiar name I went by. 'Cherry' sounds to be a friendlier name than 'Charity' to the common ear. It was my rule in the course of any inquiry never to admit ignorance, or speak a word that would suggest it, so I always pretended to full knowledge on every and any subject, however queer and out of the way it might hap to be. Suggestions on my part that I stood in doubt would have weakened faith in me, so I claimed to know all about it, however fantastic. I never showed amusement or astonishment at anything I might hear, but only displayed sympathy and understanding. There was a lot of outrageous opinions surviving among us in those far-off days; yet, up to that moment, I had never heard of an 'inkybus', though I took good care not to confess it.

"Fancy!" I said. " 'Tis quite a time since I thought upon such things, though well acquaint with them, of course. How did you learn there were such creatures, my dear?"

"I never did, miss," she replied, "but, in his own opinion, an inkybus has overtook my Sammy, and he's broke the bad news to me."

"Dear, dear!" I said. "Ugly news sure enough, but calling for attention without a doubt, Nelly."

"And marriage almost in sight now, you might say," she went on, "because they tell at Vitifer Mine how there's talk of bettering wages all round, and, if that happened, Sam would be in a position to take me. But now this dreadful thing has fallen upon us and it's borne in upon him he's got an inkybus."

"However did he come by that, I wonder?"

"He heard about 'em from his old uncle, Jeremy White, when he last went to see him a month or more ago. And I wish the mischief he had kept away. But the ancient man's a bedlier now and somebody told Sam he ought to go and see him now and again, so he went. What sense his Uncle Jeremy has left always takes him back to the past now. He only remembered Sam as a babe and didn't know that he'd grown up the huge chap he has done. But his uncle took an ugly view the moment he set eyes on him because, in the records of the White family, there's a beastly tale that, when a man child is born with red hair among 'em, then, so like as not, before he grows to twenty-one years old, he'll be catched by an inkybus. And he warned Sammy, that he's now got to an age when he may soon feel the thing to work inside him and be called home in six months if not sooner."

The poor child wept and I nodded at her solemnly.

"Yes," I said, "that's how they act. But they are very rare monsters to hear tell of nowdays. Did his uncle give Sam any details ? Had the old man ever seen one himself?"

"No, not with his own eyes, Miss Cherry; but Uncle Jeremy's grandfather saw one. An inkybus slew a red-haired young White a hundred years ago and his uncle told all particulars about the beast to Sammy and, of course, he was wishful to let me know 'em; but I wouldn't let him, because, if I hear horrors, I get bad dreams. So I can't say what it looks like nor behaves like. At first Sammy was minded to mistrust it, because his uncle is old and cranky and apt to wander in his mind now, so he went to other old folk at Moreton and found a good few that knew about inkybusses and felt no reason to doubt they were true as gospel. And though I've told him it may be nonsense and a good few men have laughed at his trouble, he knows better himself and now takes a fearful dark view of it."

I heaved a sigh and put a match to my pipe, which had gone out.

"It's natural for people to doubt why such an evil should overtake a man like him," I suggested.

"A powerfuller chap was never seen on Dartymoor, or any place else," answered Nelly, "but while this is hanging over him, he won't wed. Strong as a lion, but his brain is a very simple fashion of brain, same as mine. That's what drew us together, I reckon. We agreed from the first that we wasn't bright, but very well adapted to live with each other."

"And now he thinks you'd do wiser to part, along of his inkybus?"

"He don't think : he's positive certain, Miss Cherry. He

31

says it would be a wicked piece of work for him to take me and leave me a widow the next minute very likely."

My mind always looks at a question from half a dozen angles at once—a rare gift. I well knew that the biggest fool can be sharp as a needle where his own interests are concerned, so, for a fluttering moment, I wondered if Sammy White had changed his mind about Nelly Blake and chosen this rubbishy tale as an excuse to jilt her and escape.

"I must learn a bit more, Nelly," I said. "There's always wheels within wheels when you're up against a mystery, and an inkybus is one of those secrets of Nature that make us wonder—begging His pardon—why God ever made them and suffered the wretches to flourish. Suppose Sammy is right and has got one of these bodeful beasts hard and fast within him, would you still want to marry the man?"

"Yes, I would," she replied. "If 'twas only to cheer up his death-bed I'd take him and brighten his dying gasp. I love him."

She said those three last words as though they covered every aspect of the subject. I nodded and did not answer for a minute. It was just one of those awkward problems I loved to sharpen my wits upon, but felt little more could be done before I saw the man.

"We must keep an open mind for the minute," I told her presently. "Bide patient, but don't throw up the sponge. I'll consider the line of action when I've had a tell with your sweetheart."

"You wouldn't say it was hopeless for us?" she asked.

"Certainly not, Nelly. No mortal have a right to say any trouble is hopeless because he has lost his own hold on hope. I'll learn what Sammy's got to say, and if one of my clever strokes can be struck for the pair of you, then I'll strike it."

"God bless you, I'm sure, miss, and so will Sammy when he hears tell," she assured me. "He's very fond of being alive and very fond of me also and would be most willing for us to continue together ; and if you was able to discover it's all moonshine about his inkybus, then he'll bless the day. And if money can do it you would have his savings and mine also. We'd

32

sooner dwell in an empty cottage without a stick of furniture than lose each other."

"Companionship's better than furniture," I agreed, "though I've known folk who found their old furniture a darned sight more companionable than their old friends."

"When shall he wait on you, miss?" she asked.

"The sooner the better," I answered. "Bid him come tomorrow night, when he gets home from work, and order him to wash the mine dirt off him before he comes."

She showed proper gratitude and went her way; and on the following evening, dressed in his black Sundays, the huge bulk of Sammy White bore down upon Owl Pen. He was a commanding figure and one of Nature's wanton tricks, for into his fine body she had put the modest wits of a mouse. Sammy was a peaceful, pious lad and quite indifferent to the strength of his great frame. Truculence, or pugnacity, or pride in his brawn and muscle never entered his head. He could crush a pewter pot with one hand for the amusement of a public house, but to clench that great fist and smite another man with it would have been a most unthinkable idea for him.

"Come in, White," I greeted him. "Sit here and smoke your pipe and answer some questions."

"That's right: that's why I'm here at your commands, Miss Crymes," he answered, and then went over the situation and explained how his conscience directed him to face it.

"The facts look to prove I'm one of them men called to be took off at God's will, but not my own, for reasons unknown to myself," he said. "The like has already happened before in my family and the signals are hung out for me to see. My Uncle Jeremy it was who put me on the fatal track, because I knew nought myself. But the upshot is that if a man of the White race is born with red hair, then 'tis fifty-to-one, in betting terms, he'll go early by inkybus."

"And how do you suppose you ought to act, Sam?" I inquired.

"Put my house in order and stand up to it," he replied very earnestly. "My first duty, as I saw it, was to tell Nelly Blake and break off with her in common justice. That was the most cruel wrench, needless to say; but she's still disposed to kick against the pricks."

"Quite right too," I declared. "Don't you think I'm scorning the inkybus, but there's no call yet for you to take it lying down. They are the same as any other vermin and we must fight 'em and conquer if we can."

"Thank Heaven you ain't like most others, miss," he said, "and don't flout the inkybus. All I get is silly laughter when I relate about it. Even his Reverence took that line and commanded me to use what little sense I can claim to. 'Rubbish!' he called it."

I shook my head.

"That's not the way to respond," I replied, "and the holy man should know better. It's just by not believing in 'em that the creatures get their power over us. The Devil likes humans to say they don't believe in him, because that's the sort who fall quickest into his clutches. Now tell me exactly what this fatal worm looks like to those who have seen it. They are parlous rare in any case and, though I've never actually had my eyes upon one, I know their habits and the way they work."

Even as I spoke my mind was contriving, for I'd summed the young man up by now.

"Uncle Jeremy got the details from his own grandfather and kept 'em in memory," answered the young fellow. " 'Tis but a small thing, miss—nine to ten inches long and tailing off like the tail of a rat. Set in its head is a pair of fire-red eyes, which never shut, and it has got a sharp nose like a bird's beak. The creature's very thin and needs to be, because, once it's got in you, it curls up around your liver till there's nothing left for it to feed upon. Then you both fade out and die."

I nodded gravely, but showed no surprise.

"True enough," I said. "That's what you may call the life history of them; but I can tell you more, Sam. You'll be wondering no doubt how they creep into a victim unbeknownst."

"Uncle Jeremy reckoned they got in your drink when they was no bigger than tadpoles, and then grew up inside of you," he replied, and now, having summed him up and decided he was the sort to believe anything, I made answer.

"No," I said, "they pick their hour and wriggle into you when you're asleep. They work in the small hours, Sammy, after they've marked you down by day, and if you hap to be slumbering with your mouth open, down they pop!"

"I do sleep with my mouth ope. I waken up at the noise of my snoring now and again," he confessed.

"That throws light," I agreed. "That's what has fallen out most likely."

"There you are then!" he exclaimed. "So near to certainty as don't matter, Miss Crymes."

"Let me think now, Sam," I said. "We must get our foundations laid firm, my dear man."

"By all means think so long as you mind to," he begged.

"Give me a spot of your tobacco," I asked. "I'll light up, because baccy always clears my brain."

"So it do mine," he declared, and then took a worn tobacco pouch out of his pocket.

"My shag ain't too strong for a lady?" he asked.

I helped myself, filled my pipe and told him I liked it strong.

"Now there's a question you must answer first and tell solemn truth about it," I went on.

"I always tell the truth whatever may overtake me after," he promised. "My second nature, Miss Crymes."

"A good habit, and the question is this: do you honestly believe yourself under the dominion of an inkybus?"

He nodded.

"So help me God, I do."

"Then we know where we are and what steps lie before us, Sammy. We must follow the old practice which, in my hands, may conquer if not too late."

"You wouldn't advise to mark time for a bit?"

"I would not," I assured him. "They that mark time, instead of taking time by the forelock, seldom thrive. There's no half measures open for you now. 'Tis war to the death and you've got to slay him or be slain by him."

35

I could see he hated the idea of fighting even an inkybus, but he granted the need to do so.

"If there's any hopeful thing to do, I'll do it," he said.

"The line of hope lies in a weakness they are known to suffer from," I explained. "You can trap the little horrors if you know the charm to use against them."

I was on dangerous ground now, but he only gasped and believed.

"Trap 'em!" he cried out. "How can you trap a varmint curled up alongside your innards, miss? You can't let down a trap into your vitals."

"No, but you can set a trap to fetch 'em up!" I declared. "You can lure 'em out in the small hours after midnight, Sam. 'Tis well known when an afflicted man slumbers, his inkybus is very apt to crawl up from below for a breath of air and then go down within him before he wakes. If the sleeper moves a finger, then the creature's down his throat again like lightning; but given the proper charm, it may be took."

Sammy grew excited at such a fine thought.

"Fancy that!" he said. "Then tell me the proper bait, Miss Crymes, and I'll make shift to find it if in human reach. I'd set the trap on my pillow and pray God to find him catched some fine morning!"

I shook my head.

"No, Sam: a secret shared is a secret no more. The charm is my business, and there's not another wise woman knows it on Dartmoor but me. I'll work the charm, but I wouldn't reveal it for money."

He turned this over in his slow mind and then another idea occurred to him.

"If it comes up for an airing of a night, after I'm to sleep, why shouldn't I pretend to be asleep and then, after it's crept out, nab it myself?" he asked.

I laughed at that.

"It isn't so easy, my boy," I replied. "The point of the charm is that when that's working, the inkybus *must* come up! Given the proper charm, once you're dead asleep, it rises willy-nilly. If it's there, come it will."

"And if it don't come, then you could go so far as to say it can't be there," suggested Sammy.

"Very well argued," I said, "but seeing's believing, Sammy, and for your peace of mind and my own good fame, it would be a lot better if I got it out."

"It would be the most triumphant thing to happen if you could," he agreed. "I'd help heart and soul, Miss Crymes, if you don't command any job of work against my conscience," said Sam.

"Your conscience is on our side; because, if we can contrive for there to be one less inkybus in the world, then we are doing all our fellow creatures a good turn," I explained to him; "and what I ask you is to sleep out of your own bed for one night and no more, because, at the appointed hour, I must be at hand watching over you with the spell, so you'll need to spend that night at Owl Pen along with me. And you must sleep terrible sound and, after midnight's struck, I'll play my part."

"I always sleep sound," promised Sammy.

"And mind: not a word to a soul; and if Mrs. Tozer— where you lodge——"

"Fear nought for her," he interrupted. "She goes to her bed at eight-thirty winter and summer, and won't know a thing about it till breakfast next morning."

"Good," I answered. "Then the coast is clear as to her and you'll be back before she wakens. But you must keep mute as the grave over our night's work. The result is all that matters to the neighbours. Fetch up here on Wednesday night and I'll have a bed laid for you, and all you'll need to do is to take off your boots and jacket and get into it. Turn up around ten o'clock and don't be drinking a lot of beer at the 'Hearty Welcome' before you come."

"I'm tee-total, Miss Crymes," he said. "I drop in the pub off and on for company, not beer. I take one dry ginger and no more."

Then, with a faithful promise to keep shut about everything, he went his way.

After that I sat and talked to myself aloud, as I sometimes do of a night, when there's nobody but the cat and dog and the hearth crickets to listen.

"So be it, Cherry," I said. "Seeing is believing all right with that young man; but the Lord loves His fools and will often call upon us wise ones to get them out of their troubles."

So I set about to weave my spell before the young man returned to me, and though I say it myself, no witch, whether black or white, ever hit upon a better bit of sorcery. Yet it was of the utmost simplicity, as masterpieces often are. In my clear-sighted way I planned every item of what would happen, and with Wednesday night-time, all was ready.

A starry sky hung over Owl Pen when the hero's heavy feet arrived at the door and my sheep-dog lifted his eyes to my face with an inquiring growl. But, seeing I was not alarmed, he welcomed Sammy, though he felt in his doggy mind such a late visitor to be irregular. A comfortable bed on the floor of the house-place awaited the young man, though I was not in any instant hurry he should retire. He exclaimed to find a fire in the room and I told him that warmth was needful.

"The fire's a part of the spell," I said. "They are much addicted to heat and we need to think of all that betters our chances."

The cup of tea I gave him presently was laced with a drowsy herb and, after he had drunk it, I bade him to doff his cravat and shoes, lie down, think of nothing in particular, shut his eyes and go off to sleep. Which he did do without many more words. Then I extinguished my paraffin lamp, banked the fire and left him, but listened till his gentle snoring showed that he had fallen unconscious. And until half after five on the following morning he remained so. Then he was wakened by my shrill demands. I drew the window blind, stirred up the fire and bawled to him to be stirring.

"Wake up! Wake up, boy!" I cried in a loud and triumphant tone of voice. "Rise up and come to your senses and thank your stars! A red-letter day has dawned for you, Sammy, and I wish you joy of it!"

He heaved up and panted and rubbed his eyes.

"What be you telling?" he grunted out. "Sleeping like a dead man I was."

"Providence saw to that," I told him. "But I wasn't

sleeping! The charm worked and all went so well that I could scarce believe my own senses."

"Was—was he there, Miss Crymes?"

"He was there all right. I sat beside you when you slept, all knit up to seize my chance when it came. Still as a mouse I was with every nerve alert, and then—half after twelve—out he crept as I foretold! He marked the fire burning and slithered off your bed down to the hearth to bask in the warmth with his little, wicked eyes glittering like sparks of flame. I felt in a bit of a tremor at such a hideous sight but knew what to do and strung myself to do it. All was ready needless to tell and I lifted my stick and struck with all my might, same as you'd kill a snake. I got him good and hard and he squeaked awful and made a most valiant try to get back inside you and save his life; but all was in vain: I struck once more and broke his neck and he was a goner!"

"Thank the living God, miss! And where's the wretch now?" asked Sam, breathing hard and rising up.

"Seeing's believing as I always say, so I've kept his corpse for you to see. Look under that glass bowl, but don't you touch him."

Something was in the house-place that hadn't been there when the young man went to sleep, and I pointed to a little table with his inkybus upon it, safe beneath an upturned glass bowl. Then Sammy stared open-mouthed. The inkybus lay there curled up in a circle with its head lifted and its ruby-red eyes shining over its black, birdlike beak; while so full of life did it still appear that the beholder doubted.

"By Gor!" he exclaimed. "Be you sure 'tis dead?"

"Dead as a nit, Sam: and now you've seen it for yourself, into the fire it goes, because the air around such a creature is full of poison and parlous to any living thing that breathes it."

He expressed a regret.

"I'd like to show it to parson and a good few others who laughed at me," he said; but I acted swiftly.

"Not on your life, Sam! You might so soon spread the plague as trail it all over the parish. Tell Nelly what you've seen and none else. Let all men know salvation has come to you by the mercy of your Maker. Blaze that abroad by all means, but

39

not another word as to the details. That was your faithful promise, remember, and never you forget it."

As I spoke I turned over the bowl, picked up the inkybus by the nose and cast it into the fire.

"Throw open the window and let sunrise in upon us," I commanded him.

He obeyed and then witnessed the destruction of his enemy. It twisted and writhed a moment or two, then turned to dust and vanished for ever. A work of rare handicraft sure enough and I felt sorry to lose it. 'Twas fashioned with the skull of a jack-snipe, two red glass beads and a leather boot-lace.

"Now begone to your breakfast and your day's work, and let the world know the cup is taken from your lips and you're as likely to live for a hundred years as any other man," I said, shaking his hand and beaming upon him.

"You should get the credit for this, by rights," he replied, crushing my fingers in his great paw. " 'Tis your wonder-working under Providence have saved me alive, miss."

"That's so," I agreed, "but all you need to do is to feel properly grateful and have your banns called out so soon as you mind to."

That evening the lovers visited me, with Nelly full of thanksgivings.

"We'll name you in our prayers for ever more, Miss Cherry," she said, "and we ordain to call up ten pounds out of our savings if you say that's proper; but if it ain't enough, because no money could equal what you've done for us, then we'll pay you all we've got, which is thirty-two pounds, nine shillings."

"I'll take five and no more, and you can pay the rest in your prayers on my account," I told them.

"Thank Heaven there's one less of they awful things left among us, be it as it will," cried Sammy.

"It may even be the very last of them," I promised him.

"Oh, I do hope so, I do hope so, dear miss," declared the girl, "because then, if our first boy was to be a red-head, we shan't go in fear for him, shall we?"

They were as good as their word and never told the little they knew. That was ages ago, when I first went into practice, as you might say—just one of my earliest, simplest efforts to use my gifts and make a living by them. A trifling affair compared with much to come, but tending to show the mastership that was in me.

III

I HAVE heard folk, including a good few ministers who served our parish in my time, declare how no good results ever came out of a bad action : and I have never opposed that opinion because, if I did so, I should lose credit. But I can put down here and now in safety that you must go a lot deeper behind the question than that, for all depends in the first place on what you count to be good or evil. One man's bread is another man's poison, and you also need to bear in mind that what looks evil today may turn out a most virtuous piece of work when looked back upon tomorrow. Heroes properly hated by their own generation will, as like as not, get marble statues put up to them by the next.

Thinking upon which reminds me of another piece of my early mastership that served to bring calm out of turmoil and peace out of war. It also gave me a complete confidence in myself which never deserted me afterwards. I was once faced with a proper confusion of interests, yet all so bearing upon each other that I doubt if many women, or men either, would have made sense of the mess, or found a way through to master it ; but I rode the storm and brought all the vexed parties into safety. A job it was that called for craft, no doubt—some fools might have said for witchcraft ; and it was then—for the last time—that I availed myself of what my mother had left me— items of her outfit, often used in her days, but very near gone out of fashion in mine.

The characters to be dealt with were two women and two men, namely Widow Triscott and Benny Owlett, Peter Hacker, master of Little Merripit Farm, and old Jack Fern ; and it all began when Martha Triscott came up to see me one June morning round about noon. A bright and cheerful day, and I had a bright and cheerful visitor already with me at the time ; but Widow Triscott was not by nature bright or cheerful and never added to the joy of her neighbours in living knowledge after her life's partner dropped. Now the first thing she heard, when she knocked at the door of Owl Pen and I called to her to open and step in, was laughter, and the first thing she saw was me making a pie for myself and Benny Owlett nibbling bits of my rhubarb for the pie and sitting swinging her pretty legs on my kitchen table. Benny was one of those tiresome, beautiful, joyous girls that make you fond of them, yet make you wonder why you can waste your time listening to their empty chatter and smiling at their nonsense. Lovely she was, with no more brains than a barnyard hen ; but I forgave her for her foolishness, because she carried such an air of grace and hope and good willing. A selfish piece at heart and many a time I would dress her down when she declared her wilful thoughts ; but then she'd just laugh and put her arms about me and kiss me, and where was I ? She had played with a good few men in her time and was at this moment keeping company with Peter Hacker. Indeed the farmer regarded himself as engaged to her and prided himself upon the fact ; but Benny's father—John Owlett, the water-watcher—well knowing her vagaries, was not so certain, though very wishful it might happen because Peter was a man likely to keep his wife in order and calm down her high spirits. Now the chit spoke to Mrs. Triscott before I had time to do so.

"Bain't it too bad, Martha ?" she asked. "Here's Cherry, the cleverest woman on Dartmoor, and famed for knowing all about the future, and yet she won't befriend a poor girl and look in her crystal and tell me my fortune, though I'm offering her a crown if she will."

"You push off, you saucy wench," I said, "and don't waste any more of my time. Your fortune will look after itself, and it don't want a wise woman to tell the fate of such a good-for-nought."

She went away laughing, and then Martha looked after her with melancholy eyes and shook her head.

"I could have told that stupid puss something to change her laughter into tears," she told me, "but time enough for that. Can you list to me for half an hour, Cherry ? I'm in cruel trouble as usual and don't see no way out this time ; but I'll gladly pay you if you can give heed."

"I'll hear what you've got to grumble at, of course,

43

Martha," I answered. Her past history was already known to me, but now she travelled over it again and told some details that were new.

"When my dear husband was alive, he worked for Peter Hacker's father at Little Merripit as you know," she began, "and old Mr. Hacker often said to my better half that, when he had paid rent for his cottage for fifty years, he should live the rest of his life in it free, and me after him if he went first. That's common knowledge, and Triscott had paid the last year of it before he passed over. But now Peter Hacker says there was never no contract regarding me, and he's going back on his father because he wants the cottage for his new cow-man, so I must clear out at Michaelmas. Hard as moor stone he is and, even when I told him all that hangs on my holding the cottage for my life, he won't change or let me bide."

"What does hang on you stopping in the house, Martha?" I asked her, and she dabbed a handkerchief to her tearful eyes.

"Why, Jacky Fern hangs on it, my dear woman," she answered. "We're keeping it close for the minute, but ordain to be wed, and why not? We're both lonely souls and we've both lost a good partner and it was very convenient that we should join up. Granted he's poor and a tidy lot older than me, but he counted for security along with me, and he reckoned my cottage at Little Merripit was so good as any other place for him to close his eyes in, but now—— ?"

"He will close his eyes when and where the Lord wills, Martha," I said.

"That's as may be," she answered, "Jacky's seventy-two and claims the right to look forward to a few years of rest before his finish; but now he's heard of this wickedness, he says he's off me. He says 'no house, no marriage'; and he's a lot put about. It's terrible difficult for him to get a spot of work anywhere now, and it would be a lot more dignified if he stopped trying and just retired and smoked his pipe and took his fag-end of life along with me."

That was before the days of old age pensions, of course, and I quite saw what Jacky Fern aimed at. He had always been a lazy, unnoticeable sort of man and lived a shabby life,

44

picking up a bit of rough work as he could; but he was harmless and very good to his first wife and never known to get into trouble.

"That being so, with Jack and my lifelong home gone," concluded Widow Triscott, "the future's properly ruined."

"Let's see where you stand then, Martha," I began. "First Peter Hacker is going back on his father's word and Fern says that if he does so he don't see his way to join you. And you have got no strong friend or well-wisher that can stand up to Hacker and knock some sense of justice into the man."

"Not a soul to care a brass farthing about it," she sighed.

"What price your nephew, Nathan Coaker?" I asked. "He was always your supporter."

"He was," she agreed, "and many a good piece of my silver money he's had in his time. I fell for Nat, like all the women did, old or young, and he was properly fond of me. A terrible good-looking chap and a master with horses. Second whip to the Mid-Dartmoor Foxhounds, he was; and when an Irish gentleman, over here for sporting, took a great fancy to Nathan and offered him better money than he was getting here if he'd go to Ireland as first whip to an Irish pack, he went."

I nodded, knowing all about young Coaker.

"He was one of those after that girl who left us just now," I said, "and I understood long ago from Benny's father that they were engaged. In his opinion Nat only went to Ireland to make a bit of money and counted to come back presently and marry Benny."

"That was my nephew's intention when he left this country," agreed Martha, "and I told him at the time he was mad to think a girl like her would keep true to him once he was out of her sight. But she did mean to wed him once. That's why I said Benny was going to hear something to stop her laughter before she was much older."

"He's married somebody else," I suggested, but Martha shook her head.

"He's partly why I came to see you, Cherry. That's another misfortune, as if one wasn't enough." She felt in her pocket and brought out a letter.

"I had this from Ireland," she said, "me being the only

45

relative his master knew he had. Nathan Coaker's dead. He's broke his neck hunting, and they are sending his watch and chain and a few of his sundries to me. But it's clear he died a single man, else there would have been a widow."

My brain, when at its best, works like lightning, and I took in these facts and sorted 'em out with my usual nice attention. And while I thought, I spoke a few comfortable words to Martha.

"That's sad, sure enough," I said, "a most unfortunate end to all the young man's hopes for a happy life to come. And a cruel stroke for you too, Martha."

Her thoughts ran on her nephew for the minute.

"Only thirty-one he was and a great breaker of horses. Never known to fear anything or anybody, on two legs or four. That girl shed a bucket of tears when he left England, because he was the top flower of the bunch for her in those days, as well he might be. But now Nat's forgot, and they say she's promised to take Peter Hacker. And a frosty look out for the likes of her if she does."

"Farmer Hacker's no friend of mine," I told her. "An over-bearing chap and far ways inferior to his father. Not so long ago he dared to say I'd overlooked one of his bullocks when it died three days before Moreton Cattle Show."

"Hacker's riches have made Benny forget Nathan's quality; but now he's in his grave——" began Martha.

"Stop !" I said. "Keep your nerve and listen a bit. You have come to me and told all you came to tell, and now give heed to what I think best to be done. There's wheels within wheels turning against you, Martha, but you can't be expected to see any way to escape 'em. Nevertheless you were clever enough to seek me and find out if I can. So I will turn to your affairs. I'll centre upon them and I may surprise myself into finding a way, because, with a brain like mine, surprises can always be counted upon. But time must be allowed and time's money. If I fail you, then not a penny shall I ask or expect ; but if you presently find yourself safe in your house and a married woman again, then I'd be interested to know, as a matter of business and plain dealing, what you might feel my fee should be."

I said this because Martha was judged a lot more comfortable than she gave out.

"If there's any road pointing to my salvation and you can find it, I'll give you twenty-five pounds the day I'm married to Fern," she told me.

"Enough said, my dear," I replied, and then, with my wits now at full blast, I asked another question.

"Touching this sad affair of Nathan Coaker, what manner of man was he in his nature and his appearance?" I asked her, and she seemed surprised for me to switch back to her nephew, him being dead and out of mind. But I saw far deeper than she could, for circumstances often arise where the dead take a leading part in the business of the living. There are times when a corpse has often made a greater stir from his coffin than ever he did when he walked the earth.

"Nat was a dark-skinned chap with curly black hair and wonderful, shining, white teeth," said Martha. "A joyous, cheerful fellow, very strong and not so trustable as some, but always a most good-hearted and well-meaning man."

"Well, now we know how the land lies," I wound up. "Have you told of his death to any person yet? That's a great point."

"Not a soul but you."

"Good," I said. "Then don't do so, Martha. Something is telling me that it will be a very wise thing to keep close for the minute about this sad affair. If you want to talk about him, then come up here and talk to me. I'll gladly listen; but keep silent to everybody else. I feel most strongly about that and if you can trust me, which is the first thing, then you won't regret it."

My tone of voice heartened Mrs. Triscott.

"I don't see no light myself, but I trust you to find a gleam if there is one," she said.

"Time and again I've known hope to triumph where you'd least expect victory," I reassured her, and then she took her leave; and when the day's work was done and the world at peace, I lighted my pipe and turned over her situation.

I have always found myself very gifted at knitting the

known to the unknown, and so contriving to see deeper through a stone wall than common people. But, though a complicated job of work, there were no danger signals in Martha's mess and I had my plan of campaign pretty well worked out before I slept. It looked to be one of those watertight cases where I needed to rely upon the skill and nerve of one person only, and that one by good chance was myself. Benny Owlett looked to be the keystone of the arch, as they say, and my impulse tempted me to summon her and get on with it; but I knew a better way than that, because what I now ordained to happen must not be laid to my account, and it is always clever to act at the wish of somebody else; then none can blame, or suspect you, afterwards. So two days later I let her set the ball rolling. She came at a time when she knew I was most like to be home, and she brought me two, nice, half-pound trout fresh out of Dart river.

Now, while she chattered, I had only to wait for my chance which I knew would soon come.

"There are gypsies on Wallabrook Common, Cherry," she said. "The same caravan of them that was here last year, and I can tell you what I'm going to do. The old mother gypsy has got second sight and she's a famous fortune-teller. So now, since you won't pleasure me, I shall go to the gypsies, because I never wanted to get a glimpse into my future more than what I do just now."

She played straight into my hands, you see, because to tell her fortune was just what I now intended. But I shook my head as usual.

"I'm too fond of you to do it, child," I assured her. "There's a very solemn side against peering into the future of young people, especially them you cherish and think well of them as I do of you. The gift is mine and I exercise it same as my mother did and was never found to be wrong; but I'm set against so doing in your case, because, if anything ugly was waiting to overtake you, then I should always feel I'd marred your happiness."

"You might see it coming and put me wise so as I should escape from it," suggested Benny.

"No, my dear. What's coming will come, and who am I to

48

knock the heart out of a lad, or lass, and tell them what's coming, if it's going to be evil?"

"I've heard you say how a brave man, or woman, can often beat the cards," she argued, and I dare say I might have told her so sometime. I twaddled on a little longer, then gave in.

"If you must have it, then better you should from me than a gypsy," I said. "No right gypsy was ever trustable. They come from the Egyptians, according to history, and no good ever came out of Egypt but the fruits of the date palm. But if you are set to face it, Benny, in a proper spirit, then I'll do it, though it goes against the grain."

"Thank you dearly," she said. "I'd be glad to get firm ground under my feet, because I've decided for Peter now. He's close-fisted, but he's like to wear very well and there's Little Merripit Farm behind him and my father's very wishful to get me off his hands."

I answered nothing to that but made my preparations in a solemn and serious manner.

"Draw the blind," I bade. "The crystal only answers to flame light and a true wax candle which I have got."

Then I lit a candle which didn't throw much illumination but was very fitting to a deed of darkness, and next I fetched forth my mother's crystal—a lump of glass from Lord knows where—and a pack of playing cards that she was wont to use along with it. I polished the crystal upon a silk handkerchief, laid out the cards and told Benny to sit in a chair on my left hand, keep quiet and pay heed to every word I might say.

"Don't you speak or make a sound yourself," I warned her and put on a very mystical air with a wild and faraway look in my eyes. What my mother might have done in her time I had no idea whatsoever; but no more had Benny Owlett, so I just proceeded very solemnly and dealt out the cards face upwards. Then I set the Jack of Hearts beside the crystal to the left and the Jack of Oaks[1] to the right and made play with them. Next I gathered the rest of the cards, put them by and fixed my eyes upon the crystal.

"It's coming!" I said. "There's a picture shadowing out of the glass."

[1] Oaks = Clubs.

So I stared into the crystal and Benny stared very steadfast at me; and what she saw upon my face was the important thing, because in sober truth I saw nothing at all. I threw a blink of light on the situation then, to tune her mind for what was coming.

"You marked me set aside those two knaves," I said, "and we shall see what they stand for in a minute."

I allowed a minute to go and then let an expression of alarm and doubt creep over my face as I concentrated closer and closer upon the crystal.

"You must be brave; you must steel yourself for what looks to be coming!" I told her. "They are declaring themselves, Benny!"

Still glued to the glass, I went on after a pause:

"Trouble brewing so sure as fate, I fear. The Jacks are explained now. Two men they stand for. A dark man and a fair man—both after you—and, according to the cards, the dark one's got the properest right to you. A brown-faced chap with black, curly hair and flashing, white teeth, and growing fiercer now he's roused. That's Jack of Oaks."

Then Benny forgot my orders, jumped to her feet and cried out wildly:

"Oh my good Powers! That's Nathan Coaker—Nat sure as death, and I thought he'd forgot me years agone!"

"Hush! Hush!" I said, lifting my hand. "Sit quiet and for pity's sake be silent, else you'll spoil all. No, he hasn't forgot you seemingly—far from it."

The girl went white as curds then sat with her hands pressed over her heart to hear what I'd see next.

"There's Jack of Hearts showing up now," I exclaimed, still on the crystal. "I'd hoped they wouldn't meet, but they have, they have, Benny! They're at each other like dragons! Heaven save us—there'll be murder done!"

Then, after a fearful moment or two, I fell back exhausted in my chair and breathed and panted like a porpoise and put my hand to my brow.

"They've gone!" I said. "A great wave of darkness came over the scene and swallowed up the end. Only one thing looks to be clear: there's going to be blood flow when those two men

50

meet. Oh, why the mischief, girl, did you make me look into the future only for a horror like that?"

I sighed for a few moments, then I blew out the candle and let in the daylight, hustled away the cards and the crystal and turned to Benny. She was showing how badly the adventure had told on her, but I bade her dry her eyes and be brave. Little by little I allowed a feeble ray of hope to lighten the darkness, but was in no hurry to cheer her very far.

"My instinct is always to put up a fight against all the Powers of Darkness if need be when I feel my case is good," I told her. "There's a cruel lot to face for you, Benny, but you have got a tower of strength in me behind you. I don't want to hear any names, only to get your situation clear. What I've seen is two men both dead set on you. One pale and well-to-do seemingly and like to be a very sound partner for such as you; while the other is dark as night and fierce as a lion—a very fine figure of a man without doubt, but most like a tartar to live with. Which do you want? Which do you hope will win when they come to meet, as meet they surely must? Tell me no names: just say dark or pale."

"I want the pale one," sobbed Benny. "I thought and believed it was all off with the dark one years ago, and I'm so good as tokened to the pale one now."

I nodded and played with her for half a minute.

"We must see if I can tempt Providence to take a hand on your side," I said. "Meantime put your trust in me and don't lose hope. There looks to be very little time to spare and no doubt the dark one is on his way; which being so we've got no more than a few hours to prepare."

So the lass went off in a terrified state, counting to meet Nathan Coaker at every step of the road for certain, and little knowing the poor lad was sleeping harmless enough in his Irish grave. Benny ran straight to Little Merripit Farm and poured her woes into Peter Hacker's ears after she left me; and she could have done nothing better, for he was my next mark in any case. But now he saved me the trouble of seeking him and took the line I should have wished. He rode up to Owl Pen next morning and he was in a rage and full of temper and big talk. He bawled out sitting on his horse and bade me

51

come to him, and I stood at my door, calm as calm, and said that if he wanted speech with me, he could get down off his horse and tether it outside and walk in. I wasn't going to put myself about for Master Hacker. So he lighted down and fastened up his horse and marched in very high and mighty, smacking his leggings with his riding-stock.

"What's all this tomfoolery you've been telling my girl, Charity Crymes?" he began. "For two pins I'd set policeman on you!"

Well, I was never one to stand insolence from man or mouse.

"Stop bellowing and blustering," I said, "and know your company better, you young ape. Begin at the beginning and let me hear what tomfoolery Benny Owlett heard from me, because I'm not famous for talking tomfoolery in Packhorse Bridge, or any place else."

"She's told me what you saw in your crystal, which was that Nathan Coaker's coming back from Ireland all set for a bloodthirsty row with me, and how she promised in the far past to marry him, but has long forgot all about it."

"And who are you to dare say what I told her was tomfoolery?" I asked. "I didn't put any names to the men I saw in my crystal. That was her work: mine was to look into the future on her account; and when a sensible creature hears what is going to overtake him, he'll generally be at the trouble to escape it if he can."

"Stuff and rubbish!" he answered me. "Fortune-telling is forbid by law and I'd be in my right to inform against you."

I smiled at that. "You'd best to set about it then, Hacker," I answered, quite calm and dignified, "because I'm sorry to say what's going to happen to you will spoil your usefulness for a month of Sundays when it comes. So sure as Christmas Day is Quarter Day also, you've got something mortal ugly waiting round the corner and you'd do a darned sight wiser to look after your own affairs than meddle with mine. And now clear out of my sight."

But I could see his cowardly heart was quailing, though he tried to bluff it.

52

"I'll hear more of this before I go, please," he said, and stuck to his chair and continued.

"Benny Owlett was contracted to Coaker in a childish sort of fashion—a horse-stealer or little better and a devil of a rogue anyway. And he went off years ago, and a good riddance to all concerned. But now you look in your glass and fiddle with your cards and pretend to see——"

I shut him up then and rose from my chair and put on the airs of a proper tragedy queen, which I can do if need be, and my eyes flashed fire upon him.

"Shut your mouth, you godless dog!" I cried at him. "How do you dare to talk about 'pretending' to the likes of me—to me, the honestest woman in this parish? Begone, you wilful, ignorant wretch! I'll neither list to you, nor lift a finger to help you now!"

He caved in a bit before my fury and allowed he'd gone too far.

"All right, all right. I'll withdraw that and I'm sorry I said it, but what's a man to think?" he asked.

"I'll pardon you since you're sorry," I answered, though still heaving a bit with indignation. "Now you can go on, but watch your tongue in future."

"It looks as if this scoundrel might be coming back from Ireland," he said.

"That's so, and little doubt about it seemingly," I agreed. "I can't call him to mind myself, but Benny knew the man in a moment from what I reported from my crystal. And if she's forgot she was promised to him, he surely hasn't, and by all accounts he's the sort to overmaster a man like you mighty quick. So likely as not he's made money out there and is coming home in triumph to marry her."

"She's going to marry me, however."

"So you think; but what if there's not enough left of you to marry anybody when a savage like him has done with you?"

Hacker began to get his tail down before my fierce picture.

"You can buy off that sort if you don't want to have a rumpus with them," he suggested.

"Can you buy off a flash of lightning when the thunderstorm's on top of you?" I asked. "Can you buy off a raging,

53

lawless man when you come between him and the woman he wants? There's stronger things than money—a charge of heavy shot with gunpowder behind it, for example. But more likely, from what I hear, he'd meet you face to face in the open and wipe the street with you."

"She's my side, however."

"She may say she is, but wait till she sets eyes on him again. He's well known to be as handsome as Apollyon."

The farmer was beginning to sing smaller and smaller now.

"A thousand pities the brute can't be kept away altogether," he said.

"For your sake and for Benny's sake it certainly is," I admitted. "A thousand pities. She loves you well enough to marry you, no doubt; but you needn't think to trust her far if that man's curly black hair and shining white teeth and masterful manners turn up here again."

"How to stop it? What to do to keep them apart?" he asked. "Can it be worked by craft, Miss Crymes?"

"There's few things that can't be worked with brains," I assured him, "and when a wise woman and a resolute man pool their wits, they are so likely to conquer as not."

"Help me then if you can," he begged. Which gave me my chance.

"I can't work for nothing," I said, "but since this looks to be a job on which your future life and happiness may well depend and I feel the answer to be in my hands, I'm willing to work for you and reckon you'll find a generous fee. It's in a nutshell: if I succeed, then, on the day you're safely wed to her, I shall ask for fifty pounds—no more and not a stiver less. But if I fail, then I doubt if you'll be alive to pay a penny in any case. Still, given oceans of trouble, I do believe it lies in my power to make you a winner."

He tried to haggle, but I would not bate my bargain.

"No more as to that," I said. "And now tell me what you know about this man, for the more I learn, the better my chance to keep him off your throat."

Then Peter explained how his enemy was nephew to Martha Triscott, the widow of one of the old hands at Little Merripit. But he didn't mention that she was under notice to leave her

54

cottage, and little guessed the pattern I was weaving and what would come out of it in my own time.

I sprang another surprise on him now, with very fine results, after he had said Widow Triscott was Nat Coaker's aunt and the only relation he'd got, to anybody's knowledge. I stared upon the man with consternation in my face and a great light of revelation also.

"Good Powers!" I said. "Why, now you can see a dead certainty before you and another reason for Coaker to be on his way. It's well understood that you intend turning Martha out of her cottage, and that's your business of course; but don't you see what's arose from it? She has most surely wrote to her nephew and told him what you ordain to do, so, thinking a lot of her as he always did, Nathan's coming over full of threatenings and slaughters! And he's got a good case mind you, because there's many think you are doing a wrongful thing by breaking your father's promise to Martha's husband and firing her as you intend to do. And, as if that weren't enough for you to cope with, back comes Coaker and finds you've not only took Martha's cottage from her, but stole his sweetheart from him!"

"The more comes out, the more it looks as though he'd a lot better be kept away," said Hacker, with growing misery in his eyes.

"Yes, that is so," I granted, "but, though hidden from your sight, there's a shadow of hope for me and a growing possibility to keep him away. One thing you can't fail to see for yourself—the first step which ought to be taken this instant moment. I must see Mrs. Triscott before another day passes and tell her that you've changed your mind."

Then he showed how he belonged to the folk who can put a ruling passion even before their own destruction.

"Why should I lose money on my own house?" he asked.

"If you're that sort of fool, you are scarce worth answering, or yet helping," I said. "But if you really want to know, then you should do so for two reasons: your father's good name and your own skin. To make Martha free of her cottage is half-way to keeping Coaker in Ireland. Can't you see that much? Let her write to him that you have changed your mind and are

55

going to do the rightful thing by her and then he'll have no more quarrel with you, because he doesn't know about you and Benny yet, and he need never know, if you hurry up and marry her. She sees now the ugly danger of delay and will be thankful to take you with no more shilly-shallying."

He gave in then, though with small grace.

"So be it. I'll visit Widow Triscott today," he said; but of course I wasn't wishful for him to call on Martha till I had. As likely as not in her joy at hearing the good news, she would forget all about everything else and very likely let the cat out of the bag about poor Nathan.

"I'll see her," I answered. "You can leave her to me. What you need to do is to get after your sweetheart, because, in ticklish matters like this, an hour's time may make all the difference between good and evil."

"So be it," he said again, and then he walked out and got on his horse and went after Benny Owlett without a word of gratitude for me.

When I saw Martha, I told her how she stood and that Jacky Fern and her dwelling-house were both secured at one stroke.

"But," I added, "Peter Hacker naturally thinks your nephew is still living, and the longer he believes that, the better for you. So take mighty good care not to name his end to anybody. And what you need to say, if poor Nathan should come up in conversation at any time, is this: that, as soon as you let him hear about Hacker's change of mind, he decided not to come home for the minute."

Human nature is a most perverse contrivance, for Martha had her pet passion, which was always to tell the truth and nothing but the truth.

" 'Twill be parlous near a lie, Charity," she said, but I overruled her, same as I had overruled Peter.

"A white lie," I explained, "and a white lie in this case is a far better tool than the naked truth, because it will help a good many people round some tricky corners. So I'd advise you to tell it if need be, my dear woman."

Which she did do when cause arose, and got the house for her life and Jacky for his life also. They wasted no time about joining up, and neither did Benny Owlett, for she and Hacker whirled into matrimony by special license, being feared to wait for weeks while their banns were called. She soon found out what her husband's reigning weakness happed to be, but turned out a very fair partner for him and grew more reasonable than when in her single state. Seventy-five pounds I made by that piece of work—the largest reward I ever took at one stroke in all my life—though I did far greater feats of cleverness for smaller money time and again afterwards. But, when I think upon those people now, the one that stands out most clearly in memory is young Nathan Coaker, who, after he was dead, did a finer job of work for his fellow creatures than ever he accomplished in his short and fiery life.

IV

As you work out the pattern of your days and make your life go in tune with your living, you must above all keep close, watch over your motives. Motives are the bedrock of action, and that wiseacre who said hell was paved with good intentions missed his mark, because it is bad intentions that are evil and the good ones, unfortunate though they may be, are doubtless taken into account on the Day of Reckoning. By satisfying yourself as to motives, you can save a lot of trouble, both with your neighbours and your nearest neighbour of all, and that is your conscience. It's took years sometimes for me and my conscience to turn friends again after a quarrel; but my motives would mostly come to the rescue and, looking back, it is comfortable to mark how Providence nearly always crowned my operations with success.

You hear talk nowadays of a 'three-year' plan, or even a 'five-year' plan, and also find that plenty of such contrivances end in talk and no more; but though I never ventured to trust the future for five years, I have looked before leaping many times and seen the future work out for people much as I planned on their account. Not always, of course, for there home among us a misfortunate folk who were born unlucky and doomed to defy our best attempts, while others again, without any reason for their success, find things always go right with them, though the stupid, wilful creatures never deserved their good luck.

Such was Benny Owlett, and she reminds me of an adventure in which her father, the water-keeper, was involved and, like his daughter before him, came to me for light upon his darkness. A trifle to me, yet it confounded the parties most concerned till I straightened all out.

John Owlett was a solid, hard-working man with a cheerful countenance and friendly to all save the salmon poachers. He stood for his masters and protected the fish and was a good-looking, tough chap turned fifty-five or thereabouts. But it overset his home comforts and methodical way of life when Benny was married, so he hit on a plan to live orderly once more and invited a woman he knew well—a friend of his daughter—to take her place and look after him and his food and his clothes and his dwelling-house. Mercy Bassett was her name and she had no near relatives and was serving as maid-of-all-work at the vicarage and very pleased to exchange from the rather stern rule of Mrs. Walpole, the parson's wife, for the free and easy habits of John Owlett. He had long been accustomed to his own feather-brained child, and Mercy Bassett, though a good bit older than Benny, happened to be just such another—lighthearted and joyous and carefree and fond of the men. She enjoyed a lot more liberty now and, being very popular for her cheerful nature, never lacked for masculine company, and now she had a lot more time on her hands to gallivant than when she served the vicarage. She was a plain woman with a good figure and merry brown eyes that made you forgive her face, for with her everyday appearance there went a quality that satisfies men more than beauty—especially men getting up in years. She was thirty-five and, for all her frivolous mind, began to grow occupied with thoughts of a husband, for she well knew the time must soon come when it would be now or never.

It was after working for Owlett best part of two years that her ideas took shape and she began to consider what offered. You might say her chances were reduced to two and no more by now, for, though she had turned down many hopeful ones in her time, now she felt the hour had come to stop fooling and tune herself to business. Nothing more chills a male, in love and deadly serious on the subject, than to find the wished-for female making a joke about it; so, when with Amos Butt, or Ernest Ford, Mercy now followed a different line, watched her step and steered a safe course between them. They were both reliable men. Ernest was a miller and a widower, and Amos unmarried with a prosperous shop-of-all-sorts, far ahead of such places as a rule. He had a mother to look after his interests, and the custom of Packhorse Bridge behind him. But Mrs. Butt was growing very old and making mistakes in the shop and losing money by them, so Amos felt his wisest course would be to take a wife and train her to succeed his parent. He was not a very fine figure of a man, being in-kneed and a thought askew in his right eye; but Mercy Bassett liked his nature and liked the idea of reigning over his business and keeping shop. As for the miller, thought to be a very snug man, it was in his family's tradition to grind the people's corn, which Fords had done for a century. He had lost his wife five years ago, and now taken an obstinate affection for Mercy and was determined to marry her. People always said a vapour of flour dust hovered over Ernest Ford except on Sundays, when he worshipped in black and carried the alms-dish at morning prayer.

The parish wondered in a mild sort of way which of those contending men would prove victorious; but then happened very curious things, for both of them got sick and tired of waiting for her, so the woman was thrown clean off her balance and driven into doing an idiot thing the like of which none ever heard. There fell out two fierce and final attacks upon Mercy inside one day, and she had only just settled accounts with one of them when she got a broadside from the other and came near losing the little mind she had between the pair of them.

It was late upon the evening of this day when I heard a summons at my door and found that John Owlett, the water-watcher, stood there. He brought Mercy Bassett with him, and such was her state that I thought John might have done wiser to take her to doctor, and told him so. Owlett was fortunately a man who never lost himself under any passing vexations.

"Use your craft to calm her down," he said. "She's all right in her body, but has made such a damned mess of things, poor soul, that she's lost her reason for the minute. When I heard her fantastic tale, Miss Crymes, I couldn't see the right step to take and it looked as if a mad house was like to be the only future for Mercy; but then I had the good sense to think upon you, so I brought her here, to tell her own jolter-headed tale."

It was such a situation as I liked to tackle though I little guessed what the woman would unfold. I calmed her down and

60

cheered her up while Owlett sat quiet and smoked his pipe and watched my methods overcome Mercy's spasms and bring her to a state when she could give an orderly account of all that had overtaken her. In half an hour she was tolerable collected, and when John had also spoken comfortable words and patted her hand and told her that she could very well leave the future to my wisdom, she reached a pitch when her eyes grew dry again and her bosom at peace and she even gave a feeble giggle or two, though, from her point of view, there was mighty little left to giggle about.

"Things with me have come to a climax," she began. "I've often wondered exactly what a climax might be, Miss Crymes, and now I know. There's no doubt I've been keeping Mr. Butt and Miller Ford up and down like a seesaw, God forgive me, but now I'm punished for it. I was at the shop-of-all-sorts getting some gadgets for Mr. Owlett this afternoon, and Amos Butt opened a bottle of his raspberry wine for me at my request, but he sounded a trifle sour himself I thought. In fact I was just off when he bade me stay and listen to him. Then he hastened to shut up his shop, so there should be no interruptions. Next he bade me to sit down and give heed, because his patience was exhausted. In a fierce and desperate state he was and worked himself up into a proper tempest and swore he couldn't stand another month of delay nor yet another week of it. He used coarse language and behaved very unlike anything I'd seen or heard from him before. He said he'd got his character as a leading man to think upon and wasn't going to be played with by a woman like me. He said I might fiddle about and look sideways and downwards and upwards and anywhere but into his face; but he was going to have 'Yes' once for all before I got out of his sight. He said I wasn't the only pebble on the beach, although I appeared to think so, and then he ran on in a quieter tone and poured out his advantages and prospects. He said he was going to open a butcher's meat department presently; and then he reminded me I wasn't getting any younger and that, between two stools, it was well known many silly people often found themselves on their backsides. He also mentioned that there was far better fish in the sea than any caught yet, and so on. After that he turned to

61

Ernest Ford and poured scorn upon him and said the miller was running after a widow to Moreton and his business affairs were a lot more doubtful than was known, and his age far older than he said it was. And I sat and listened, feeling drawn to Amos closer than ever I felt before. At last he'd said all he could think upon and drew out his gold watch, and told me he'd give me fifteen minutes to make up my mind. 'No sense waiting any longer,' he said. 'Marry me next November, when I'm going to London to get my Christmas novelties, and you shall come along with me and see the Zoological Gardens and the Tower of London and the famous waxworks and Westminster Abbey and even go to a playhouse so like as not.' Such items was too much for me and I couldn't stand up against him no more, so I told the man I supposed he must have his way and took him once for all and for ever. His last word was that the banns would be called out next week."

Mercy stopped and stared at me helplessly.

"Well," I said, "and what's the matter with that? If Butt was the climax, then it's a very fine climax."

" 'Tis only the first half of the climax," explained John Owlett. "Go on, Mercy."

"The proper crown of the climax had yet to come," she continued, "because so soon as Amos was out of sight, something deep down in my mind began to work against him, and my thoughts instantly turned to wondering if there was any way of escape."

"Your natural instinct is to make men miserable," I pointed out pretty sternly, "and now, when you've got one of them into a contented and happy state, you turn miserable yourself."

"Let her run on, my dear," begged Owlett. "You haven't heard the half yet."

"What followed went like this," murmured Mercy. "Miserable I certainly was—never more so—because my spirit had turned dead against Amos by now. I came home and brewed myself a cup of tea and wished Mr. Owlett was back, so I could consult him how to escape ; but it happed to be one of his late nights and I was sitting in the dark, too overcome even to light a candle, when there fell a knock to the door and I opened

and found how Miller Ford stood there. I said Mr. Owlett
was not at home; but he answered that he had come to see me.
'So you can light your candle and pay respectful attention to
what I shall tell you, Mercy.' Then I grasped the awful situation, that Ernest was bubbling over with the same savage
affection as Butt and come upon the self-same errand! There
was me—all battered and bruised after Amos had bullied me
into saying 'Yes'—and now I'd got to face up to the miller.
He began by saying he wasn't going to be toyed with no more.
He declared that enough was as good as a feast—not that I was
a feast by any means, but only a middle-aged fool that didn't
know her luck. Still he wanted me notwithstanding and was
going to have 'Yes' before he went home."

Mercy broke off to get her breath, and then I asked her
what happened next.

"Next," she answered, "before I knew what he was up to,
the man dragged me upon his lap, and very near squeezed the
life out of me and swore, by Almighty God, he wouldn't let
me down till I'd named the day! He bellowed again and again
and kissed me between every bellow. In fact, what with the
row he made and the love he made, he showed himself to be
a grand spectacle of devotion no doubt. Anyway he dazzled
me for the moment and, being by now fearful of what he might
do next, my mind got in such a mizmaze I must have thrown
up the sponge and taken him, for what followed was hearing
him say there could be no going back now and I might
thank my Maker that I had shown sense at last."

"Just her brute instinct for self-preservation made the
poor fool do it," explained John, "and I wish I had got home
sooner to send Ford packing and tell him he ought to be
ashamed of himself; but he'd gone before I got back, to find
her yowling her head off."

" 'Come Sunday the banns called'—that was nearly his
last words he said," concluded Mercy; "but he also told me
that he was just come from the 'Hearty Welcome', where he
had heard Amos Butt give out in the bar I had took him
once for all! 'I'm no law-breaker,' he said, 'so I merely told the
little snipe he was a cross-eyed liar and left the pub and
tramped straight to you!' Then Ernest marched away, full of

63

pride at what he'd done, and I sat and faced the mad situation —how I'd promised to marry two men and hated both of them worse than sin!"

That was Mercy's monstrous tale, and, having told it, she heaved a pitiful sigh, while Owlett also sighed.

"Her only way of escape looks to be an asylum where she'd be safe from tormenting men for ever more," he said, "but you're such a wonder that I've brought her on the chance you may see light in the darkness; and I'll pay for it willingly if you can."

"I've never heard of anything quite so near to flat lunacy as this, John," I confessed.

"Nor anybody else," he agreed. "No such piece of work ever happened in a Christian land to a Christian woman, I'd say."

Then Mercy got lighthearted again and began to titter faintly.

"When they both go to parson, he might tell them to toss up which is going to have me," she suggested; but my brains were running at full steam by now and taking the high line which puts them in a class beyond competition.

"No," I said. "There must be no laughing at your situation, Mercy, if you are going to get out of it without becoming a public laughing-stock yourself. There must be no talk of getting you certified and put away, nor yet of your being tossed up for. Steps must be taken at once, and it is for you to take 'em."

"Is there a chance," John asked, "that, when they find what she could sink to do, both men will chuck her and thank God they have escaped? That's the best could happen."

"They won't," declared Mercy. "They are hankering after me far too bad to chuck me."

I then discoursed, while they gave heed, and it was long after midnight before they left me. I showed Mercy how it looked to a mind like my own, and much astonished and bewildered her with the view of a road hid from her narrow vision and beyond her imagination till I unfolded it. Then they went off together.

"I shall be glad for your own sake, Mercy," I said, "if you

64

see it as I do, for that's the only way to clear you and polish up your faded credit in the public eye."

"Safety is all I want, dear Miss Crymes," she declared.

"And more than you deserve," so John told her.

The affair got out quick enough as such things will, and the very next day, when I travelled down to the village, I heard how both Butt and Ford were blazing out their victory. Amos told me the news himself, when I went in his store for a box of lucifers; while returning home, I met the miller's head man, who said his master was the winner and planning to wed Mercy Bassett at once before she changed her mind again. Packhorse Bridge stood divided as to what might be the outcome and which man his Reverence would call out on Sunday next; because all were agreed the choice must lie with him and, seeing Mercy had served Mrs. Walpole in the past, many reckoned that lady would cast the winning vote as to who was going to get her. Everybody liked the wayward woman very well and the people took a sporting interest in her fate.

I met John Owlett the next Friday. He drank at the 'Hearty Welcome' and, after telling me he had come round to my way of thinking and approved of it, he said the last time he went in for a pint that betting ran ten to one on the miller, because most felt certain Ernest would get parson's support, being Church of England, whereas Butt favoured the Wesleyan flock, which ran the Establishment pretty close among us. As for Mercy herself, she was reported to being seen going to the vicarage; but nobody could get a word with her, for she kept very close just then.

There came a bumper rally of neighbours to worship at Morning Prayer when Sunday arrived and I took my place among them. Ernest Ford was to the forefront as usual, bearing all the appearances of victory, and Amos Butt, in strange surroundings for him, sat humbly under the shadow of the font, and I do believe the Reverend Walpole, when he came to the appointed place, licked his lips before he gave out his bit of news. Anyway he kept up the excitement till the last minute and went so far as to name the woman first and hide the man till the final moment.

"I publish the banns of marriage between Mercy Bassett, spinster," he began, and paused for half a minute to gaze upon the assembly. Then he went on, "And John Owlett, widower, both of this parish."

Next he challenged anybody who knew just cause or impediment to declare it, and added that was the first time of asking.

There was a queer sound, like a covey of partridges rising, and everybody looked across at the pew where Mercy was used to sit with Mr. Owlett of a Sunday; but neither of them appeared.

I met Toby Snell, landlord of the 'Hearty Welcome', a day later and he told me what followed at the inn after service was over.

"We had a good laugh," he said, "and congratulated Owlett, who dropped in for his usual as soon as I opened. For all his grey hair John is only fifty-four; but he never thought to take a second until Mercy Bassett got in that fix and you struck one of your masterly strokes to get her out again. Then she never hesitated for a moment, but was down Owlett's throat like a frightened rabbit going to earth, and he gave way."

No doubt the Reverend Walpole had seen eye to eye with me that, of those three men regarded as a husband for Mercy, the water-keeper was most apt to succeed. And we were right, for as I remember she made John a capable wife. It was rumoured, early after their marriage, that she threatened to break loose once more; but she bore him a brace a year later and her twins anchored her hard and fast to a very good man.

Just one of my lesser flashes that was, but one to be welcomed at the time and leave its mark on a future generation. For I always took an interest in Bobby and Teddy Owlett, feeling to some extent responsible for them coming into the world. Those dangerous women, with the fatal habit of matchmaking for their own amusement, seldom look ahead in their scheming, or spare a thought for the unborn. But the real success or failure of the wedded state full often depends on whether the offspring make or mar it. None can tell how any parental blend will turn out, because what may hold for kine, or sheep, don't hold for humanity. I've often marked very bright fathers and mothers to produce a brood of born fools, while on the contrary the most everyday, commonplace folk may possibly hatch out some changeling boy, or girl, to set the sieve afire and beggar belief.

V

NOT long since I had light on a story that always interested me greatly and of which I thought the end was common knowledge. Yet it only came to me in truth two years ago and then blossomed out from the lips of an ancient man at the point to die. By rights this queer tale belongs to my mother, and many a time she related it to me, but she never let out that herself was at the root of the matter, or said a word to link her craft with the adventure. It concerned a lot of the upper people and gentry now in their graves, though very much alive in their time. Yet there my mother was—the linchpin of the entire affair—though so great her foresight and caution, that she kept close shut on the subject all her life.

Now, bedridden and crushed down by weight of time, did Joshua Merry send a message to me and told me he was wishful for me to visit him. He also bade me to respond quickly before he went to earth, which he hoped to do very shortly. For years he had been the veteran of the parish, where he was born and to which he finally returned. He lived to the age of ninety-six and I'd known him all my life as a friend of my mother and kept in touch with him for her sake; but he lacked for friends after he turned ninety, because his generation was all dead by that time and his dark view of things in general could not commend him to many among the middle-aged, or be anything but right down hateful to the young. He lived in one of our small alms-houses and looked after himself till he was called to take to bed; but now an old woman, still spry and with her wits about her, spent most of her time along with him, and the parish nurse tended to his requirements.

It was some five-and-forty years ago that I received his last message and went at his command, expecting only the usual acid views he was wont to utter, and hear him curse his aches and pains and the universe at large and everybody in it, for if the Lord ever put any milk of human kindness into Joshua Merry, it was long ago dried up to the last drop. His views of the quality were not such as I could repeat, but what he had to tell me concerned them for, from boyhood, he had worked at Oaklands, and though those who ruled there in his youth were long sped, he remembered the old days and the small part he played at the manor all those years agone.

"I'm come to your commands, Joshua," I said, "and brought you a bit of shag for your pipe."

Then I put it in his hand and he nodded and I sat down at his bedside.

"Thank you, Cherry," he answered. "Only parson ever brings me a pinch nowadays."

"Very kind of him."

"He comes in and we talk of fox-hunting. For a devil-dodger the reverend gentleman's tolerable well up on that subject: better riding to hounds than in his pulpit most like."

Then he went on how he was wishful to tell me the old tale, and I said I'd heard it many times from my mother, because it happened within her memory when she was still a young woman.

Joshua hardly looked his age. He was very thin and his eyes were clouded by cataract, but false teeth had preserved his mouth from falling in and his snow-white hair, though scanty, was still evenly distributed upon his poll. He was underhung and you could see his big chin through the remaining tatters of his beard. He wore a red, flannel bed-jacket buttoned up to his neck and his bed-linen was clean, his chamber tidy and his peat fire burning bright.

"Yes," he said, "it happened in her memory all right when she was yet a maid, but there's details she was pleased to forget when telling about it, and they will be lost for ever with me if I don't hand 'em down. Load my pipe, Cherry, and I'll discourse. My tubes be clear for the minute and I can talk."

Mrs. Bolt, who watched over him, came in at this moment with a glass of hot milk.

"Let it down, Joshua, before you start, and don't smoke till you've finished," she said. "When you talk and smoke at once you always choke yourself."

"Be off, woman," he answered. "I'm telling secrets with

69

Cherry Crymes, but not for your ears nor any other chatter-box."

Then Mrs. Bolt laughed and went her way.

Then he started with the old story, in which as a boy he took a place none now ever remembered but himself.

"Before your time, naturally, and very near before mine, for I was only twelve years old when it happened—a stable-lad at Oaklands, where the Scobell family lorded it then. A very fine race, but it was said that a bad Scobell always followed a good one. The bad would lay waste and ruin with his dice and his women, then the good would turn up and devote his days to paying debts and healing sores and getting the ship on to an even keel again. But bad and good are only words, and if a man's a sportsman and plays the game, whether he's the rake-hell sort, or the pious, 'tis all one," declared Joshua, and then he set about his tale.

"Well, there's two men in it, and a horse, and, of course, a woman. There's Oaklands where Captain Gerald Scobell ruled then, and there's the manor of Clyst St. Mark, which marches with Oaklands and is let nowadays to a tobacco merchant. In my youth, Sir Norman Voysey had just followed his father at Clyst St. Mark. He was a baronite and a good lad and well thought upon—a plain dealer, a fair landlord to his people and promising to spend his money like a gentleman. My father and mother belonged there, father being head woodsman and mother dairymaid at the home farm, and Sir Norman Voysey's mother was very well addicted to both my parents. As for me, it happened that Sir Norman's neighbour wanted a stable-boy for the minute and father applied for me and Captain Scobell let me have the job. He was counted a bad member of his race, with the sort of badness about which there's no two opinions. I mind him well enough for he was a hero to the young. I've felt his hunting-crop on my back, but never very hard, because he found I was clever with horses. Horses were my gods, and as good gods as any others, and I'd stand up to horses that frighted most youngsters, but never frighted me. My master had an evil temper, yet lacked the virtues that often go with they fierce and fiery men. He was bone selfish and lived for his own comfort and amusement alone. He had only one quality

70

you can boast upon, and that's courage. He'd fought well against France and never ceased to brag about the foreigners he'd slain in his time; but when peace returned, he came home to rule at Oaklands. He'd outface the county in dangerous sports and left a great record for horsemanship behind him; but a lot of cruelty went with his pluck and he didn't care if he tortured a horse to death so long as it carried him to some fresh triumph. He was a great shotsman too, and never such another as him with a pistol, for he could write his initial letters at twenty yards on a barn door, or so it was said.

"Round about thirty-five years old he was—a lean, tough customer with good thighs for a horse and wonderful hands. A brown, weatherbeaten man, with a drooping lid over one of his black eyes and a blue chin said to be shaved twice daily. But such friends as he had knew how to get round him, for he was terrible vain and liked his butter laid on thick. He spent his time in sporting and kept a close eye over his money. The man took a lot of care of his body and didn't drink nor yet smoke, for smoking wasn't the rage in those days that it has grown to be now.

"So that was Captain Gerald Scobell, and of course he knew his neighbour, Sir Norman, and they pursued the same fashion of interests and enjoyed the same amusements, except that Voysey lived a quieter and honester sort of life and was better thought upon. The Captain had a lot the most money and the bigger estates, but they carried on in friendship and each kept his opinion of t'other to himself. Lady Voysey, the baronite's mother, looked after her son and daughter and Clyst St. Mark, and a very good sort she was said to be, but Scobell lacked any kinswoman to keep his house and said he'd be damned before ever he went in chains to a female. He tried a mistress at Oaklands for a bit, but his housekeeper and his butler and one or two other old domestic servants gave warning at that and he got wind how the county was making an uproar against him, so he sent the woman packing and played for safety; but was never forgiven by the bettermost."

Joshua took a minute's rest and lighted his pipe. He cut himself off from the present and was silent and buried in the past for a few minutes, then went on with the tale.

71

"It was round about then that I first came to Oaklands as a nipper and had my fill of blood-horses and was suffered to put a leg over one for the first time. They soon found I was born for the job, and the Captain, after seeing me take a young horse over hurdles, showed a bit of interest. He raced at West Country Meetings and he let me ride an old 'chaser' on one such occasion. I won by a length and he was pleased, and I took a lot of pride to pleasure a man who rarely had a word of praise for those he employed.

"That's how it was when there came a Mr. Philip Waverley to Hill Crest—a moderate-sized property two miles away."

"A smart place once, but a ruin now," I said.

"That's so. There was Mr. Waverley and his widowed sister and his daughter. That was the family. He had retired from trade and come to live alongside Dartmoor. A go-by-the-ground sort of man and nothing accounted of, because the gentry didn't know shopkeepers, retired or otherwise, in them days. But young men will always be very willing to know a pretty girl whatever her havage, and Ann Waverley was a lot more than pretty. There are painted pictures of her yet, I believe; but no man ever painted her within a mile of truth. The most amazing piece of female loveliness, enough to make common folk believe there might be something in the talk about angels. I saw her often when I came to manhood and always got the same creepy feeling about her. A fair girl, light built, head carried high, big grey eyes, a lovely mouth and a fearless nature, which she showed in the hunting field, because she was a brave huntress.

"Well, Philip Waverley, with an eye to her future perhaps, was said to have had Ann educated a good bit above her station; but be that as it may, there's no doubt her natural gifts and fine order of intellects would have put her beyond most young women in any rank of life. A creature such as her couldn't be hid under a bushel anyway, and the first time she rode to hounds she created a proper sensation at the meet and woke a powerful interest in the company assembled.

"Mr. Waverley, whatever he was by trade, had an eye for a horse and a clever understanding of them. He came to his first meet of hounds along with his girl and received the usual civilities of the hunting field, and he conducted himself quite correct and showed he knew the sport. He rode hard and he rode well and cut a very fair figure for a man not born and bred to it. And Miss did all right also, and the huntsman of the Mid-Devons in those days told my father after, if ever he'd seen an angel on horseback, 'twas on that occasion. But Ann Waverley weren't the sort just to fill the eye of one man here, or one man there: she had a quality of beauty that king or tinker alike must bend to."

Old Joshua mused upon that vanished vision, which was evidently still clear to his fading eyes, and then he rambled forward again.

"These things, of course, were all hid from me at the time they happened, but I heard tell about 'em from my mother's lips when I was allowed home to Packhorse Bridge now and again to see my parents, and it looked very clear to the parish that Sir Norman Voysey, from the first day he catched sight of Ann, was shook to the roots. Twenty-five years old then and had never thought to wed yet awhile, so when he begged for his mother to call upon the newcomers, Lady Voysey began to be anxious and put about and felt she need to grow watchful on her son's account. But Sir Norman's sister, Miss Linette, she was called, put her brother before all the world and held he could do no wrong. She met the Waverleys in the hunting field and had speech with Ann and told her mother that the maiden was a fairy changeling and no less, and did ought to be seen and heard before judgment could be given against her or her family. The young ones kept at their task and, in the upshot, Lady Voysey drove over to Hill Crest with her daughter and called upon Miss Waverley and the aunt that lived with her. And her ladyship was properly received and couldn't deny but she had got a seemly welcome, and couldn't deny that all she had heard about Ann looked to be true. The families got to be good friends and Miss Linette lost no chance to serve her brother. Indeed the two maidens soon found themselves to be very addicted to each other from the first and Mr. Philip Waverley, when he came before her ladyship, conducted himself in a dignified manner.

"Then came the tremendous news from Oaklands that

Captain Scobell had fallen for Ann also and had cast his famous opinions about women to the winds, meant to marry her and weren't going to let man or devil come between him and the girl! And, knowing what he was, few but reckoned he'd darned soon cut out Sir Norman and carry off Ann Waverley from under her father's nose if he had to do so. For once I could bring a bit of news home with me, because I heard our head groom at the stables talk to the butler, who had got it from Mr. Waverley's own valet. Captain Gerald was far too downy from the first to rub Ann's father the wrong way. He went about his job very clever, started to win over Waverley and sold him a very fine horse, up to his weight and at a rubbish price, for friendship. He made much of Waverley's ladies also and had 'em to Oaklands and showed 'em the fat of the land. For nobody could play a part better than the Captain when he was set to make a new friend. Not that he often laid himself out to please, for he'd got all the world could give him and money counts more than manners with most folk. So it soon came to be known that Philip Waverley smiled upon my master and wasn't going to stand in his way so long as the settlements went to his liking and Ann found herself satisfied with the bargain.

"It was then I first saw the lady close, and my boy's wits were sharp enough to mark something else and see it weren't all over bar shouting by any means between her and my master. There came a day when the Captain brought Ann into the stables to look over his splendid horses, and I led out half a dozen of 'em for her to cast her eyes upon. And even then I could mark she wasn't so pleased with the Scobell as what he was with her. A lovely sight in her dark, bottle-green habit and ostrich feather in her hat. She'd ridden over with her father to take luncheon : sunshine on a dark day.

"Then the master had out his great hunter, by name of 'Baal'—a black stallion with a temper like hell one day and so good as gold the next. He hated his master, who'd broke him in himself, and Scobell knew he hated him and liked to best him. He sauced the horse before Ann and told her what an uncertain brute he was and what a wonder; and then he slapped 'Baal' on the cheek in a contemptuous fashion and

74

took liberties with the great horse to show he didn't fear him. But, like all of us, he kept clear of his stern, because 'Baal' could whip a kick short and sudden as a pistol shot, like a half-arm blow at boxing, and he'd killed a good fox-hound that way and broke a groom's leg into the bargain, before the boy was warned.

"And then I saw out of the corner of my eye that Mistress Ann didn't like Captain Gerald's behaviour. She flinched when he slapped 'Baal's' jowl and bade him, in a voice so cold as ice, to give over. And she told him to his face how she hated to hear a man saying insulting things or doing insulting things to one that could not answer back. And when Scobell spoke to her again presently—very humble with his tail between his legs—she didn't answer a word, but looked at him out of lovely grey eyes with just such a look as I'd often seen his horse give the man. And I grinned in my heart and thought what he'd store up for her if ever he got her.

"That's how it was when the next piece of news came from Hill Crest, and the parish heard that my master had offered for Ann and been declined. There was a brave upstore about the business, because her father put Scobell's wealth above all comers and as good as promised the maiden to him. He took no chances and got her father's support first; but Ann Waverley refused to take the man once and for all, and her reasons appeared soon after. She'd fallen in love with Sir Norman Voysey and was wishful to wed him; but when the baronite paid a duty visit to Mr. Waverley, after all was settled between him and the maiden, he got a blunt refusal. Which events were noised abroad through the Waverley serving staff and soon came to be known far and wide.

"Of course you can see what next happened behind the scenes. Philip Waverley and the Captain got together and Scobell heard what he was up against, but told Ann's father that he would darned soon deal with Sir Norman, and the next step could be left to him.

"A tricky job of this sort was well in the Captain's powers to handle, and being a man little used to opposition, he reckoned that once Sir Norman and his nonsense was swept away, the girl would come round to him. He was too vain to think he'd been fairly bested, but imagined no doubt that Ann was took by a title and would very soon change her mind. Because he doubtless reckoned that a woman with the brains and foresight of Ann was not such a fool as to put the baronite before a man like him."

Old Merry pictured the scene and looked to be figuring out the matter pretty much as it must have happened.

"They say all's fair in love," he went on, "but that's another of them smooth lies we're prone to. Once folk are properly sunk in love and mad to share it, they ain't masters of themselves any more. The Captain well knew there wasn't any straight or sportsmanlike way to conquer Ann if she truly loved Sir Norman, but he was faced with just such a bit of dirty work as he cared best to handle and he didn't waste no time about it neither. But for a bit he burrowed like a mole out of sight, and laid his plans unbeknown to his neighbours.

"How much Sir Norman and his sister knew about what was going forward, none can say, but they wouldn't hear nothing from Ann, because she wasn't the sort to let out another had offered for her, and though no doubt by then Sir Norman understood very clear Ann's father didn't want him for a son-in-law, he only felt himself and Ann faced with a demand for patience and the hope that Waverley would come round, given time. 'Tis clear that the young man had no idea who was fighting against him, for Captain Gerald kept as friendly as usual with the baronite and hid his game very close till the crash burst on 'em. That fell out when a dinner-party was given at Clyst St. Mark, and my master was one of the guests; and the next bit of spicy news burst out from there.

"A small company assembled—twelve all told, so we heard—and Scobell rode over on an early November afternoon to take his place thereat. Then, after the females were gone from the table and the men left to their walnuts and drinking, the bolt came from the blue.

"'Twas after port wine had gone round a brace of times that the Captain took his first step, and the ladies hadn't gone more than half an hour when he differed sharply with his host over some trifling opinion, and said sneering words to gall the younger man. Cool as a cucumber he kept, no doubt, and edged to his plot and then, being crossed in argument, pretended to let his fury go. A footman was in the room at the moment and saw what happened. He'd come in with more wine, when he heard the rising babel and everybody talking at once and rising from their seats and the wax candles flickering a bit under the row. Then up leapt Scobell and told Sir Norman he was a damned liar and flung a glass of wine across his face.

"Well, in those days you couldn't insult a gentleman at his own dining-table—not if you was a gentleman yourself—without risking your life for it, and as the Captain very well knew, there was only one way out of that rumpus. He also knew that Sir Norman was going to be the challenger, and so he himself would have choice of weapons.

" 'Get out of my house, you dirty dog!' roared Sir Norman at the man. 'You'll hear from me tomorrow!' And the Captain said he couldn't hear too quick and told the flunkey to bid 'em fetch his horse round, and so went forth from the company.

"It was a plant, of course, and that had happened which the scoundrel meant to happen; but old Mr. Watts, an uncle of young Voysey, who was visiting Clyst St. Mark at the time and the only man who had kept his head and watched the row, said afterwards that it had been provoked of set purpose and for one reason only. He declared that if the case was set before a jury of gentlemen, they wouldn't have let young Voysey go out; but of course Sir Norman wasn't that sort and would never have took a lesser stand than a duel. Such things were kept quiet, unless they ended in death for one or other man, and was never known to the public.

"Then came what I saw myself, on a rough morning seven days later, and it was the cream of the tale, though only one tongue but mine could have told it."

"And what man still lives who knows as much as you do, Merry?" I asked and he showed vexation.

"Don't be shoving your oar in," he snapped out. "Keep your mouth shut and list to me."

"Sorry, my dear," I answered. " 'Twas very bad manners to interrupt you."

He forgave me and went forward again.

"Silence settled down over all concerned then, but the

77

challenge went and was accepted and the place of meeting determined and a doctor given the office to be there. Exactly when and where they were going to fight none knew but themselves, and not a woman guessed what was afoot; but the fate of Sir Norman hung over his servants, for he was well liked among them and all felt a good bit put about that he should be trapped to his death in this fashion, for nobody doubted how it must go.

"The day before the adventure my master came to me and said a queer word. 'Have "Baal" saddled and ready for me at half after five o'clock tomorrow,' he ordered. 'Keep your mouth shut, Josh, and don't tell a living soul.' He pitched me half a crown and he knew he could trust me, but little guessed that I was aware what he ordained to do next morning. He would go forth to shoot Sir Norman, and I felt so sorry about it as a child could be expected to feel for the troubles of grown-up people. The Oaklands men were talking that night, though they didn't guess the fight would come off next morn, and I heard them say that the duel would be fought out with pistols and that Captain Scobell was never known to miss his mark, but Sir Norman, though fond of sport as any man, was no great hand with firearms. So I went to my cubby-hole downhearted and restless and in no mind to sleep. The stable clock rung out the hours but I didn't hear 'em till it told five, and then I rose and looked after 'Baal' and set about him. That was always my work and I felt very jealous of it and nobody ever envied me, but it had long been discovered the horse, though not friendly to many, felt kindly to me and liked for me to talk to him and liked me around him better than the rest of us. The Captain had soured 'Baal' a bit, I reckon, and the creature couldn't be trusted very far at best of times. But he loved hunting and understood in some queer fashion that, when he was going to be rode by a man in pink, there would be sport for them both. He was asleep on his legs when my lantern and my voice awoke him, for the dawn was just offering to break and stars still shining out of a clear sky and the owls answering each other on their way home. He didn't much like being roused up so early and still less favoured being fetched out and saddled for a bit of work. I offered him an apple, which was his favourite food, but he wouldn't bite to it and I could feel he didn't take kindly to the morning. I walked the horse up and down for half an hour and then took him to the upping-stock at a spot under the chestnut trees outside the forecourt, where his master always mounted. There I saddled him just as Captain Scobell arrived, and to my astonishment the master wore his scarlet hunting-coat! For a moment 'Baal' stood in two minds between seeing him in pink and seeing him at all, for he hated Scobell even on his most amiable days. But it was the fashion always to wear black if a man was going to fight a duel and I didn't hear till long after that Captain Gerald meant to ride to his destination clad for hunting to pleasure 'Baal', and then put on black to murder Sir Norman.

" 'How's the brute this morning?' he asked me.

" 'He didn't much like being roused up, your honour,' I answered.

"The Captain gave his usual, cruel laugh and said, 'Well, we'll go hunting.'

"With that he mounted the upping-stock, while I held his steed so steady as I might and, the moment he'd got his leg over him and was in the saddle, ran for my life. But Scobell didn't laugh no more that day."

Joshua kept silent for a minute now and lighted his pipe once again, though he only took a puff or two and then set it down.

"The way was clear," he continued, "and 'Baal' danced off on his hind legs, threatening fire and fury under the trees and there was light enough now to mark his antics. Down he came presently and then bucked and bucked again, and, child though I was, I could see the man upon him was going to have his work cut out if he meant to stop there. 'Baal' didn't behave that way at his worst as a rule and I saw that his master himself was a good bit astonished. At another time he would have enjoyed the battle and kept cool and fought it out to a finish; but this was a morning when he'd want his nerves quiet and his eyes clear and his pistol hand steady, so he was vexed with the horse from the start.

"But the Captain kept his temper for a bit, though 'Baal' was properly mad from the start and acted as if every imp out

79

of hell had got in him. All over the shop he was and going from bad to worse; and very soon Scobell knew that he'd have a job to keep his appointment that morning. There was a proper tug-of-war now, and I could hear the horse screaming with rage—a scream I'd never heard from any horse before and a very ugly sound to hear if you was sitting upon him at the time. And then the certain thing happened and the man got angry too, and when a bad-tempered man and a bad-tempered horse clash together, it don't take long for something final to happen. The Captain tried to quell him and get him going and put the fear of God in with a bit of sharp agony, so he leant forward and hit 'Baal' with his hunting-crop across the side of the face. With all his might he struck twice; but he loosed his rein hand for half a second with the blow and the horse's head was thrown up and his neck would have broke the gentleman's neck if he hadn't been swift as lightning to escape it. But in that flurry 'Baal' had got the bit clamped in his teeth, and started to gallop, and I wondered where he would take himself and his rider. It wasn't going to be far, because the horse, blinded and raving, turned up the slope into the spinney outside our forecourt like a streak of darkness through the autumn blaze of falling leaves showing their colour under the morning light. And I ran after them so fast as I could, because I knew that ten seconds or less under the trees was going to see the end of man, or horse, or both. They were swiftly swallowed up in the wood and, before you could tell it, came the devil of a crash and one shout and no more. A brace of pheasants flew high overhead with a rare clatter, and then all still as a church-yard.

"I crept in and soon found the man all squashed in his pink coat and crumpled up face downward beneath a hugeous bough that had taken him breast-high and smote him off the horse; and ten yards farther on was 'Baal' fallen on his side, with his right foreleg broken under the knee and very near torn off his body. He had run into a tree-bole head first and was near dead. He would have to die in any case now and I mourned for him and tended him and took the saddle off. He opened his eyes and heaved a bit but didn't move again. And then I had a look at the Captain and saw his neck was broken and his breastbones driven in. But I didn't lay a finger on him: I ran back and woke up the house and told what had befallen.

"A parcel of men came running in no time at my direction; and one got on a horse and rode for doctor and others fetched a hurdle and brought in the corpse. Then Will Ford, head groom—a merciful man by nature—got a fowling-piece and loaded it with ball and finished 'Baal'. It was just after that when two gentlemen came galloping up the main drive. They were the dead man's seconds for his duel, and they'd been waiting for him by appointment at a cross-roads three miles off called 'Milly's Grave', because a noted witch was buried there many years ago, being denied holy ground.

"Finding Captain Scobell didn't arrive, the gentlemen had rode over to seek him and I was pushed forward to tell them the tale; and when they heard tell, they had a look at their friend, then went off, hell for leather, to where Sir Norman and others were waiting for the morning's work.

"And that was the finish of Captain Gerald and his merry innings. The Crowner sat on him and the jury fetched in 'Death by misadventure'.

"Before another year was over Sir Norman done two things. He took up a mastership and married; and, as Master of Fox-hounds and husband of Ann Waverley, gave a good account of himself.

"I went back to Clyst St. Mark after the Captain was done for and got work at the kennels under the baronite and was a whipper-in at twenty-one and a second huntsman at thirty-one."

"That's all very well, Joshua," I said, "and you have told the story very clever; but 'tis all old stuff, my dear man, and nothing new."

I rose up a bit disappointed, but he bade me list a little longer.

"Sit down," he said. "I didn't send for you to hear no old story but the end of this one, because only your mother and me knew the end, and now you shall. You see, that beastly soldier, Captain Scobell, didn't die what you may call a natural death, because it was me that killed him, and I've laughed in my sleeve for many long years to think how a rubbishy stable-boy could alter the face of Nature and make history and keep one man in the land of the living and send another where he rightly belonged—to hell. Very amusing, if you look at it the right way, and a great source of satisfaction to me all my life."

I peered into his dim old eyes and he grinned as he spoke.

"Go on," I said. "I doubt you're lying, my dear man, but tell on."

"This is where your mother comes in," he answered, "and I ain't lying neither. Why for should I? Too late to hang me now. Hark back to me that night, when I couldn't sleep and kept saying to myself that my master was going to kill a better man than himself next morning, and didn't ought to be allowed, and must be stopped at any cost if I could only find how. It was then your mother rose up in my mind, for though but a young woman she was noted for cleverness and had done things I'd heard the people praise."

"Her gifts came down from my great-grandmother and she handed them on to me," I told him.

"Be that as it may, the thought of her drove me up and out and off that night. It wanted best part of three miles to Owl Pen, but I got there. By night I went and beat on the door, and your mother looked down from her window to know who wanted her at such an hour, and I told her it was me come on a parlous business from Oaklands to learn what I should do. She knew all about what was afoot and came down and heard how I stood and was terrible interested in all I had to say. She gave me food and drink and told me what looked to be a very fine thing to do if I had the nerve and strength to do it. 'There's danger for you,' she said, 'and I shan't think none the worse of you if you dare not; but if you dare, then you'll do what you want to do and be a·bit of a hero, and the right man may be killed instead of the wrong one.' She properly strung me up to fighting pitch and I set my mind on doing what she told me to do, no matter what might come of it. I went back that night full of the plot; but kept my nerve till the right moment came, and then, as I saddled 'Baal', put three chestnut burrs under the saddle and drew home the girths so gentle as need be. That meant hell let loose so soon as the Captain was on him; but the end I couldn't know and all turned for me on

82

what was going to follow, and how chance-ordained it should turn out. A dozen different things might have overtook them but I felt from the first it was long odds I'd get out of it safe. I had planned to disappear for good and all if ever the truth came out, because then I was going to be a doomed boy; but everything went dead right and Providence looked after the details and took care of me well enough. The man perished but a stone's-throw from his own gateway and I was there on the spot to nip off the horse's saddle and hide my work from every eye. Your mother praised me to the skies afterwards, but she warned me solemn enough never to let vanity and thirst for fame loosen my tongue to any living creature. And never it did till this minute."

Joshua had shot his bolt by now and grown tired and sleepy, so I thanked him very heartily and said how he'd given me a lot to think about.

"Nobody could have found that tale better to the purpose than what I do," I told him, "because it shows my mother had just the same fine craft and quality as my great-grandmother. And in my turn it is handed down to me. A feather in her cap it was to hit upon such a clever feat, and just what I might have done myself, Joshua. And greatly to your credit too—just a green boy as you were then."

"I reckoned you was like to take it in a proper sporting spirit," he answered. "A smart old devil like you was sure to give me a pat on the back, and when I'm gone you can let it be known. I could tell you another fine tale about Lady Ann some day if I live to do it."

"I'll see you again before very long," I promised him, but never heard him croak out another adventure, for a fortnight.

VI

IF YOUR mind is built to take the long look forward and never content that tomorrow shall watch over itself, then, like me, you are one who views the future as child of the present.

Which shows how often it requires a very gifted and long-sighted mind to weigh actions in the balance, measure their promise of success against their threat of failure and convince your reasoning powers which course is most trustable to perform, or likely to miscarry.

In the matter of Abednego Bragg, who was one of the most interesting human creatures of my experience, a further challenge appeared in the problems that man created for me, because he was not as other men, and there is nothing more difficult to deal with than a crippled mind and the gloom that so many half-witted people throw around them.

The nature of Mr. Bragg's plight always formed argument among folk at Packhorse Bridge, for he did not go under total eclipse all his time. Today he might be like everybody else, or even more intelligent than the most of us; tomorrow, so likely as not, he'd wake up mad as a hatter, though never at any time a peril to his neighbours; and when he stood in a middle state, he sufficed to puzzle everybody, because, in those bygone days when he lived, all the direful things that put a curb on the wheels of reason were not understood and conquered as now they often are. But when Abednego first came for me to throw light on his stormy wits, he might well have beggared any doctoring. Indeed, from my bird's-eye perch, I'd say that his case was more in keeping with the present, feverish and hysterical times than in those steady-going, sober-sided days. For there is a lot more madness in the rising generation than there was among people at large when Bragg went his haunted way.

To learn the situation as it came before me, I must set out the story of the man himself and his history before these strange things overtook him. He was middle-aged when he revealed his wounded mind to me and the amazing tangle where it had landed him. Bragg was a moneyed man, the only son of a publican famous in his day. Noah Bragg kept the 'White Lion' at Moreton, made good money and had a big following for many years; but when he died, Abednego sold everything and came to live at Packhorse Bridge. He was round about thirty-five then and not very fond of work, but liked peace and quiet and a bit of fishing, which was his only sport. He married Mildred Parsons, and it was not until he'd been wed ten years that his mind began to rock and show symptoms not to be mistaken. Everybody liked him because he was gentle and kindly by nature and generous to help a good cause when he met with such. Not a few amongst us argued that, if he had kept single, he would also have kept sane. They blamed his downfall upon his wife, because Milly Parsons never took him except as a matter of business and only for his money and the position he could give her. She always slighted the man himself, but claimed to do her duty by him and try to teach him that his virtues of friendship and good-willing were a weakness and apt to be bad business. He was no fighter but a lot too humble-minded in Milly's opinion, and his men friends were also the humble go-by-the-ground sort and so no use to her. Women friends she wouldn't let him have in any case.

'Bed', as the people always called him, struck up one curious friendship, which his wife hated, and that was with the sexton of the parish, a man called Weston Churchward. He was a nice enough chap and, after a year or two, Weston and Bragg grew into a great regard for each other, shared the same prime pleasure of fishing and enjoyed each other's company at all times when possible. The River Dart was their playground, while such was their attachment that, when Churchward was too busy about his work to go after the trout, 'Bed' would wander down to the burying yard and sit and watch his friend grave-digging and such like. The sexton was a widower with one son, and 'Bed's' affection extended to Willy Churchward, a very nice lad of twenty-one years old who helped his father at the churchyard. The Braggs had no family, but an orphan niece of 'Bed's' wife dwelt with them and ministered to their needs. Susan Crocker was her name and she liked her uncle well enough, but feared her aunt. Indeed there is no doubt that Mrs. Bragg was a fearsome type of person. She was mean beyond all decent bounds of thrift and, when the cloud rose over her husband, she would have liked to put him away but dared not attempt such a thing, though she made a lot of it and told everybody that it was a cross put on her by the Lord and must be borne with patience. But she exerted more and more authority over him and made him work in the garden and docked his old liberty as far as she might. It was in the garden that a side of his queerness first appeared, when he took to mixing flowers and vegetables and have sweet peas ramping with his runner beans, and marigolds in the potato patch and other wild touches like that.

But what his wife dreaded most was about 'Bed's' money, because she'd long wanted to get control over that and hated him to be openhanded and giving. So now, with the doctors and lawyers on her side, she got his income and savings in her keeping and was satisfied that he would not be able to write any last will and testament against her. 'Bed' was willing enough and quite contented with a pound a week for his tobacco and fishing and nightly round at the 'Hearty Welcome', while she tightened the reins very gradual so that he should not feel the pinch too sudden. But he didn't like his wife by now, being quite sane enough to know she proclaimed him a cross from God ; and when a man's better half looks upon him in that light to the whole parish, it is only human nature, whether sane or lunatic, that he should lose his affection for the woman.

The poor chap was always sane enough to know himself mad and marred by his Maker through no fault of his own. He'd tell anybody who had time to listen that it was a most ill-convenient thing and he wouldn't have had it happen for a fortune if he could have helped it. And again and again he'd break out with such sensible opinions that many vowed he was sane as the best and a lot wittier[1] than most. But then suddenly, upon his steadiest hours, would come his fatal weakness and his eyes would roll and he'd utter vain opinions, such as that

[1] Wittier=Cleverer.

his wife was turning into a house spider under his eyes, or that he'd marked the apple trees were all bearing pears this year, and so on.

He went his harmless way and found abiding happiness along with Weston Churchward. Then came round an early spring morning when trout-fishing was lawful once more—a red-letter day for both men which they had looked forward to all the winter. So, armed for their sport, they set forth as usual, full of the hope that never deserts the angling kind. But conditions were all against them that morning, because rain had fallen in fierce and obstinate fashion upon the Dartmoors for a week and their river—the East Dart, swollen into a proper torrent, was flooding the vale and choking the bogs round about and foaming and shouting and filling the air with a riot of noise that echoed back and forth amid the tors. The men were masters at throwing a fly, of course, and they knew every stickle and hover where the best fish homed; but a fly was out of the question that foul morning so, while scorning to use worm as a rule, they knew it must be done on this occasion if they didn't break their record of never failing to kill a fish on the opening day.

So they fished with worm and soon got their reward though always somewhat shamed to take their victims with that mean bait. They quickly had enough and were just going to wind up and return home when, as destiny would have it, they must throw a last line at a spot where the river was used to tumble over an apron of granite boulders into a deep run below always good for trout. But today the fall had changed into a proper cauldron of cherry-coloured water lashed with yellow spume. The usual conditions were all altered and the banks overflowed so that even an experienced eye could not say where the verge of the stream ended and the foothold was no longer trustable.

Then their accident overtook them and in a moment, as he hove his worm into the welter, 'Bed' outstepped the brink and was in the river with no bottom for his feet and nought to lay hold upon. He got swept out into the main current like a straw and with no better chance than the wriggling worm upon his hook; but Churchward just caught a glimpse of his terrified face as he opened his mouth and gurgled out a shout of terror.

'Twas do or die then, and the sexton, a brave man by his nature, acted instanter, cast off his heavy coat and went in after his friend, to save him, or perish along with him as fate might will. Both men could swim in a fashion, but it was good luck and not skill that saved their lives at the time, for, as Weston got swept to 'Bed' and gripped him, both reached ground with their feet where the river shoaled again and Bragg held on to a tree branch above their heads and Churchward held on to him. In another half minute they were both out of danger and standing dripping on safe ground.

The spot so near to being fatal lay well down East Dart, on the way to join with her sister river at Watersmeet, and the men had most of a mile over the rain-swept valley to get home again; but they made it at the best pace they could muster in their exhaustion, and Bragg left his friend at his cottage and then travelled home himself, where Milly and Susan Crocker looked after him and got him into hot blankets and made soup for him and listened to his tale. Elsewhere his son, Willy, ministered to his father and put him to bed and sat up with him all night because Churchward showed signs that the cold water and the exertion and the long tramp home had done something evil to him.

Next morning 'Bed' rose up none the worse and thanked God for it; but he wouldn't take his breakfast before he went to see if all was well with Weston. Yet he soon returned home stricken and cast down beyond measure, for he found a kinswoman with the sexton and Willy gone for the doctor.

"He's parlous sick and wandering in his mind," so Bragg told his wife, "and something tells me that the man's going to die. Then I'll be called to answer for murder as an infamous character that slew the man who saved him, because to slay the man who saved your life is a deed of treachery worse than Judas!"

The poor fellow was difficult to handle, no doubt, and when his fear came true and three days later Weston Churchward did die, of lung troubles beyond the skill of the doctors to cure, 'Bed' wandered the countryside like a lost dog, crying out that he had slain his only friend on earth and shouting to know why the people did not lay hands upon him and crucify him for a wicked rogue beyond the forgiveness of heaven or earth. Henceforth he dedicated himself to the dead man's son and set Willy first and highest in his remaining worldly interests.

Beside Weston's grave in the burying plot, 'Bed' rested not until he had secured the next pightel of land for himself when his turn came, and there he spent no little of his days in future. Willy Churchward had always felt kindly to his father's friend, and after the young man was suffered to fill the sexton's place, dig the people's graves and tend the little yard, he would welcome Bragg and let him help to keep the spot decent and in order.

When the time came to lift a memorial to the bygone man, 'Bed' begged his wife for a little money to set up a fine tombstone and, with much difficulty, extracted five pounds from Milly, since there were no members of the Churchward family who could furnish the cash to do so. She little liked to disgorge so much, but for peace consented and also promised her husband to pay for an exactly similar stone over his grave when he should go. Mrs. Bragg had it all her own way with the family fortune by then, and being a miser by nature, liked better to hoard it beside her so she could touch it and count it now and again. She mistrusted investments, but while more than half her husband's money was out at interest, some thousands Milly kept beneath her own roof, piled up in secret against her future freedom, when 'Bed' was taken. She always contemplated the luxury of riches in days to come.

Folk expected that his terrible upset when Churchward died would quicken 'Bed's' weakness of mind, but though he hid himself a lot from his fellow men for a time and was no more seen for months at the 'Hearty Welcome' and never forgathered at the bridge for a talk with neighbours upon Sundays according to local custom, yet he continued kindly and gentle as usual. He took up his fishing again, though never more known to angle in the fatal pool where Churchward had got his death-blow.

Then there rose a situation that was commonplace enough in itself, yet, by nature of things, made for trouble in a small way. Susan Crocker, who lived with the Braggs and served them, fell in love with Willy Churchward and he fell in love with her. They suited each other very well and both had youth and energy and a great longing to join up and clear off Dartmoor and enter upon a united life where prospects looked to be more full of promise. So they announced themselves to be tokened and fired with hope of a united career away from Packhorse Bridge and maybe far away from their native land and in foreign parts if all went well. But they found there was going to be sharp opposition both from 'Bed' and his wife, though for different reasons. Mrs. Bragg proved dead against it from the beginning, and declared horror that Susie should lower herself to think twice about a penniless grave-digger; while young Churchward found Abednego in deep concern at the prospect of losing him for ever.

Willy told me in after days, when I took a hand in his affairs, how matters stood with him and Susan.

"There came a morning, Miss Crymes," he said, "when I was opening a pit for a baby in the yard, and Mr. Bragg sat beside me and smoked his pipe and watched me at my work. And we went over my hopes as to Susan and our future. I told him that Mrs. Bragg had got a proper down against Susan for loving me, and a proper down against me also for daring to fall in love with her. Though why she must needs want to keep my intended beside her I couldn't say, for she feels no more friendship for her."

Then the boy explained what troubled 'Bed' so cruel was the thought of Willy's hunger to go foreign. Because he felt that if the young man passed beyond his reach, then there was nobody left on earth to care a wren's feather for him any more.

"But you wouldn't stand in my way, 'Bed'," Willy had said to him, "and Susie's more set on it even than I am. She'd love to get off to Canada, where there's room to turn round, and see me digging at something more cheerful than people's graves. And if I was to fetch off to the West, I'd get good work, because Canada's cruel short of labour and can do with millions more men and women. But," continued Willy to me, " 'Bed' reminded me I'd got nought, so could not emigrate, and he reminded me that Susan had got nought either and never would have a penny in the future if she crossed her aunt. He said he dearly liked Susan himself and would have been well pleased for me to marry her some day if no question arose of us leaving Packhorse Bridge."

Then Willy told me how he had sounded his father's old friend and suggested a scheme. "If I agree to stop in England within reach of you," he had asked, "are you prepared to pay me for the sacrifice with money enough to marry Susan? If I could come before Susie's aunt with a backing of solid cash, then it's most like that Mrs. Bragg would change her mind and suffer me to wed Susan, which would be far more to me even than going to Canada."

"And what did Mr. Bragg say to that?" I inquired.

"He grinned all over his face and was a good bit amused," replied young Churchward. "He said no doubt that was Susie's own idea, and I said it was, and he granted how my sweetheart might be a downy piece of goods, but not near so downy as Mrs. Bragg. He went on with one of his curious speeches and told me that even the cleverness of the cleverest woman ain't equal to the cleverness of a madman. He said: 'You see how it is with me, Willy. I'm cracked, and the rights of a lunatic to his lawful money are taken away from him by the Law. Therefore I can't pour a lot of golden sovereigns into your pockets in secret and make you rich enough to wed Susan. I'd do it willingly, but the power is taken from me. Nevertheless,' he went on, 'I'm all for lending you a hand because I owe a great debt to your blessed father, Weston, who laid down his valuable life for no better purpose than to save my useless one. Which being so, I'd do anything within my power and valiance to pleasure you and help you to get Susie.' I thanked the poor old chap very heartily for that kind speech, Miss Crymes. I said we were strong and full of work and had no vices whatsoever, and that it would a lot better for me fighting a big fight in Canada than poking about here doing an old man's job with nothing to it.

"Just at that minute," continued Willy, "Susan herself came into the burying ground, where 'Bed' and me were talking, to call him to his dinner. He was apt to forget meal-times and, when missing, would generally be found amidst the

91

graves with me; so now Susan came for him and heard the last thing I'd spoke to him. And she backed me up. 'That's right,' she said, 'what woman wants to see her future husband digging graves for babies, Uncle 'Bed'?' Then she told him his dinner was ready.

"But he continued to dwell on the matter in hand," went on Willy. "He turned to Susan and laughed, and said, 'We'll hatch out a fine plot against my better half some day, and learn her to feel kinder to the pair of you!' And then," concluded Willy, "I warned him he must do nothing rash, and he promised to wait for one of his sensible intervals before he did anything at all. Then he told Susan he didn't want any dinner that day, but would come home to his tea later on, so she and I left him and wandered away and he sat on there by himself."

That was the end of young Churchward's talk with me, and a good few months passed before things came to their climax.

Through the following winter 'Bed' was reported to be restive, hard to neighbour with and fonder of his own company than of old. He'd walk by the river for hours alone and do queer things and say queer things, and sometimes his little oddities were told to his wife to vex her. I was friendly on the surface with Mrs. Bragg and knew, in a general way, where the shoe pinched; and then there came a morning when she, much to my surprise, paid me a visit and asked for a bit of advice. She didn't like me any better than I liked her, but she knew my fame and thought, no doubt, to pick my brains without paying a fee for her trouble. She was one of those hungry women—charming and pleasant, but sharp as a needle, with her glances always peering round about her to see, in a neighbour's house or garden, if she could ask for anything, or scheme for something to be given her. She never liked to go from anywhere empty-handed, so I knew she'd called for a bit of my wisdom gratis.

She didn't waste time but edged to the subject of her husband after saying what a lesson of energy and good willing I was. Then she dwelt on the martyrdom of being 'Bed's' wife and how hard she tried to carry on bravely and bear her burdens with Christian courage.

"No cross, no crown, Miss Crymes," she said, and I answered that was the general opinion.

"What galls me above a bit," declared Milly, "is to hear all these strange stories of my poor man's vagaries. They cast me down just when I feel a rising hope his mind is offering to mend and, by God's will, he's coming back to his senses. It's well known that life is often darkest before dawn and so, after a long spell of grief, I'll feel that brighter days may be in store for me ; but then my heart faints to hear things about him that show he's getting worse rather than better."

"What manner of things ?" I asked.

"Stark mad things," she answered. "He's always with young Churchward now, because the boy has grown to be his bosom friend since Weston went. Willy's a poor, slack-twisted creature and worthless in my opinion, but Abednego will bring him into my house, and he's had the impertinence to offer for my niece, Susan Crocker. But the young man sees a lot of my husband and only yesterday he told Susan that her uncle has took to doing a piece of nonsense every time he goes in the churchyard now. Not content with putting a flower on Weston's grave, when there's any flowers to be had, he also sets a flower on the plot next to his friend, where he's going to lie himself ! That has been promised to him by the vicar, and he takes a great interest in it ; but he always says he isn't wishful for me to go in with him when my call comes. 'You must be teeled[1] some place else, Mildred,' he says to me."

"Think nothing of it," I advised her. "Just the idle chatter of an afflicted soul."

"You can't hit upon any line of action for me to take, I suppose ?" she asked. "I do every kind and thoughtful thing I can think upon, but all in vain seemingly."

"How would it be if you let him have the run of a little more of his money ?" I suggested. "Maybe, if he felt he had control of more of his cash, it might bring a bit of pride to him and make him feel he was somebody still and win back his self-respect."

She tightened up at that double quick.

"My dear woman," she said, "he already has the run of a lot

[1] Teeled = Buried.

93

more money than he knows what to do with. They tell me he's always giving sixpences to the children and he's shown me time and again that he don't know the difference between a florin and a half-crown. Then, when his allowance is gone before pay-day, he cadges tobacco and beer from other men."

She didn't let me reply to that but ran on.

"And now there's another stone of stumbling, because he's obstinate and foolish about my niece and this boy. The poor soul thinks it a very suent thing for them to wed and even go to Canada if they want to do so. He can't see the different stations they occupy and that a common labouring man is no partner for Susan."

Her eyes were scouring round while she spoke and she spotted a basket of eggs on my dresser; then, after a little more talk leading nowhere, she sighed, expressed her regret that I couldn't throw light and rose to depart. Next she put on an act, pretended to have seen the eggs for the first time and asked for a couple.

"I wonder if you'll crown your kind and useful words with a tiny gift, dear Miss Crymes?" she begged. "I didn't ought to ask, but I'm not thinking of myself, only my husband. He does love an egg to his breakfast above all else, so you'd be doing the poor man a proper kindness to spare him just one or two."

"Sorry," I said. "Nothing would have pleased me better and I'll keep in mind he likes them; but these are for his Reverence—an order to be paid for according at market price. Mr. Talbot's very addicted to my Barnevelders."

So off she went and drew a blank every way, but nothing she could pin a quarrel to. Then the wheels slowed down a bit with her, though they turned pretty busy in poor 'Bed's' scattered wits, and a few months later he paid me a visit himself. He sent a message by Willy Churchward that he'd take it kind if I would give him a hearing and named a day when his wife was going to be out of the way. So I agreed to see him on a certain afternoon and he came.

I bade him to smoke if he willed and offered him a glass of milk, or cider, as he might prefer. Then he said he would like a cup of tea better than either, but was come before all else to consult me on a tricky piece of work, where he wanted to be guided by the gumption for which I was so famed.

"They praise my cunning, Cherry," he began, for he was always familiar with me and called me by my popular name, "and I grant you that great craft is in me, because, though mad, my madness will often put an edge to my wits and give me finer thoughts than any that come to more sensible men."

"I can well believe that, 'Bed'," I answered. "I well know you think good thoughts now and again, just as you do many kind actions."

"That's right," he replied, "and now my wishes have come down to two only, and how to follow them out to their proper ends is the problem before me. How best to make them come true is what I want you to clear up. Something tells me they ought to fit into each other, same as the blades of a pair of scissors, and yet they do no such thing. Instead of clicking home together, they yawn apart, if you take my meaning, and defeat each other instead of completing each other."

"Very interesting," I declared, "and nicely put. Life's full of such quandaries by reason of our contrary human natures, 'Bed'. They say two wrongs never yet made a right, and some believe two rights never yet made a wrong; which ain't true, because two rights often end up in a hopeless mess and prove as wrong as can be."

"Both my intentions are dead right," he said, "and I'll take 'em in order. If I was free and had my wits, the one would follow the other without any fuss at all; but it's just the tiresome mischance of being mad that creates the hitch. The first idea is that I ordain to kill myself, Cherry, but that's for your ear alone, mind."

I never let any bit of news, however fantastic, to put me into disorder, so my mind went on its even way, and in truth 'Bed's' idea did not surprise me overmuch. There was nothing very amazing if he thought to cut his own thread, for he had long lost what made life worth living, and even many a sane man has destroyed himself for private reasons amply sufficient from his own point of view. Therefore I didn't fly out to hear poor Bragg say such things. A sane man would, of course, have expected me to do so and taken a sort of left-handed

95

satisfaction at seeing me horrified; but I just nodded and answered with no more emotion than if he had told me he'd got a toothache.

"You can trust me to keep your intentions to myself," I said, "and every man has got the right to call his life his own; but to quit our bodies is a very final piece of work, 'Bed', because we can't get back into them once we take our leave. I wouldn't be in any great hurry if I were you, and maybe your second big thought could only be carried out with success if you stop here to look after it."

"It all turns on that," he explained. "If I was sane and free to leave my directions like other men, then the second thing would follow upon the first all in order and no complications at all; but, being of infirm mind, I can't make a will or dispose of my money, or anything else, just for the tiresome obstacle that I'm off my rocker. Milly would see to that. And yet I cling to the second thing as a lot more important to my comfort than whether I live or die."

He looked troubled and I saw he was getting out of his depth.

"Then tell me what you are aiming at, my dear man, and what is the second thing on your mind," I said. "Perhaps you can find a way to compass it without taking any fatal steps whatever."

"The second thing is to do Willy a proper good turn while I'm here to do it," he explained. "I'm wishful to serve the boy so that, when I meet his father again up aloft, I can take a bit of good news to my old friend and tell him all's well with Willy and he's going to marry Susan Crocker and carry her off to foreign parts. Then I'd let Weston know it was for his sake that I found the money, so that the young people could start life together with a thousand pounds between them. And that news will make Weston's home in the Happy Land a lot happier than at present when he thinks and wonders about Willy. So, before I pass out of here myself and join up with him again, for which no doubt he waits and longs, same as I do, I must complete his happiness in that manner. Therefore the snag is how to screw the money out of my wife before I take my own final steps."

96

"You can't trust Milly to feel your wishes sacred and do as you wish when you're gone?"

"Not a dog's hope! If I don't do it, then it will never be done. She hates Willy and she'll want Susan for her own future convenience more than ever when I'm gone. So Willy must be made a man of substance before I go."

"Then you should feel in no hurry, 'Bed', but take your time: that's the first thing," I assured him; but he shook his head at that.

"You might think so," he admitted, "being a sane woman, Cherry; but my madness knows different."

"It's your madness comes between you and the good deed you want to do: that's what we need to get round," I explained.

"You look at it wrong," he said. "The problem is that I can't see the way to link up my coming death with the money for Willy. Something tells me that the one depends upon the other. Upon my going depends the boy's legacy and future prosperity, and how to order that I don't see; but give you time, Cherry, and I'm hoping you will see."

"The money must be free so it shall be his after you go?"

"No need that he should know about it before I go, and better that he shouldn't; but I want to be dead sure that he has it safe after I go, and can bear the good news to his father. No use carrying pious wishes to the next world. You must take certainties, else they won't believe what you tell 'em."

"The question is how to do it. That's what you want me to consider."

"And mind you consider them in their proper aspect," he warned me. "The money's mine and to get it into my hands won't be a criminal job of work, because you can't steal what's your own, and though it's denied me under the law of man, that don't mean it's denied me by the law of God, who made me mad, so it wouldn't bar me out of heaven to take it. In fact, between ourselves, Cherry, I'm tolerable certain my Maker's on my side."

Of course that remark promised to simplify the first part of the problem, so I jumped at it.

"You mention a very important fact," I said, "and I quite agree with you so far. The money is yours, so when we take action, there is no need your hands should be tied in that matter. And I'll go further and say your Creator would agree the money was yours, because He gave it to you. I can't dictate how it is going to reach the destination you plan for it, but I do agree that the money is your own and the first step is to have it in your pocket. One thing at a time, 'Bed'. I don't want to put any spoke in the wheel—far from it; but I'm very wishful to see you accomplish your purpose and also live to enjoy your triumph after you have accomplished it."

He was a good bit disappointed at this idea however.

"My triumph is to get back to Weston," he answered. "There's no triumphs for me down here. I've never triumphed over anything in my life bigger than a trout. I'm sick of being mad and my triumph is to get sane again along with Churchward in eternity."

I saw then that he was getting into one of his wild moods and brought our conversation to an end for the time being.

"Keep tight hold over yourself and take first things first," I warned him. "The future will unfold as it always does; but it's for us to look after the present and you have got plenty of wits still to help my wits. Just look at it as if you were going fishing: but the fish this time isn't hid in the river; it's under your own roof! Can you catch that fish? Have you got the tackle to play it and land it?"

You can often speak in riddles like that, and though a sane man may not understand you, a mad one will. At any rate 'Bed' took my meaning quick enough. He grinned and nodded and rubbed his hands together.

"I see what you're aiming at," he said, "and I've brooded a lot already as to that point. I know a lot more than what somebody, who shall be nameless, thinks I know."

"Enough said as to that then," I answered.

"More than enough," he agreed. "If she thought I knew her cubby-holes, she'd have a fit, poor woman; but you can't live along with a wife and not learn where her heart is. There's the surprise of her life will burst on Mildred Bragg when I go, Cherry!"

We were on properly dangerous ground now and I had no mind to be involved in what lay ahead. I knew Abednego

98

couldn't look so far into the future as myself and that while to get his money was one thing, to put it safely into Willy's hands would be quite another. We met again a week later and I told him his affairs were working in my mind; but then he said an astonishing word that showed him for the moment as intelligent as you could wish.

"All's in order," he said, "and my way grown as clear as sunshine, though it will be for you to give the finishing touch after I'm gone. I'll leave a masterpiece behind me, Cherry, and you must carry it to perfection."

Then he trotted off full of business; and that prophecy was the last word I ever had from his mouth.

A fortnight later came the opening scene of the mystery he had woven from his disorderly wits. There was an annual celebration at Packhorse Bridge, when brakes were engaged and the school-children had their holiday party and were conveyed away down to Plymouth to enjoy a feast and gather on the Hoe to play games and see the ships and the Sound. It was a festival long looked forward to and many grown-up people went with the boys and girls for their kindred favoured the outing as much as the children. Our vicar always went too. In those days he was the Reverend Talbot, a very popular minister with his flock and large-minded to human weakness, and not too old, like many holy men, who have forgot what it was to be naughty themselves.

Away they all drove in their four-horse vehicles with a blue sky above them and promise of a triumphant day. Indeed all went well and the festive party didn't come home till after nine o'clock at night, when they drew up at the 'Hearty Welcome', singing and shouting, to find a rally of neighbours assembled as usual to welcome them back. Mrs. Bragg and her niece had taken holiday with the rest and they expected to find 'Bed' waiting for them with the assembled company; but he wasn't there and nobody had seen him. More unusual still, on getting home they found the place empty. But he had left the fire burning and the lamp ready to be lighted and their supper hot in the oven. So they hunted round about and lifted their voices, yet met with no response. It came on to midnight then and Milly Bragg was feared, so she sent Susan to wake up

99

Policeman Arscott and tell him that her husband was missing. And, waiting there alone for him to come back with her niece, no doubt she wondered if by good chance 'Bed' was taken off at last and her cross lifted off her shoulders by some kindly act of Providence. But she had something else to wonder at before the policeman came, for, going to cheer herself with a peep at her money, there burst the shock that her husband had foretold to me and she found one of her hiding-places empty. She screamed at the direful sight, but there was none to hear, and so she hasted to other hidden hoards unknown to all but herself—or so she thought. One other had been rifled ; the rest were safe, and she quickly figured up that round about fifteen hundred pounds of Bank of England notes were stolen. Milly's mind moved quick enough then and, when Susan and the policeman arrived together, she had her theory mapped out, and Susan let me hear what she said.

"He's mitched with more than a thousand pounds," her aunt told Policeman Arscott, "and he only cleared out a short time before I got home, because the fire was alight and food hot and waiting for me ; so it's up to you to blaze it abroad and lay hands on the man before other people get hold of him and rob him. And that's where you stand now, Job Arscott."

But guardians of the peace don't much favour the opinions of the public : they better like to form their own, and Arscott didn't want Milly's ideas thrust upon him. He was a big, black-bearded man with a very orderly habit of mind, who held that slow and sure was the right way to approach crime and capture criminals. He objected to be hurried even where speedy action was shouted for. Excitement he always strove to quench.

"Be calm," he said, "and stick to facts and leave the case in my hands, to be examined in a proper way. It's far too early to throw the blame on Mr. Bragg and you have no right to say he stole the money without any proofs that he did so. And further-more, you must bear in mind what is known before you start guessing at what is not known. One fact is well known. Which is that you choose to keep a great deal more cash in this house than is needful or orderly. And I tell you so to your face here and now, Mrs. Bragg, and who can say how many nefarious characters are well aware of it? Thieves might have watched your husband's movements as well as your own and broken in when his back was turned, or worse even than that could have fallen upon him: he might have come back to catch them at work and lost his life trying to save the money. In their rush to escape they'd so likely as not put a bullet into him to silence him for ever. Or, at this very moment, he may be hot-foot after them and will catch them yet. A lunatic's craft will often accomplish what a man with all his senses cannot. In fact the case looks tolerable thorny and we may be called to put in a lot of work before we clean it up."

Milly was dancing with impatience and anger by now.

"It's no use wasting time and babbling stuff like that," she snapped at Arscott. "Proper thieves would never have found a penny if they'd turned the house out of windows. He's kept a watch on me and nosed it out and marked my goings and comings; and now, when my back was turned, he's took the money and made tracks with it."

"He may have done so, or he may not," answered Arscott, "and since we all know the money was his own, it's well within reason—him being out of reason—that he should still reckon it was his. I shall raise hue and cry for him up and down the country tomorrow and we may count to find him in another twenty-four hours if he's alive; but if he's not alive, then we certainly shall not find him so quick, because murderers would take a lot of trouble to hide his body. I'll send for Atkins tomorrow. He's a very clever thief-taker. And now I should shut up and go to bed if I was you; but if you get any news before morning, then let me know."

Atkins was a Moreton man, well thought upon for his successes against crime, and the next day he came to Pack-horse Bridge, waited on Mrs. Bragg, saw the places where she had stored her treasure, studied the ground round about and made search for clues. He kept dumb as to what was passing in his mind and said little to Milly or Susan but, when alone with Arscott afterwards, inclined to believe the vanished man was responsible and had probably done pretty much as his wife thought. Mr. Atkins showed special interest in their family history and suspected that Susan Crocker might very

101

possibly know more of the situation than appeared. He also visited the 'Hearty Welcome', took a room there and settled himself for three days. His inquiries yielded no fruit, however, and no explanation of 'Bed's' doings was forthcoming, which inclined Arscott more than ever to cleave to his own theory: that Abednego had fallen in upon the robbers, lost his life and been hidden for their own future safety. The likelihood of suicide was not entertained. "If," declared Arscott, "he ordained to destroy himself, he wouldn't have wasted time to take the money, unless, under his mental breakdown, he had got some straw in his head that it would come in useful where he was going."

For my own part, though there was no occasion for the policeman to question me, I felt tolerably sure from the first that poor Bragg had kept his promise and taken his own life, but that didn't help to show what he must have done with his money. Then I wondered if Willy Churchward knew anything. Nobody had named his name in connection with the matter, but it was understood that Atkins put a lot of questions to Susan which she couldn't answer, and I knew very well that if in truth the girl knew a morsel about it, she wouldn't have hid it from Willy. So I waited my chance and got a message to the young man and asked him to come and see me at Owl Pen for a minute. He came, and very down in the mouth and miserable he was. The disappearance of his friend and the doubts as to his fate had properly upset Willy; but he convinced me easily enough that he knew no more what had happened than anybody else.

"The policemen are most like to be in the right of it," he said. "Some cut-throat devils caught him in his home, well knowing he'd be all alone there. And then they tortured him till he told where the money was hid, and then they killed him and took him away with them and hid him."

It was an ugly picture for all concerned, but nothing happened either to contradict or confirm it for several days. Wide enough search was made for the vanished man, but no evidence pointing to his whereabouts could be found.

Something told me none the less that 'Bed' was responsible and I saw his hand in it, though none else did, except Mrs.

Bragg. But she believed it for a different reason from mine. She was positive that he had took the money and cried shame on the law for letting a lunatic beat them; while I believed that he was dead, but not before he had taken the money. Still, for all my usual penetration, I couldn't explain what he had done with it. What he wanted it for I well knew, yet since Willy could throw no light and had heard nothing, I found myself properly at a loss for once, not guessing how the core of the business had yet to come and demand my attention when it did.

Not till five days later definite news broke upon us and then the light shone and the vanished man appeared. It was poor Bragg himself who saved any further trouble and a fisherman found his body floating in the river. None ever thought he was like to be there, though I did, knowing of his intentions. The first thing to find out next was what 'Bed' had died from and whether he had been slain and then sunk in the water, or gone into it by accident. Both Arscott and Atkins were much disappointed when the doctors announced the dead man had been drowned; but not a sign of the money rewarded a proper search of the corpse, or the water, or the margents round about. The Crowner sat upon him in due course and his jury brought in that Abednego Bragg had killed himself, being of disordered mind at the time and not responsible for the rash act. Some doubted whether the victim would get Christian burial and, if not, where they would bestow him; but the Reverend Talbot made no bones about that and declared the dead man was going to get a Christian burial and lie where he had always wanted to, in his promised grave beside Weston Churchward. So Willy's work lay before him and, at early dawn in the morning after the inquest, the sorrowful youth set about it. His father had always favoured sunrise for a sexton's work and the young man did likewise as a rule. He'd cut the turf off by four o'clock for, in mid-June, there was plenty of daylight by then; and yet, strange to tell, less than half an hour later he'd dropped his tools, left the yard, taken a beeline up to Owl Pen and was knocking at my door! Not a soul moving so early as that, of course, but the heath larks overhead singing, because they waken early in June and go upward to catch the first rays of the rising sun.

I was asleep at the time but awoke in a moment to his summons, looked down from my window and saw him standing beneath. I didn't waste time asking silly questions but told him I would be down house in five minutes, and when I descended, there he was still panting after his run and in great turmoil of mind. I couldn't read his face and bade him come in and sit down and get his wind back before he told what brought him at such a freakish hour. Then he grew calmer and produced an object from his inside pocket—a tidy-sized, round tin. It was a familiar object to me because Amos Butt, at the shop of all sorts, got some of his goods in these cases and, when he'd done with them, would always sell them, for three-pence apiece, to any customer who might have a use for them.

"One of Butt's tins," I said. "What the mischief have you got in that, Willy?" Yet even as I spoke, so quick was my mind ever to flash forward, that I felt to know the answer.

He made no reply for a moment or two, then related what had overtaken him.

"I was at work on Mr. Bragg's grave at peep of day this morning, Miss Crymes, and there felt to be something soft about the earth after I'd took the grass off, and I thought it might hap to be a mole's run, because they do work there by night sometimes. But no—it was this tin, set there by dear 'Bed' where only I was going to find it and safe from every eye but mine."

"The money!" I said.

He took the lid off and put the tin in my hands.

"Read what he says, Miss Crymes," he directed.

The tin was tightly packed with a roll of paper money—mostly five- and ten-pound notes, and at the top lay a scrap of paper with 'Bed's' writing upon it. Thus he wrote:

For Willy and Susan all but fifty pounds for Cherry Crymes. Take the money to her and do what she ordains. From Abednego Bragg with his good wishes.

Willy spoke while I sat silent deep in thought.

"He bids me come to you, miss. Is that all right? Or did I ought to take it to Mr. Arscott?" he asked.

"Not on your life, Willy!" I answered. "Would you dare to disobey your best friend's last message? This has nothing to do with the police nor any other living souls but you and Susan and me. For love of your father, 'Bed' did the thing your father would above all else have wished to do, and that was to better you and help you to face the world come presently. And he knew there would lie difficulties about this money beyond your power to cope with, so he sent you to me, well understanding that you and Susan were safe in my hands and I would take good care none dared to come between you and the money."

"Thank God you'll take it on," said Willy, "because Mr. Bragg was right there. He knew me and Susan wasn't clever enough to hang on to it; but a woman like you would be, Miss Crymes."

"Waste no more time here," I said. "Get back to his grave and keep dumb as a newt for the present. After the funeral I'll fasten upon the subject and find the way, but don't whisper a word—not even to Susie yet. If the law got wind, it would be down upon you like a hawk and pluck you bare and rob 'Bed' of all his fine plans."

"Where's the money going to be dead safe against Mrs. Bragg?" he asked.

"Here," I said. "It's as safe with me as if it was under the churchyard grass, Willy. He knew that, else he wouldn't have put it there for only you to find it. He saw the future as only a dying man ever does see it, and you can thank the Lord for all His mercies and just lie low and bide your time. If poor 'Bed' could trust me, you can, and the safest place for the present lies with me. It belongs to you and Susan, but according to the letter of the law, it belongs to Mrs. Bragg, so we must use craft and not let the law rob you of what is yours."

He expressed his gratitude and went back to work, while I took an early breakfast, fed my hens, then lighted my pipe. There was a tricky job of work before me now and Abednego knew it would be difficult and had left me good payment

105

accordingly. What he said at our last talk came back to my mind. To fight and conquer the law had now become a solemn duty; while to fight and conquer Milly Bragg was an easier task and no more than a pleasure in any case.

I like best to work alone and especially when there is a side to my transactions open to misunderstanding in small minds; but now and again I have used an accomplice when the case was beyond my strength. So, when I discovered it lay beyond me to do the dead man's orders without a confederate by my side, my first step was to think upon a trustable and high-minded ally who was going to look at the problem from the same angle as I did. That occupied my wits for quite a long time and, strange to say, it was only thanks to a sudden prompting, after I began to despair of finding the right one, that I came to final choice. To be up against the law has a mighty crushing effect on people and, though they may be as brave as you please and will stand up to dangers and risk all manner of peril for the sake of justice, yet when it is a question of breaking the law of the land, they flinch and lose heart about it. Because in their minds law and justice are one and they lose heart if they know the law is their enemy. I passed over the local characters without hitting upon one of them to meet the case, and for a few days I stood in doubt. Then came Abednego Bragg's funeral and a good rally of neighbours crowded round his grave when he sank into it.

Willy Churchward stood by, and the coffin was elm, not oak, and Mrs. Bragg did not take the chief mourner's place. She had given out the certain conviction that 'Bed' was responsible for his own death and for the robbery of her money and never forgave him.

The vicar read the burial service in a manly and moving manner. He had always liked the dead man and been kind and friendly to him, and his Reverence made a fine figure at the graveside with his surplice billowing in the wind, like a ship in full sail. Then, as I listened to him, there flashed into my mind that I'd set him the task to help me. A sudden impulse woke in me that in Parson Talbot, if in anybody, I might trust to find the needful qualities of pluck and fairness called for. He was a sportsman and also a most fearless and largeminded man in the pulpit, so although a bit of a gamble to put the story before him, yet something told me none could be better trusted, then, after considering the matter for inside a week, I felt my inner voices to be right. Parson was very approachable and I felt no doubt that he would be willing to see me in his own time; but he had a lot of work to do and, as he was never known to give a parishioner more than ten minutes for an interview, except when he was christening them, marrying them, or burying them, I waited until I met him in the open one day and told him that I was wishful to say something of importance but it would take every minute of half an hour to do so. Then I begged him to name a half-hour when he could listen to something a good bit out of the common, though not, in my opinion, proper for any ear but his own. The gentleman knew me and was aware of my fame. In fact he'd had a taste of it, for I cured a fine mare for him, after the horse-leech had said she was going to die, and he'd given me a guinea for so doing. Thus he was well-intending to me and bade me come to the vicarage at nine o'clock the following night.

"And bring your tobacco pipe, Charity, if you mind to," he said, "and I'll fill it with leaf of good Virginny."

So I went at the appointed hour but didn't take my pipe. I brought the tin of money and burnt my boats, as they say, and laid all before the holy man.

He always favoured action and now, after he had listened without a word to the story from start to finish, he spoke in his usual downright way and gave me a taste of his quality and summed up and made clear his own intentions.

"A remarkable narrative, Miss Crymes, and you have done well to bring it to me and learn my opinions," he began. "You could have chosen no better confidant, for I know all the parties concerned and have already had them in my mind and wished that I knew them better. But you have filled the gaps in my understanding and I need ask for no time before I pronounce an ultimatum. You and I are faced with two alternatives. We might sit on the fence between them, and pretty poor figures those generally cut who occupy that position; but nobody can sit on a fence indefinitely, or descend upon both sides. Our dilemma, so to call it, awakens in me a reflection on

107

which I design to preach on some future occasion, and it is this."

The gentleman then launched out into some deep ideas, but linked them with the matter in hand before he finished.

"Now in the case before us," he summed up, "God-made equity and man-made justice are at variance, and the law, if permitted to do so, will act clean contrary to the divine direction. It will restore our dead friend's bequest to his wife, rob those entitled to their legacy and commit a gross wrong. Had poor Bragg's purpose been unjust, or unreasonable, then his fellow men might have been right to ignore it; but nothing can be considered more humane and praiseworthy than to bestow upon the son of his dearly loved friend, Weston Churchward, a beneficent gift which will enable that young man to face life with the handsome support of this bequest. The means that the deceased took to attain his object are open to deep regret, but we must remember the difficulties that faced him. And though his self-destruction is to be deplored it cannot be denied that he availed himself of that crime with considerable ingenuity. Such things could hardly have been accomplished by one not out of his mind; but, though he was no longer trustworthy or normal, his inveterate good will remained unimpaired and, for my part, I shall do nothing to confound his purpose by any attempt to defeat it."

The Reverend Talbot stopped to take breath, while I expressed my pleasure to hear his opinions.

"Thank you for these fine words which only you could have spoken, your Reverence," I said. "To the last moment I trembled at coming before you, and it isn't much happens ever to make me tremble, but you show how wise I was to come, and you never took a heavier weight off a creature's mind than what you have taken off mine this minute."

"Good!" he answered. "We shall be conspirators in this excellent deed of darkness. The word 'conspiracy' sounds sinister, but we conspire in a Christian tradition that can cast no stain upon us. There is one who will suffer and only one."

Of course I saw the person he was aiming at, and feeling I had got to know the vicar quite well by now, expressed a fearless opinion upon Milly Bragg.

"As you go through life, dear sir," I said, "you will be pretty sure to run up against some people who make you wonder why God ever made them."

To my surprise he met this remark with a loud laugh.

"True," he answered, "and doubtless we also run up against many people who wonder why the Almighty wasted His time making us, Miss Crymes!" then I laughed too.

"The true value and reason for any of us is only known to our Creator," he said, "and in the case of Mrs. Bragg, the object of her existence may only be hidden from her fellow creatures for the moment. Perhaps it has yet to appear, and meanwhile a more interesting subject confronts us, namely the future of Willy and Susan and how best to handle their money for them. We must approach this challenge with craft and some measure of righteous cunning. We must be patient and wait until the clouds roll by, so that none can associate these young people with the death of our late friend, or the disappearance of this cash."

"That's where the situation beats me, dear sir," I confessed.

"The needful steps must be taken with caution, and you need do no more than preserve silence and watch me take them," he replied. "I had been thinking of Willy Churchward for some time before these events took place, and have felt that now he should be engaged on a more fruitful and promising task than digging the last resting-places of my parishioners. Indeed a first step is about to be taken and it means that he will soon be translated from a village sexton into an under-gardener at the Manor. Such advancement need create no wonder of any kind, and there he can remain for the present while knowing that he is destined for better things."

The vicar then went on to tell me that he favoured going to the colonies for young men and women and that emigration was already one of his private activities. He had powerful friends in London who worked for the same cause and, when the time came, he could promise that nothing would be easier than to launch Willy and Susan, because they would have good money backing.

"The authorities are glad to help those who can help themselves in that matter," he told me, "and all details of the transaction I shall be in a position to supply. I shall now speak with Willy and unfold his destiny, imposing upon him silence until the appointed hour has struck. His money will be invested on his account; your legacy you can take with you, Miss Crymes."

Then he counted out my fifty pounds and put his hand on the money and blessed it, and I went off into the night with my heart at rest.

All happened as the clever old man had planned, although he allowed two years to pass before he moved. Then Willy noised out that he was going to marry Susan and go foreign; but not even the police ever joined that trifle to Mrs. Bragg's vanished money. His Reverence married the pair and they were soon sped for a life beyond the sea. Their children may thrive out there yet for all I can tell and the vicar had a line from Willy now and again in the following years. But after the good man went to his reward, long ago now, nothing was ever heard of the Churchwards again to my knowledge. Only the name lingers on in the burying ground where 'Bed' lies tucked in with his faithful friend beside him.

And here looks to be a fitting place to say a word on my own behalf and report a good advertisement for myself which will be hid for all time if I do not set it down. The Reverend Talbot has got to be thanked for it and, under his own hand, did he record the words, though little dreaming the world at large would one day set eyes upon them. After he was taken, his old wife—sorting amid his papers and sermons and odds and ends—came upon a writing by her husband at some moment of his leisure. And it served to show his manifold cleverness, for he penned in rhyme that ran as suent as any Church hymn. And there, set down by that remarkable and Christian soul, was his opinion of myself! Any lesser woman than Mrs. Talbot might well have torn up this fine piece of poetry, but she did otherwise. She reckoned that here was a great treasure for me and so gave it into my possession.

There were always neighbours that liked me little and some, out of their ignorant and jealous hearts, would even dare to lie about me; but here was the noble reply that this righteous man made to the parish on my account, and every line of it true as Gospel.

CHARITY CRYMES

A right white witch, as any of her kind,
Who never cursed, or cast the evil eye,
    Or did a mite of harm,
But toiled for troubled man and beast to find
Some safe way out with wondrous remedy
    Or mediaeval charm.

By night, 'twas said, shaped like a hare she'd go
To join the pixies at their junketings
    And lead their moon-lit fun,
But never soul could swear they'd seen her so,
And if the woman did such clever things,
    What odds to anyone?

VII

SOMEWHERE between fifty and sixty years ago, my dear
doctor—a most understanding man, who practised his craft
at Widecombe, among other places, ordained for me to take a
breath of sea air if I could venture down off Dartmoor to the
coast and taste the wind blowing over the Atlantic Ocean for
a spell. And such was my trust in the gentleman that I agreed
to do so and travelled so far away as Cornwall, where friends
of mine had a married son who dwelt nigh Marazion, in
Mounts Bay. He made his living as a carpenter. The man and
his wife received me well for my modest money and I found
them to be nice, sensible people ; but, among their neighbours,
was a Mrs. Rose Tregenza and, strange to say, I found she
stood to Marazion much as I myself stood to Dartmoor and
the folk in it. So there was offered the uncommon case of one
wise woman meeting another. We found ourselves much in
tune to each other's opinions, as you might expect wise
women to be, for she was a tolerable deep thinker, though
lacking my power to face any problem, great or small. However I found she could furnish me with examples to prove her
not called a wise woman for nothing. Her adventures had
mostly to deal with seafarers, who are apt to look at life from
a wider standpoint than incountry people do, because for them
there's two elements that encompass their hopes—the sea and
the land—whereas for us, who dwell beyond sight or thought
of the ocean, the manners and customs of solid earth are all we
know about.

We were sitting taking the air together on a sunny
afternoon and watching the fishers' fleet from Newlyn
out to sea upon their business, when Mrs. Tregenza put a
question.

"Would you say," she asked, "if such gifts as you and
me can claim are put in us for a purpose, or happen by
chance ?"

"For a purpose surely," I replied to her. "In my case, they came from my forbears."

"Why I got my gifts puzzles me more than where they came from," she explained. "I was well up in years before I knew my qualities and only discovered 'em in a most fearful manner. There's the power to ill-wish your fellow creatures and the power to good-wish them and, God's my judge, I never knew I had the dark powers to bring evil upon anybody until I found myself actually doing so!"

I didn't contradict her—she being many years older than myself—but I did venture to ask how she came to find out such a horrible thing.

"I'll tell you," she said. "You know that the best of us will sometimes lose our temper with a stupid or obstinate person and express our vexation in impatient words. We may wish the offender 'at Jericho' or, if you hap to be rough-tongued, you may say, 'Go to Hell', or some such rude speech. But once in my case I snapped out words I never used before, and they were certainly put in my mouth to say, for I wondered at the time why passing anger with a beast of a man should have made me curse the wretch. But that was nothing to my astonishment to find inside twenty-four hours that the curse had took shape!"

"Fancy!" I said. "No doubt such a thing learned you never to curse nobody in a hurry again."

"It did. I'd not wished death on man, woman or child before that fatal night, and I never have done so since; but I hoped that if I'd got such a perilous gift as that, I might also have the opposite and be able to wish blessings as well as cursings. And I took a lot of pains to discover. Yet I soon found that it wasn't so. My good wishes came to nought."

By that time I began to fear how Mrs. Tregenza must have a bee in her bonnet.

"Tell me the details, if you can reveal them without doing any harm," I begged, "and I'll decipher it if in my power. You Cornish people are said to have the second sight, and some tales I've heard about the smugglers and tin-miners down here sound as if there may be bad spirits working among you beyond your powers to reckon with."

She agreed that was so and told her tale.

"It happened on a winter's eve," she began, "with a red sky overhead and frost in the air. And for the moment there was a pinch of frost in my heart also because I'd just had cross words with my late husband, Albert, about some silly matter, and I walked upon the quay—not far from where we are sitting now. I was on my way home at the moment to make it up, and I knew that Bert would be glad enough to do so—such a one for peace as him. A few men were coming down to the boats—inshore fishermen who would be working by night at a ridge of rocks not much more than a mile to sea, and it was a spot only safe for fishing on such a peaceful and moonlit night as promised that evening.

"Among the fishers came a famous drinker—a godless man of bad character named Patrick Pengelly. He was a widower who had lost his first and, being of very low reputation, couldn't find a woman to let him try again. He lived with his son, a child of seven years old, and a sister, who kept his house for Pengelly and stuck by him in exchange for the home he gave her.

"Now he was on his way to work and going down to his boat, where it lay by the quay steps with one or two others. The tide was running and the night winged down peaceful and good fishing for certain promised. Pengelly was just short of drunk, but he could carry a lot, and after wasting his money in a public house the cold air revived him and his sight cleared. In his mind was to make for the 'Devil's Gullet'—a deep inlet amid the rocks down south, famous for heavy conger at this season of the year. Fantastic tales were told of the fish that harboured there.

"Pengelly was nearing the pier, his legs unsteady still, when, just as he passed me by, his right foot failed him and in a moment he would have fallen. I was carrying a couple of small flat fish, I remember, and, as he slipped, the man threw up his arm and clutched me by the shoulder. The action saved him a fall, but brought me to the ground in a heap, sent my fish flying, knocked my fisherman's cap off my head, hurt my arm and woke my temper into a right-down rage. I was more frightened than hurt, but often fright will breed anger and I

114

rose off the ground and shook the dirt off me and found myself cursing the man with all my might. 'You drunken swine!' I cried out. 'You hulking, God-forgotten beast! Get off the land! Go forth upon the sea and cast your line and catch your death!' That shook him a bit, and it shook me too, because my voice sounded ugly to my own ear and not the way I was used to talk. 'For two pins I'd pitch you into the sea, you damned, black witch!' he said, and glared at me like an angry ape. Then he turned and went down the steps to his boat."

"Who would have thought it in you to talk like that, my dear?" I asked. "But I've known both men and women under pressure to use language that was foreign to them until the moment came. Yet, to their own surprise, there it was hid under their tongues and ready to bubble forth if called upon."

"What was lying in wait for Patrick Pengelly I little guessed," continued Mrs. Tregenza. "For the minute, both shocked and shamed, I went home and made it up with my husband; but next morning, going in the public house for his half pint, Bert met Pat and heard all about it.

"After you had cussed him as you told me, said Bert, he went out to the rocks and he was particular anxious this morning, when he came back, for you to hear the tale yourself, so he took pains to tell me to bring it clear before you, Rose. Away he had gone and presently, upon the offshore breeze, put up his sail and slipped down to the ridge. And he said that all the while there echoed in his mind the curse you had spoke against him. Then he got into the 'Gullet', where he ordained to fish, and dropped his anchor. Under the rocks it was growing dark by now and his thoughts continued to be ugly, because when a little coaster ran on the reef not twelve months agone and sunk there with the loss of several lives, it was reckoned the congers caught since must be man-eaters.

"Then he baited his hooks with cuttle-fish and began to ply his trade. He lighted his lantern and forgot all else but his lines, for though a poor sort of creature, he was a very skilled fisherman. There didn't seem to be much moving for a long spell and Pat had already got it in mind to try farther south and quit the 'Gullet'; but then, just after he heard church clock tell

115

ten and counted the strokes note by note, a line at the bow of his boat throbbed against the bulwark and grew so taut as a harp-string. He hurried to the line and soon found by the strain upon it that he must be into something extra. Striking gently to make sure the fish was well hooked, there came a fierce answer, and so the battle between them began. Foot by foot, so he told Bert, Pengelly got his line in and his blood boiled with excitement, because he knew that, if his gear held, there was a giant eel down below with only an hour longer to live. The conger fought like a demon every inch of the way, but it came up at last with a rush to the surface and was presently struggling alongside the boat. Then the victorious man made the line fast and lifted his lantern to see what manner of creature it might be that he had hove up from below. And there, churning alongside Pengelly's boat, he saw a huge black snake that twisted and looped and, under the light of the lantern, looked as if it might be twenty feet long. It was by far the biggest conger he'd ever set eyes upon; but by now he'd lost any sense of fear and knew he was going to be a winner if he stuck to it and kept his nerve. He coaxed the fish a thought nearer and made the line tight so it shouldn't dive again; then he fixed his lantern to show what he was doing and got out his gaff."

Mrs. Tregenza rested a minute and then continued.

"By now, so Pat told Albert, the great eel was lying like a log in the water exhausted after its first bout with him, and Pengelly took his time, waited for a favourable moment and then stabbed in his gaff half a foot below the creature's gills. He planned to hold it thus with his left arm and beat in its head with his right before dragging the thing aboard; but his gaff woke the eel into all its strength and fury again and it made another tremendous effort to break loose. Pat heard his line snap, but the gaff held and he got both hands to it and, when the fish heaved its head high out of the water with a mighty effort, the man dragged it bodily out of the sea and pulled it into his boat on top of himself; and then the gaff broke at the head, so now the eel was free in the boat and twining round Pengelly, one on top of the other, in the well of the little craft, and threatening to sink her between them. Once

116

the conger got on top for a bit and Pengelly told how, during the next half a minute, it was anybody's fight and him still as like to lose as the fish. He said the creature made deep-sea sounds and grunted like a wolf, and crashed his jaws together, but never got home, by good chance, else it would have torn his throat out and killed him for certain.

"The man felt it wind ice-cold rings round his body once and counted to feel his ribs cracking under the pressure, but he wriggled out of that and just saved his hand as the fish struck at his wrist. He couldn't get any grip on the beast because it was too slippery and too strong, and if that eel had got a brain, it could have killed him no doubt; but it was fighting against another animal unknown to it, while Pat had a brain and knew what he fought against. At last he found himself clear and scrambled up on to his feet and climbed upon the little foredeck of the boat. He was bruised and bleeding by now, slobbered over with slime from head to foot, half blind from a blow across his face and raging with such passion against the conger that he could hardly steady his hand to strike a match. Great silence fell between them for a little while. The lantern was overturned and out, but moonlight helped Pat creep to his locker forward, while the eel lay motionless and silent down below in a tangle of rope and fishing line. The barb of the gaff was still in its body and its life near spent; but as Pengelly drew an axe from the locker, then turned, measured his distance from the foe and crept a thought nearer, he could see its head streaked with moonshine and its eyes watching him as if it knew what he was up to.

"You see, the man had got it at his mercy now," went on Mrs. Tregenza, panting a bit with the force of her story, still clear in her mind despite the years that had passed since it happened. "The eel was done for now, and he pinned its body under two blocks of ballast and then chopped off its head with his axe. He confessed to Albert that he shouted like a maniac with joy and laughed so loud that he made the rocks of the 'Gullet' ring with his noise. Then he came to his senses, lighted his lantern again, stopped a leak his boat had sprung and, with what strength was left to him, got his anchor and hoisted his sail. It took him three tacks to make harbour; but

117

he and his prize fetched home at last and came ashore before dawn."

"A grand victory," I said. "You tell a fine story and I can well believe how thankful you must have felt at the time when you heard about it. He did indeed cast his line, and he came awful near to catching his death and making your curse come true; but, thank the watching Lord, he was saved by the skin of his teeth."

"So it looks to you," Mrs. Tregenza agreed, "and I did thank the watching Lord and took to my soul the warning; but wait till I finish: there's more to astonish you yet, Miss Crymes."

Then she went on again.

"Thirteen feet long that fantastic monster measured by the light of day, and such a conger had seldom come from the sea in living memory. The beast brought eighteen shillings in money and, even so, Pat Pengelly kept a pound and a half of the tail for his own eating, because he had a fancy to taste the flavour of it. He was a bit of a hero after everybody heard of his battle and saw his catch, and his sister cooked his dinner when the time came for it, and he and his little son sat down to table in very good spirits to enjoy their feasting. Then the triumphant man piled his own plate and placed a few morsels before the child. Both set to work and Pengelly doubtless plied salt and pepper and vinegar and fell to. They were alone together because Pat's sister had nipped out for a minute to fetch a jug of beer, so just the next thing that befell will never be known because no human eye was there to mark it save the child's. But with my mind on the past, I see everything as clearly as if I had been on the spot.

"What overtook them was this, Miss Crymes. Feeding his fill, the man suddenly started and clutched at his throat and the little boy stared when his father rose up off his chair and dropped his knife and fork and run for dear life about the room. And for dear life he was running, because, gulping his fish, he'd let down a bone along with it, and that bone had stuck hard and fast and he was choking. They found afterwards how one of the small back bones near the end of the conger's tail was got in along with the meat and come between

118

Pengelly and the breath of life. He growled and gasped and fought, same as the conger had fought; then he fell down and his little boy rushed screaming into the street. But the man was out of his trouble when people got to him."

Mrs. Tregenza broke into a perspiration over the end of her tale and I could see she was living it all over again and picturing everything she described. I also saw the point of the story now and how it had struck upon her with a force none could feel but herself.

"As I see it," I said, "either you had nothing to do with the fisherman's death, in which case your angry words only sound as if they meant something, or else—all unknown to yourself— you have a gift to will things to happen, like the Bible prophets of old. In my opinion I should say it was very unlikely indeed that any quiet, go-by-ground woman like you should have been given such a fearful power as that, and still more unlikely you should have gone so long without knowing it. So I'd say you might well feel for your comfort that you have got no deeper witchcraft than I have got myself, either for good or evil."

"And no hand whatsoever in Patrick Pengelly's death?" she asked.

"No hand at all," I declared. "You lost your temper and wished him dead, and the queer fact that he did die so mortal quick afterwards was only one of those accidents without any hidden meaning to them."

"Then you'd say nobody's got any right to charge me with unholy craft against my neighbours?" she asked.

"Yes," I answered most forcibly. "Powers you have got, of course, but not unholy ones. No evil spirit can enter into us unless, of our own free will, we open the door for it; and you are a most unlikely woman to do any such thing."

Mrs. Tregenza declared her gratitude to me for my words and promised that henceforth she was going to cleave to the same opinion; but, at the bottom of her old heart, I knew she felt a little disappointed. She had long clung in secret to the thrilling belief there was a gift of enchantment in her, and won a fine sense of power out of the thought; but the bleak truth, that she was only a commonplace person, like everybody else,

119

would have cast her down beyond measure. No, no—I'll stake my own fame that to her dying day Rose Tregenza treasured the thought how she had killed that bygone fisherman and was a mighty deal more wonderful than her neighbours imagined.

VIII

A FRIEND once asked why I never seemed to see anything worth laughing or weeping at, and I replied that, on the contrary, nearly everything brought under my notice awoke amusement or regret, as the case might be; but I laughed or wept for different reasons than did common people. I laugh out of sight at times when the folk are crying, and often shed tears unseen while they are cackling with laughter. But I never shed crocodile tears at any time, nor yet laugh crocodile laughter, which I always recognise very quick when I hear it.

In the case of 'Sir Thomas'—a little affair scarce worthy of my pen—all depends upon your point of view, and while I found it amusing, for others it hovered on the brink of a very tragical misfortune. The woman most involved suffered much at the time; but, thanks to my craft, no fatal harm was done and I cannot mind a case when I could say, 'To God be the praise' with better appetite. Only those caught up in the plot ever knew a thing about what was happening at the time and as for 'Sir Thomas' himself, he lived in his own little world and cared nothing about ours.

He was in fact a parrot and spent his orderly days, like many another dumb creature, quite ignorant of the turmoil he was going to make for the human family where his lot was cast. I always felt for the bird that he had not got the life he would have chosen, but balanced the security of a cage and well-meaning human friends against the joys of freedom to live along with his fellow parrots in a kinder climate and on better fruit diet than Dartmoor could offer him. He was an amiable bird and seldom lost his temper or forgot his manners, for he took things as they came and fitted in very well with the two women who made up his household. To his owner, Mrs. Rachel Haycraft, he was much nearer and dearer than any human creature; but for Jane Lintern, Rachel's great-niece, 'Sir Thomas' meant much more than pleasure; he stood for her daily duty and first anxiety. If Mrs. Haycraft could have left all she had got to her parrot, then doubtless she would have done so ; but her money and her cottage were assigned to Jane on condition she did her duty by the bird. For thirty years it had been the widow's first blessing, and she always thanked God that 'Sir Thomas' would outlive her, because their final parting in her opinion must represent a far greater pang for her than her own death was going to be for him.

His story was rather unusual, but when I and Mrs. Haycraft first came acquaint and grew to friendship, she related it to me in her own sentimental words.

" 'Tis wrapped up with my love's young dream, Cherry," she told me, and into her voice, which was hard and lacked for any music on other subjects, there crept a shadowy tenderness.

"You must understand I was tokened to a sailor man in my early twenties—twenty-four to be exact," began Rachel, "and, when he returned from the ocean after a voyage to Australia, Peter Coombes, which was his name, fetched me a foreign parrot, born and bred out in Australia, where the lovely creatures neighbour in flocks. I always feel that in some fashion, known only to him and his Maker, the bird understood what was going to be my cruel fate in the future, for he took to me and wound himself into my heartstrings in a week. Then he grew to be nearest and dearest to me of all living things. In your ignorance you might ask, if I thought such a lot of Peter Coombes as to marry him, then why the mischief did I come to feel such a passion for the parrot? It was for this reason. Me and Coombes were going to be wed after his next voyage and he promised he'd fetch over a hen parrot for a mate to mine and how we'd all settle down as a brace of married couples together and share and share alike and face what time and chance had got in store for us. He left me laughing, and I never saw him again. He sank along with his ship in a hurricane down under. I was crushed to the earth naturally, and then set in my devotion to 'Sir Thomas', for I always felt nobody comprehended my loss same as the parrot did and his worship for me grew deeper from the day Peter's death came to my knowledge. He couldn't fill the gap that

122

smashed up all my hopes and pretty plans for the future when Peter came off the sea, but nevertheless he did more than all my friends could do to temper my sufferings. A good few years passed over me before I got to care for Haycraft well enough to marry him; but between ourselves, Cherry, I never felt to him half so deep as what I felt for 'Sir Thomas'. Poor Haycraft would often say in his whimsical fashion that if he'd foretold I was going to put the bird first and let him only be an 'also ran', he'd have given me a miss. But he was trustworthy to live with none the less and I mourned him more after he was gone than I valued him while he was here."

That was Rachael's story and explained her feelings about her bird. She had lost Joe Haycraft ten years by now and her great-niece, Jane Lintern, she liked very well; but only in measure as she waited upon the parrot. For though Rachel was not exacting as to her own requirements, Jane had to keep a sleepless eye upon 'Sir Thomas' and see all done right for him, on pain of the old lady's furious displeasure if neglected. So the girl had got to be a machine to serve 'Sir Thomas' and wait upon him faithful down to the last daily detail, for he was a most methodical creature and liked every day to go exactly the same as the last. In fact he treated Jane pretty much as her great-aunt did—was pleasant and civil and kindly so long as all went well, but could be short and sharp with her if she failed of her offices. His attitude to her was very different from how he behaved to Rachel herself.

Yet, despite the stern exaction of life upon her, Jane Lintern had found time to fall in love and was now situate much as her great-aunt had been in the past, for she was tokened not to a sailor, but a soldier. Charles Cobley belonged to the Royal Marines and he had just returned from serving in the Far East when these things happened. The exact situation stood as follows. Mrs. Haycraft was gone for her annual holiday to the sea, while Jane remained at home, in charge of the parrot and the house, and Sergeant Cobley was due at Plymouth on his return back from India and would then arrive at Packhorse Bridge, where his parents lived. Rachel had sanctioned Jane's engagement because Cobley was a good lad and well thought upon; but she had made it clear that there was to be no marriage yet awhile, and the sergeant well understood that, for Jane's future hopes, obedience to her great-aunt's wishes was all important.

As for the parrot himself at this time, he continued to be in perfection of health and plumage and gave no sign of advancing years. His waistcoat and reach-me-downs were a fine rose-pink, while what you might have called his tail coat was grey. A crest he also wore, and when Rachel approached his cage he would always put up his crown feathers, like a real gentleman lifts his hat to a lady. It pleased Mrs. Haycraft no little and raised her opinion of me to find 'Sir Thomas' suffered me to scratch his poll and converse with him, because he wouldn't let everyone be so familiar by any means. He was no great talker, but he'd say 'Bless you, Rachel' at all hours of the day and 'Lord make me thankful' when he got a red chilli, which was his favourite tit-bit. For the rest he liked to imitate natural sounds and since Mrs. Haycraft would often have her afternoon nap in his company, he'd got her snore to the life. It began on a low note and rose to a shrill squeak, then deepened again and faded away with a gurgle.

Rachel would be funny about animals sometimes. She put elephants next to parrots in her scale of values.

"Because," she said, "you can set your affection upon either and know it will outlast you ; and if I was a rich woman with no cares and a sizeable garden and accommodation, God's my judge, Cherry, but I'd consider an elephant, because they are faithful creatures and models of devotion."

"So they are sure enough," I told her, "and, what's more, they are mighty workers and would be proud to labour for you. Not that there's much in your little house you could find for an elephant to do, my dear."

But now I need to tell you about a summer afternoon sadly clouded for 'Sir Thomas' and his friends. Mrs. Haycraft was away at the time, having her annual refreshment at Dawlish when, passing down to the village from Owl Pen, I was just walking by Rachel's dwelling-house as out rushed Jane Lintern in a frantic state of mind like a tragedy queen and lost to her behaviour. She had caught sight of me on my way and turned by instinct for the support of a fellow creature who, luckily for her, happened to be me. Indeed she recognised her fortune.

"Thank God 'tis you, Miss Crymes!" she cried. "Not that you can do a thing about it now."

"Don't say there's bad news of your great-aunt, Jane," I begged, and she replied:

"Worse—far worse than that!"

She was no sight for the open street, being distraught and her hair down and her face disfigured with tears and her voice out of control, so I entered in the gate and bade her tell me the worst in as few words as could carry it.

"So long as Rachel's well, there can be no cause for all this upheaval, my dear," I assured her. But even as I spoke my searching eye marked a parlous sight through the house-place window. In the back garden stood the parrot's table, where his cage was set when noonday sun shone and he took the air; but the cage gaped empty with the door wide open!

"Mercy me!" I cried out. "You're not going to tell me 'Sir Thomas' has escaped, Jane?" And then, in her reply, she told her shattering story and all the fearful things for her that were going to follow after it.

"He's not escaped," she said. "He's dead; and that's bad enough, but you may say I'm his murderer, and when great-aunt knows that, it's good-bye to me and the end of my world you might say."

Her prospects were certainly cruel grim, poor girl.

"It was John Tripe's cat," she began. "His cat and our parrot never would neighbour and I always had to keep an eye on the garden when 'Sir Thomas' was upon his table, because the cursed cat loved to come over the fence and cruise around him; and the parrot hated the sight of it. And the last thing great-aunt said to me, before she went off, was never to leave the back garden while the bird was on his table."

"Surely you never gave the cat a chance, Jane?" I asked.

"Yes I did," she answered, "and the yellow devil took it. It was like this: I'd put 'Sir Thomas' out as usual after dinner and then in came Nan Cobley, my intended's sister, to say how Charlie was back along with their mother and coming to see me tonight. Then you see what happened. It was all so cruel

125

interesting, what Nan had to tell about my sweetheart, that I stood for twenty minutes listening to her, then suddenly remembered 'Sir Thomas'—too late."

She fell to sobbing again, and never did a stricken maiden have more to sob over, for one could see the hopeless mess she was in a lot clearer than any way out of it.

"If your Marine is a good, fair-minded man," I began, "and as much in love with you as ever, he'll put your fate higher than your prospects, Jane, and it's too soon for you to despair about him. Your great-aunt will most likely cast you out because you've failed of your duty something shocking; but even that's not a certainty because she's a forgiving Christian at heart. There's plenty of time to see how the land lies as to her before she comes home, and meantime what about the parrot?"

"When Nan Cobley went off I hasted back to the scene, Miss Crymes," continued Jane. "There was the cage on the ground and that cursed creature walking round it and pushing in a paw to see if he could claw the bird; but 'Sir Thomas' lay in the midst already done for. He hadn't been touched. But the shock of finding the cat on his table and then being pitched off it, cage and all, and flung to earth—that was too much for him and he died of fright no doubt. The cat hooked it over the wall the moment I came in sight; but if I've got a man friend left on earth, he won't have no peace till he's shot that filthy beast."

I inspected the victim's body and found he was gone beyond call sure enough. There lay the poor old gentleman, and not a feather out of place.

"I've got the hideous thought that, when great-aunt hears tell about this, she'll die as like as not herself," said Jane, rich in miserable ideas. It was a harrowing opinion on the face of it, yet quite within the bounds of possibility and likely to save a lot of trouble if it happened.

"Make me a cup of tea, my dear," I begged, just to give her something to occupy her distracted mind; and while I drank it and pondered, Jane herself came out with a suggestion which was both horrid and foolish.

"Would it be a clever thing to get the bird stuffed and set

up in a nice, glass case against the day she sees him again?" she asked.

"Very far from it," I answered. "If you adventured any such indecent stroke as that, she'd hate you for ever more, Jane, and so should I. You can't flout the dignity of death like that. More tea, Jane. You must meet this like a brave girl and keep your nerve and give Providence a chance."

That was a properly prophetic word for me to speak, though little I knew it at the time!

"You have done something to cry about—granted," I went on, "but you've cried enough and what you want to do now is to brace yourself and concentrate on what to do next. We must examine every channel offering for escape."

"Escape is the only way," she agreed. "I feel as if I wanted to call on the hills to cover me."

"No," I said. "The hills don't rise that can cover a thing like this. For the moment you've got to keep 'Sir Thomas' in a cool place and greet your sergeant with smiles and a kiss when he turns up. If any light shines, I'll see you tomorrow, and till I do you can keep your mind on one bright thought, Jane. Should you find Cobley to love you as well as he did when last he went on service, then, before you break your situation to him, you'll have another true well-wisher on your side—a fighting man who may have his own ideas as to what's the next step. But hide nothing and let him know that Charity Crymes is giving her thoughts to the matter on your account."

The girl thanked me but still feared more than she hoped and I felt fearful if she'd strike the right note when her soldier made his appearance, because if she let grief for the parrot overmaster her joy for the man, then he might take it amiss. So I left her and if ever there was a case of the ram caught in a thicket for sacrifice at a critical moment, it happened five minutes later. Then, if I didn't run straight into Cobley bound for Jane Lintern! He didn't know me and I didn't know him, but my perceptions were quite equal to guessing who he must be, and every nerve in my body tingled to mark what he was carrying, because, though wrapped up and carefully concealed, he bore along what my senses told me was a bird's cage. And, amazing though it may sound, the piercing eyes of a mind like mine, that never need spectacles to sharpen their sight, told me how Providence was in that cage. I stopped the stranger, much to his astonishment.

"Excuse me," I said, "but you'll be Sergeant Cobley of the Royal Marines on leave and bound for Mrs. Haycraft's great-niece, your sweetheart, Jane Lintern."

"Sure enough—all true as Gospel, old lady," he answered. "And who the mischief might you be?"

"Jane will tell you," I answered. "I've just left her and I mustn't keep you. But I'll ask one favour. There's more in our meeting than meets your eye, Sergeant, and I'd thank you very much if you'd give me a peep at that foreign bird you've got in that cage."

He obeyed my wishes and I gazed upon a parrot so similar to 'Sir Thomas' that it would have taken a feat of magic to part them.

"The idea in my mind was to fetch back a mate for Mrs. Haycraft's parrot," he explained.

"Say no more," I begged. "Let your Jane tell you the meaning of that bird and unfold what lies before you, Sergeant. And when you hear how we all stand, you'll see that this foreign fowl may be called to play a higher part in your own future than ever you dreamed in your wildest moments. But I won't keep you longer because there's an awful lot to do now and only a very few days to do it in. Tell Jane there's high agencies working on her side, but she must play her part same as you must. And tell her she can expect me to be at her house before midnight."

I left him in a maze to know what the mischief I was chattering about, but a great idea already filled my mind and, after I had returned to the lovers at a late hour, I found that they were moving along the same lines as myself, though not so far forward as I was. It cheered both a lot to find me on their side, and when Charles Cobley heard my directions and saw my insight, he said he was going to bet his bottom dollar on my cleverness if Jane would only be quick to follow every hint I gave her.

"It's do or die," declared the young man, "and being such a monstrous thing to happen, Jane's great-aunt will never

128

dream that such a thing could happen. That's what we call 'tactics' in war, Miss Crymes."

His tactics were well on the way. He had given out at home that his bird had died suddenly, as parrots will when called to breathe cold air. He told his mother it had died of a pneumonia and he had already buried the real 'Sir Thomas' deep in Mrs. Haycraft's garden and started the new 'Sir Thomas' in the original cage. There was a notch on the dead bird's tail feathers —the only thing which the live one lacked, and Jane had taken her scissors and put the notch on the new one's tail. He was a spry bird and travelled his cage quick and took his food well from the first, and by good chance he didn't talk, so I pointed out the first thing would be to try to teach him to bless Rachel Haycraft, same as her own bird was apt to do, and rub the words into his understanding day and night.

"Keep him in the dark and repeat the words to him over and over and over again, Jane," I said. "Let him hear nothing else, and if he can be got to say 'em, that's half the way to success. And if your great-aunt marks that he's not so talkative as of old, just say that it's the same with parrots as with men: when they get up in years, they talk less and less, because they know there's nobody to listen."

Well, I will say that the lovers put in a lot of hard work for their salvation and told a power of needful falsehoods and was very thankful to me for all the priceless hints I furnished them. Through the fortnight remaining before Rachel's return, Jane lied daily on a postcard to Dawlish stating that 'Sir Thomas' was all right. She had grown desperate now and felt it needless to worry about any more details of behaviour. 'So well be hanged for a sheep as a lamb,' she said, and felt very little hope of the final issue. But her thirst for vengeance persisted and she couldn't have hated Tripe's cat worse if it had been a human being. She kept on at Charlie to shoot the creature, till I pointed out how Tripe didn't know what his cat had done and if it was slain, that would only complicate a situation, which was going to be touch and go as it stood.

A few discoveries we made as to the new parrot which gave cause for hope. For example he loved a female hand to scratch his poll, so when the widow caressed him, as she certainly would, there was no fear of tragedy. Another bright thing happened just two days before Mrs. Haycraft came home. Jane had shut the light from the cage for hours and hours, as I directed, and worked like a beaver to make the bird catch up the familiar words 'Bless you, Rachel,' and now she told me he had begun to try his hand at them and looked to be turning them over thoughtful to himself.

"Please Providence he'll burst out with them the moment they meet," I said; but Jane was always on the losing side by instinct and never felt a ray of hope.

"I'm a liar and a lost creature," she said, "and I don't deserve to succeed and something tells me I ain't going to."

Then back came Rachel to Packhorse Bridge and the new parrot, and thankful she was to be home, as folk so often find themselves after taking a holiday. She was fearful that Cobley might want to marry Jane before he returned to work, but very relieved to hear there would be no hurry as to that.

"I don't want for Jane to begin her married life in barracks, ma'am," said Charlie to her, "and we have agreed to keep company and no more under your orders."

That disposed her to him and he was full of tactics to keep her friendship till his leave ended and he went back to business. Meantime it looked as if the parrot understood his task and felt on his mettle to make a good job of it. He puzzled Rachel sometimes and revealed glimpses of his former life which were strange and not too easy to explain; but only once did that bird blot his copy-book in such a way that I wanted all my artifice to save the situation.

Dropping in one day six months after the new 'Sir Thomas' had settled down without any mishap of consequence, I found his mistress uncommon silent with a look of care upon her face. My inner voice told me the parrot had put his foot in it; but I left her to open the subject, which she presently did, after Jane had cleared out and we were alone together.

"I've had a shock, Cherry," she said, and I was sorry to hear it.

"I hate shocks myself," I answered. "They are bad for the system when you get on in years."

"It's my bird," she continued. "Last night, just as I was

putting his cover on, without a shadow of warning he said something I won't soil your ears to repeat; but it was something that no decent man, nor decent parrot either, would ever be catched saying. He don't talk near so much as he did talk, but never in his life has he dared to utter any such shameful thing before."

"Fancy that!" I exclaimed. "What they'll hoard up, Rachel!"

"He certainly never hoarded it up in all his years with me," she answered; and sighed as she spoke.

"You'd best to tell me what it was," I begged her, "because, if I knew, it might lie in my power to explain how he came to such a downfall."

"I won't say it, but I'll write it," she replied, "though I blush to do even that, but you're a woman of the world and can stand up to it no doubt. My terror is that he may fall into the way of repeating it again now it's come back to his memory and give the house a bad name, so as I shouldn't dare to ask any respectable person into it. And if I thought Charlie Cobley had learned him, then I'd forbid Jane to take the man once and for all."

"Not for a moment must you accuse the Marine of any such thing," I said. "He's far from that sort and I never heard him use a foul word, let alone teach a parrot one." Well, she wrote it down and she spelled it wrong, but there was no manner of doubt as to what the poor, ignorant bird had uttered.

"Horrible!" I said, tearing up the paper; "but don't you make too much of it, my dear, nor yet put the blame on 'Sir Thomas', any more than you do when he imitates you snoring."

"He don't do that now," she answered. "He's given that up once for all."

"So much the better," I assured her. "It was always a pity. What has happened, Rachel, is in my opinion tolerable easy to explain. We know that more than half a century ago your beautiful bird travelled to England and might well have been in mid-ocean for months along with the baser sort of sailor men. We also know how the far past will stir our memories when we grow old, and so—just by some sad accident—this stirred in his. It means nothing to him—only just an idle echo

131

from fifty years ago, and I'd say most likely it has gone for ever and you'll never hear it again."

"If I do, Cherry," she said firmly, "I'll whip him till he screams for mercy!"

But never more did anybody hear the bird disgrace himself; though a very curious thing happened some few months later, for then Jane came full of news one morning to tell me the sham 'Sir Thomas' had picked up Rachel's snore to the life and was doing it even better than the first had done! Which left no shadow of danger even in Jane's mind.

Of course she and I and the sergeant all kept secret as the tomb till the old lady went to her rest, which she did do two years later, leaving her great-niece her cottage and one hundred and fifteen pounds a year. Her will was mostly full of directions as to the support and comfort of the parrot, and he saw her die, for she had his cage beside her deathbed and closed her eyes upon the pleasant sight of him at work on a red chilli. Needless to say her great-niece was jealous to respect Rachel's wishes; but it was like Jane's poor spirit to find herself full of anxieties for the next world even though her stay in this one turned out so well.

"There's no secrets in the Happy Land," she told me once, "and when great-aunt hears our shameful plot laid bare up there, her happiness will be ruined for ever more."

But I reproved the wilful creature and spoke sharply to her.

"Paradise is not going to be a scene of nasty revelations," I said, "and Mrs. Haycraft need never know the truth about the parrot for all eternity unless you're fool enough to tell her yourself when you get there."

But Jane only started another hateful thought.

"I'm little likely to myself," she answered. "A tricky, lying piece like me don't deserve it; but many folk believe that their pet animals go to heaven and nobody can prove they don't. And what then, Miss Crymes? Why, then you've got to face the chance she may be met by the real 'Sir Thomas' first moment she arrives!"

"Well," I asked, "and what's the matter with that? She'd a lot sooner meet him than anybody else."

"It's what he'll tell her," sighed the idiot.

132

IX

RACHEL HAYCRAFT'S parrot reminds me of another bird which, though it never existed in sober truth, yet furnished a mighty queer page of human story and was vouched for long ago by trustable people. Indeed I should not have lifted a hand in the adventures that overtook the Bullstone family without help from that fabulous creature itself. Though never better than a spectre to me, it was far more for those who had seen it and suffered from the sight of it and known its ugly history for generations past.

Not very often do you hear tell of a family ghost among the poor and humble, though quite a common thing with the quality; yet while they were not quality, the Bullstone race was of long descent and had dwelt and died on the acres named after them spread in mid-most Dartmoor, since an ancestor of the clan settled there many years before living memory. The Bullstones of Bullstone they were, and still among their heirlooms they numbered many curiosities from the past, such as a musket one of their men carried in our wars against the French, and a beautiful little model of a foreign, fighting ship carved and built by a Frenchman, when the great war prisons at Prince's Town harboured thousands and thousands of the poor fellows.

The famous ghost bird of the Bullstones was in a measure like to that still more famous 'White Bird' of Oxenham, which is still renowned in the history of that noble family because, when the reigning head of the race is marked for death, their White Bird may surely be seen by living eyes at the time flying around about Oxenham Castle, or brooding with folded wings upon the roof-tree of the mansion. I have talked with not a few old folk who actually saw it when a master of Oxenham was going home; and even though he happened to be far away and not in residence at the time of his passing, yet the 'White Bird' never failed to signal when his days were ending. In the likeness of a large, snow-white swallow it came and flitted even into the

133

chambers of the dwelling-house sometimes, to tell how another lord of the manor approached his grave.

The Bullstone death-watcher was a bird also, though not what you could call a bird unknown, but just a familiar object to every Dartmoor dweller. It was known as the 'Grey Fisher'— in shape and form a common heron and an everyday sight upon our streams—and the way of his operations was this. A hundred yards from the house-front of Bullstone Farm runs Cherrybrook, a feeder of West Dart. It takes a sharp bend at this point and there's a bit of a fall into a deep reach below, with heather-clad banks on one side and a little beach of pebbles and silver sand upon the other. And here lies Nicky Pool, so called because of the fearful thing that overtook a moorman there in times long forgotten. Nicholas Gill he was called, and when cutting faggots from a furze brake one autumn eve there suddenly came a rush high above and a hurtle of noise, and he marked some great flying thing sink to earth behind the brake. Thinking it must be a skein of wild geese descended, Nicky crept to look, and there he stared upon a mother-naked witch, broomstick and all, while, what was more fearful yet, he saw that she was no less a young woman than Cora Satterly—the girl he was tokened to wed and daughter of Miriam Satterly from Packhorse Bridge! The shock of such a thing turned young Gill's brain, so his story ran. He told his tale and Cora denied it most furious, swore on the Book she knew nought about witchcraft and was a good Christian before God, and threw Nicky over. Which was the death of him, for a fortnight later he flung himself down Cut Hill Quarry and so died. But whether his sweetheart was a witch or not is hidden from human knowledge and the tale does not report what was the end of Cora.

For the Bullstones, Nicky Pool meant trouble all through their history, because as sure as the 'Grey Fisher' was seen beside it, the head of the family knew he must be called to die tolerable quick. The fatal bird was last seen a good few years ago when Fanny Bullstone lost her husband. I had long known her and her family, but it was not till after her husband's end that I entered into her interests myself. He was a weak man and far too fond of the bottle, but very kindhearted and generous, as so many hard drinkers are. Fanny liked to talk to me because I was a good listener always, and I well mind how she came and drank tea at Owl Pen and laid bare all she'd been through before her husband died. She was an uncommon big woman—fifteen stone at least—and she was like a great black mountain in my little parlour as she sat there and traversed her misfortunes in her widow's weeds, and with her deep, woe-laden voice. She went back a bit for her starting-point to show how the accursed bird had shown twice in her own recollection.

"There was my husband's grandfather first," she said. "He saw the hateful thing in his old age, when he went out to feed his pigs on a bitter winter's morning. He came into breakfast with his bad news and was gone ten days after. But my dear Henry's father never met with the 'Grey Fisher' and died a natural death, whereas there's no manner of doubt the bird brought news of my husband's end upon him. By all accounts the Fisher is only seen at dawn or dimpsy light, and it was break of day when my Henry saw him and tottered back into the house just as May and me were laying breakfast."

Then she told how he came in to his meal a stricken man.

"He was shaking like an aspen when he sank down upon the settle with the blood all flowed from his face and his eyes glazing out of his head," she said, "and I cried: 'Guy Fawkes and angels, Henry! Have 'e seen a ghost?' 'I have,' he answered. 'I've seen 'Grey Fisher' by Nicky Pool and 'tis all over with me, Fan!'"

She broke off then a minute to explain.

"My son, Richard Henry, don't believe in the 'Grey Fisher' and always makes fun of it, but my second son, Joshua, does believe in it. And so did their father, though we all tried to put heart into him and prayed for him not to be down-daunted, and thought as like as not that he'd mistook some stock or stone for the bird in the grey dawn light and never seen anything out of Nature at all; but Henry knew only too well there was no doubt whatsoever. To please me he called on his Reverence at Packhorse Bridge and had a long tell about it; but the minister told him he ought to scorn such heathen nonsense and not believe a word of it. All in vain, of course, because my husband had his family history behind him and so didn't take any comfort from that. He was cruel moped and downcast for a day or two and scarce went farther than the farmyard; but then he got reckless and rode about in all weathers and kept away from home more than usual."

I showed Fanny my heartfelt interest and inquired as to details.

"You might say in a manner of speaking, once he knew for certain he was doomed, that his coming fate changed his character," I suggested.

"Yes—exactly so," agreed the widow. "My Henry was one of them men born to be ruled, and he knew it. His mother ruled him and he lived very comfortable under her dominion until she passed on; then he turned to me, knowing the woman I was. Never, you might say, did the dear man fill my dream of a husband; but he was one I'd got to know before marriage and felt myself very well capable of carrying on and making him content. He was the sort to need a wife with a heart a bit harder than his own, and not given to be so freehanded to the world at large as he was, because there's nothing more certain to get you in a mess sooner or late than over-much generosity, and them that practise it have often to pay an ugly price for their weakness."

"You were a famous wife to him, Fanny," I said, "and a pattern of what a good partner can do for the male if he's got enough sense to listen to her."

"So was the general opinion, I believe," she replied. "Yet in my secret heart I've often compared the state of the wife and mother with that of the independent spinster, complete in herself and unattached. Better be a happy old maid than a miserable married woman, or a forlorn widow."

"Whether or no, you've got the unclouded happiness of your married life to look back upon," I said.

She shook her head.

"Not to call it unclouded," she confessed. "There was always the one weak, obstinate spot in Henry beyond my cunning to heal. I couldn't wean him off liquor and it was a battle that raged between us all his life. At his best he was a steady drinker, though seldom he disgraced himself in public

136

except on a Bank Holiday or some occasion of national rejoicings. Then he would defy me and let himself go with a light heart."

"In a measure he hastened his own end, I'm afraid, poor dear man," I said with a sigh, and she nodded.

"After that awful bird showed up, he lost all control and soaked a lot too often. In the end it finished him, two months from that fatal morning when he heard his days were done."

"Poor Henry's end was very melancholy sure enough," I said, and she agreed.

"He rode home drunk as a lord two nights running and then had to keep the house for a bit; but after that he was off again for the last time and we heard afterwards that he had drunk himself blind at the 'Cat and Fiddle', that pot-house kept by Tobias Bloom some miles from Packhorse Bridge and very inferior to the 'Hearty Welcome', kept by Tobias Snell. He left there at closing time and got on his horse, which was well used to carrying beer, and nobody feared for him till he was reported next day up at Cocks Bottom with a broken neck."

Mrs. Bullstone went over the details, forgetting I knew them all, and then carried on her sad story.

"A terrible come-along of it and how I lived through such misfortunes and the shame of them, God He knows. But so it was and such is life. Now it's Richard Henry's turn to work, for all is altered by his father's sudden end and he's called to take life serious."

"His brother, Joshua, will be your right hand still, however," I reminded her.

"That is so. Joshua is built on the steady lines of my own family and loves the land and is a trustworthy, hardworking farmer without a doubt; but Richard Henry don't shine with his nose to the grindstone. Too fond of sporting and pleasure and gadding about. However, Joshua's well content to do the work and let Richard Henry have first place and all the fun."

Joshua was a quiet, go-by-the-ground young man, more useful than showy; but he liked his elder brother to cut a bit of a dash.

"They have both turned very bitter against the herons now," said their mother, "and, though Richard Henry will have it that it was only a chance wild heron his poor father saw, he never misses a chance to shoot the beastly birds when they come in his reach."

A tidy long time passed before I saw Fanny again after that, but near a year later, riding on my donkey not far from Bullstone and evening coming down, I thought to call and ask for a cup of tea and hear if all was well and the head of the family settling to his life's work. Richard Henry was a true Bullstone—tall, handsome, fearless and lighthearted, with a joke for everybody from squire to stone-breaker; but Joshua happed to be the opposite—a dark, solid man and a slow thinker, yet steady as time and loyal to his ancient race.

Both were out when I came along, but Fanny was home with her daughter, May—a nice girl though too big in the beam for only eighteen years old and promising to be as huge as her mother some day. They were pleased to welcome me and full of a bit of news, which they regarded as doubtful, but did not much surprise me. Joshua was already tokened to a Pack-horse Bridge maiden, though his mother had ordained they were both too young to think of wedding for a year or two, but now had come the news that Richard Henry was in love also and Fanny told me about it.

"The news is a week old now," she said. "My eldest plumped it out at breakfast in his usual feather-brained fashion. 'Mother,' he began, 'you can stiffen up a bit this morning for I'm going to surprise you.' 'Not you, my son,' I answered him. 'You'll never surprise me till I see you doing a bit of man's work.' 'I have been doing a bit of man's work,' he answered. 'I've been courting, and she's said "yes" at last, and I count to get married tidy soon.' We all stared with wonder for he'd given no sign of what he was up to. May laughed and Joshua whistled and old Michael Duffy, our head man, cackled uneasily and looked at me, for he wondered how I was going to take it."

"Mother was wonderful, Miss Crymes," put in May Bullstone. "She just towered up to her full height, as she always does before anything outstanding, and gazed on Richard

138

Henry and then turned down his intentions once for all in her biggest voice, didn't you, Mother?"

"At first," answered Fanny, "I didn't regard him as serious. He has always been addicted to the girls in a general way, which is a Bullstone weakness; but there's safety in numbers and I didn't fear any danger of that kind; but now he declared he was serious, so felt it best to nip his nonsense in the bud. 'You're a long way short of wife-old,' I told him, 'and I hope you'll drop any such caper this instant moment, Richard Henry. The lazy likes of you can't keep yourself, let alone a wife, and I won't listen to it till you're a lot wiser and harder working than at present.'"

"But he was well prepared to argue it out," went on May.

"Oh yes; he put up a fight," admitted her mother. "'You didn't make no fuss when Joshua took his girl,' he said to me, and I told him there was a great gulf fixed between him and his younger brother. 'Joshua's got an old head on young shoulders and don't let courting interfere with his duty,' I said. I was glad to praise Joshua to his face, because he's the quiet sort that don't get much praise in a general way. 'No more do I let courting interfere with my duty,' said Richard Henry, 'but now that I've got to think of Nancy as well as the farm, you'll see me pull my weight all right'."

"Then there was silence," went on May, "and Joshua and Mike Duffy left the table and went to work and mother said nothing for the moment; but she and me both fastened our thoughts on the name he'd let slip. I could call home three Nancys."

"And so could I—three and no more to my knowledge," went on Fanny, taking up the tale. "First there was Nancy Veale—a homely, harmless soul, the stone-breaker's daughter. She's as plain as bread and no education and quite below Richard Henry's notice in any case. Then there was Nancy Bloom, daughter of Tobias Bloom, landlord of the 'Cat and Fiddle', and a man I hated worse than sin, for I well knew if he'd watched over my husband on that fatal night and not let him ride forth drunk to his death, Henry would have made a more honourable end."

139

"Nancy Bloom is his only child and serves in her father's bar," said May. "She's a bowerly maid, and I know some girls who like her and say she's very quiet and well-mannered for all her rough job of work at the public."

"Sly no doubt and, if a barmaid, much too common to pass muster with a Bullstone I should hope," went on Fanny. "And, lastly, there's Nancy Sweetland, Barry Sweetland's eldest at Bair Down Farm. She must be two years older than Richard Henry, but a sensible woman and a famous prize-winner at butter-making. She might have been a bit uninteresting to the male eye, but was not by nature against the men, so her father has told me. My son sees a good bit of the Bair Down people, because Sweetland is a keen sportsman, so, putting two and two together, I decided that it was her Richard Henry aimed at."

" ' 'Tis Miss Sweetland, no doubt,' I said to him, 'but I'm surprised she saw much in you.' 'And you might have been still more surprised if I'd seen much in her!' he answered. 'Why, God's truth, Mother! If there wasn't a woman left in the world, who'd have any use for that psalm-smiting old maid?' "

May laughed.

"The very words he said, Miss Crymes," she told me.

"Then I asked him as to the others," went on Fanny. " 'It won't be Nancy Veale?' I suggested. 'You bet your life it won't!' he answered. 'Have another shot.' 'There's only Bloom's daughter left that I can think upon,' I murmured. 'Only Bloom's daughter!' he cried out. 'And what in thunder can any living man want better than Toby Bloom's daughter?' "

"He said she was the pink of cleverness and loveliness," went on May. " 'She's a proper miracle,' he told us; but mother had grown firm as a rock by now, hadn't you, Mother'?"

"I had, and so I still remain," declared Fanny. "I said: 'Once and for all I defy you and forbid you, Richard Henry. I don't often put my foot down, as you well know, but once down, it stops down, and no human power was ever known to lift it. So long as I am on earth you don't marry Nancy Bloom,

140

and there's more reasons against it than there are hairs on your head, my son. First and foremost,' I went on, 'you forget that Bloom so near murdered your dear father as no matter, and if you think I'll suffer you to wed a murderer's daughter, then you think wrong. Never shall it be,' I said, 'and if you loved your father's memory as you should, then you'd never have darkened the door of the "Cat and Fiddle" again, let alone tinker up to a common barmaid, and I'm shocked to the roots that ever you could have sunk so low, and if you'd cleave to your proper work and not go mooning after every giglet wench that turns her bold eyes upon you, it would be a darned sight better for my peace of mind and your own self-respect.' "

Her daughter confirmed this.

"That's just what you said, every word, Mother," declared May. "And you heaved with indignation and went on till you got that pain in your side and was forced to stop. And Richard Henry surprised both of us, by listening very patient and not flaring out. He saw it was going to be pull baker, pull devil between him and you. But he kept his temper and then, when you got your spasm, he said, 'You calm down, my old dear ; there's a lot too much of you to grow so excited and you didn't ought to do it.' "

After that Fanny resumed.

" 'Little you care for my health, Richard Henry,' I answered him, and then he vowed he loved me more than anything in the world after Nancy Bloom. 'There's things that may happen and there's things that must happen,' he said, 'and things that may hap do, or do not ; but things that must hap will hap for dead certain.' Then he played a clever card but didn't deceive me for one moment. 'Why, bless your old heart,' he went on, 'she's your sort—just the hard-working, straight, plucky, sensible kind you say are all dead and buried nowadays ! And clever as a cartload of monkeys too. I often feel little better than a fool before her, young as she is.' 'Yes, I daresay you do,' I replied to him. 'Young she may be, but she's had plenty of practice at twisting the men round her fingers, no doubt, and you wouldn't be very difficult.' "

"Then he smiled," cut in May, "and his smile is always

too much for mother. 'You won't make me angry,' he promised. 'I know what I know.' "

It was time I got on my way and so prepared to leave them.

"I'm glad he's going to be patient and well-behaved about it," I said. "You must watch over him and watch over yourselves also—you and May. You must take public opinion into account, my dears, and consider the general opinions."

"As to that," answered Fanny, "I've aired this business round about, and all but one agree that I'm right. And that's Trueman Trinny at Two Bridges. He tells me to keep an open mind! He's all for leaving it to Nature to take its course; but I've seen a lot too much of Nature taking its course on Dartmoor and don't want nothing of that sort in my family. It would be a fatal match at best; and that's where we stand up to the present time, Cherry."

It was just the sort of tussle that pleased me to hear about, but nothing happened for a while except a brave stroke struck by Richard Henry, of which I heard from Fanny's daughter two months later when meeting her in the village. May had quite a lot of news, most of which I knew already.

"If my brother didn't bring Nancy Bloom in to tea last Sunday!" she began. "Bold as brass he brought her and, shocked though mother and me were, you couldn't deny she's a lovely piece of goods—all in her best gown with nice stockings and saucy shoes. Of course, before mother, she demeaned herself most orderly and looked after her manners and took the proper line. She was far from bold or pushing, yet on the other hand, didn't cringe before mother. She made a good tea and ate very nice and praised the cake and listened to us and talked sensibly; but you may be sure mother didn't show no yielding. Nancy mentioned that her father, Mr. Bloom, wasn't doing too well at the 'Cat and Fiddle' and had it in mind to quit and find a public in the South Hams for his health's sake; and then mother let loose and told her that, go where he might, her father wouldn't escape from his conscience when he remembered his wicked behaviour before my father died."

"How did she get out of that, May?" I asked.

"She only said that if her father thought he had any hand in Mr. Bullstone's death, he'd never forgive himself," replied

May. "She's got a voice like a singing bird, and I couldn't but rather like her myself because she was so pretty and had such lovely hair. But she didn't soften mother, and when Richard Henry had finished his tea and found he'd drawn a blank, he said they must be going now and took her off. Mother dressed him down pretty sharp when he came home to supper, but he kept his nerve about it and confessed he was sorry he had brought her and only done so in the hope a sight of her and sound of her speech might thaw mother. And soon after, if Mr. Bloom himself didn't poke his nose into Bullstone and ask for the pleasure of a few words with mother!"

"Fancy that!" I exclaimed.

"I wasn't home," continued May, "but mother told me all about it when I came back from Prince's Town. Mr. Bloom is a thin, shabby-looking man with a miserable, long moustache and feeble eyes—so said mother. He kept clearing his throat and tapping his knee with one hand and pulling his moustache with the other, and he bowed his head to every word she said to him and sighed deeply to find he couldn't make any impression upon her. But mother made a lot of impression upon him seemingly. He had come to find if he could make the engagement go pleasant all round. 'Love is love,' he said, 'and us getting to the middling stage, though you keep as young as your family always does, Mrs. Bullstone, mustn't forget what it was to feel the tender passion. I had a good wife and all the world knows you was blessed with a wonderful husband.' That was a pretty poor start, needless to say, and for answer my mother ordered him to keep father's name off his lips and it was like his impudence to dare to mention him. Then Mr. Bloom tried again and dwelt a bit upon Nancy's fine qualities and what an honest, handsome and upright young man Richard Henry was and so on. But my mother soon had enough of that and presently sent him off without any tea and a flea in his ear. 'Now you can list to me, Tobias Bloom,' she finished up with, 'and when you've heard a bit more than my son's like to have told you, you can go home to your public house so quick as you please. I'm fixed as a rock about this and ordain it shan't happen. And if my son was fool enough to go against me, he'd be a ruined man. And whether you feel

143

wishful for your girl to marry a ruined man is your business.'
And then she told him how my brother stood."

"And how does he stand, May, if you care to tell me?" I
asked.

"There's no secrets about it and we all know how Richard
Henry stands," she answered. "Father left Bullstone, lock,
stock and barrel, to mother, and mother will leave it as she
pleases, and also her bit of money as she pleases. She told Mr.
Bloom that if Richard Henry took Nancy, she would say
'Good-bye' once for all to the pair of 'em."

"Which hit him pretty hard for certain," I said, "because
no doubt, like everybody else, he thinks that your eldest
brother is down for the farm."

"Yes," agreed May, "Mr. Bloom was hit very hard. He
rubbed his nose and patted his knee and pulled his moustache
and said mother had properly astonished him. 'You're one
who never leaves anybody in doubt of your meaning,' he told
mother, 'and, of course, if that's the situation and your boy
don't inherit Bullstone Farm save by your good pleasure, then
it's clear as mud the case is altered. Because it wouldn't do for
my Nancy to take a chap who had quarrelled with his own
salvation, would it?' That's what he said, but mother didn't
trouble to answer, so he gave his knee a last pat and got up
and bade her good evening and shambled off with a walk like
a lurcher dog."

"That doubtless explains how it's got to be public knowledge," I told her. "They say in Packhorse Bridge there's a lot
of wonder as to whether your brother, or your mother, is going
to conquer."

"Richard Henry has got his tail down for the minute,"
May answered. "Joshua and I are both sorry for him, and
Joshua's downhearted too because if Richard Henry puts
himself out of the running, then Josh will have the farm; but
he'd far rather play second fiddle all his life to Richard Henry."

"Now I can tell you something in exchange for all your
news, May," I announced. "Last Tuesday, after nightfall, two
folk came to see me, namely your elder brother and Nancy
Bloom along with him."

But she wasn't surprised.

144

"As a matter of truth, Miss Crymes," she replied, "I'm responsible for that—not for Nancy, but Richard Henry. I told him a bit ago, out of mother's hearing, what a far famous one you are for knotty questions, and I urged upon him to relate his fix to you and pay you proper if you could see any way round it. And very glad I am he came."

"Yes, he came and brought Nancy with him," I repeated.

"What did you think of her?" she asked.

"In herself I think well of her," I answered. "For her age she sees very clear, and she's got the experience that a barmaid is bound to pick up. She's intelligent and modest and she's properly in love with your brother. Seeing what she must know now about his position and prospects, you might have thought she would have felt the game was up and dropped him, if only for his own sake, but so far it hasn't struck her to do that. They can't imagine any such thing as parting and were both very calm and collected about it."

"I'm glad they came anyway," said May. "And I'm glad you weren't against them."

"By no means against them—quite the contrary," I assured her. "I think they are well suited to make a good job of joining up. She's got youth and good brain-power, and might well be the sort to steady Richard Henry and learn him to work and not be a playboy any longer. She might in truth bring out the best of him, as love will often bring out the best in some natures. But there's your mother to think upon, and her peace of mind, and the dignity of the Bullstone race and the future of the farm."

"I'm sure you gave them a lot to think about," agreed May, "and I hope you'll turn it over and not turn them down out of hand, Miss Crymes."

"I gave them a lot to think upon as you say, May," I replied. "We must wait and watch what comes of it."

"To win mother is the first thing," she said.

"All gives place to that," I admitted. "There's the key to the lock, and we must go on hoping I shall find it."

But a week later everything was altered and Providence took an unexpected hand, as it is so apt to do. All changed in the twinkling of an eye and Richard Henry's prospects were suddenly lifted on to a plane where his love affairs and his other hopes and fears were all going to be wiped away, along with the poor young man himself. I chanced among the first to hear this news, for I called in at Bullstone myself with a little gift for Fanny, knowing it to be her birthday. But a black birthday she already faced and great confusion and despair had properly upset the apple cart for her and her family. A cold, late autumn dawn there had been, with heavy morning fog over the land and rain to follow; but it bettered after noon, when I looked in to hear the fateful tale.

Fanny had taken to her bed, but willed to see me. She was red with crying and her window blind drawn when I went to see her; but she heaved her huge body up in the bed and panted like a giant porpoise, and after a few melancholy words to say that all the plagues of Egypt had come upon her, she related the shocking details.

"I'd just got up and was doing my hair in front of my looking-glass with my mouth full of hair-pins, when I cast my eyes out of the window, as I always do to note the manner of my birthday weather," she began. "From this chamber you can see Cherrybrook flowing down past our crofts; but this morning the mist was heavy upon the scene. Then it broke and lifted for a while before crowding down again, and in that space of time I saw it—the 'Grey Fisher'—so clear as death! There it stood humped up, gazing down upon Nicky Pool. Then I gave a scream loud enough to shake the house and fainted, and May told me after that she heard my shriek and rushed up to find me unconscious on the floor. She fetched me round and I hid the truth from her, and hoped to God the spectrum I'd seen was only in my own mind and no place else. But though the fog soon came down again and hid all, others had seen it also. There weren't no hiding the horror from Mike Duffy, up to the cow-house, and another man along with him also saw it, and, worst of all, Richard Henry himself. He had viewed it before he came in, after we were all set to breakfast, but he tried hard to look cheerful and kissed me and wished me happy returns of the day, and brought out a gift. But everything was in vain because Duffy had already confirmed the worst. Then my son confessed and granted he had witnessed the bird also when the fog lifted. Instantly he had rushed over to see it close, in hopes to prove it was no more than a living creature; but 'twas vanished when he got to the Pool and the mist rolled down again. 'You must be brave about it, Mother,' he said to me, 'and face up to it and believe it's all nonsense'; but he was badly shook and could let down no breakfast to name. We all tried to be as valiant as him, but Joshua broke down and couldn't hide his dismay, and old Mike Duffy snivelled and wept into his porridge, and May began to yowl also. But Richard Henry rebuked the lot of us and told Joshua we were Bullstones, not babies, and must face the curse as bravely as our anticessors had been called to do. I was the first to pull myself together and order everybody to put their trust in God; but though he praised me for trying to be brave, Richard Henry agreed presently we mustn't deceive ourselves. 'There's no manner of doubt 'twas the accursed bird,' said old Duffy, 'and I knowed it the minute I set my eyes on it!' "

"A cruel wisht birthday for you, poor Fanny," I told her. "But I'm not one to belittle signs and wonders as you well know, and I've seen too many things happen beyond power of any human explanation. Yet courage is mostly given us when we need it and the cup may pass from Richard Henry, so I'd pray for you to be hopeful."

I comforted her and said it was often darkest before dawn and a few other silly things like that; but I felt quite satisfied she was all right in herself and the shock was not going to do her any bodily harm.

The news went through the parish in four-and-twenty hours and many well-wishers and lovers of sensation poured in a stream to Bullstone to pity the family; but pity's poison to a nature like Fanny's and she strained a friendship here and there by saying so. Everybody was terribly sorry for the victim himself when his family curse looked to have got him, and some flouted the tale, while others believed it and wondered when and how the blow was going to fall. Among the believers stood Fanny herself, and next time I went to see her she suffered from the hateful looking forward and the misery that haunts you when you know evil is near but cannot tell how near.

147

" 'Tis a torture to wait for death, when the doctor's coming regular and everything as it should be," she said to me. "But to have this shadow hanging over your eldest and nothing to do but to sit and wait till he's snuffed out—that's right down hell, Cherry."

May told me of incidents that had overtaken Richard Henry.

"He's a changed man, of course," she said, "and all his old pleasures lost now. He don't follow any of the ways he employed to waste time; but to our astonishment he hasn't cast off Nancy Bloom, which was the first thing mother expected and hoped for him to do. And more curious yet, Miss Crymes, she hasn't cast him off neither! She's come to tea twice since it happened, and mother hadn't the heart to do anything about it, but just let her sit silent and watchful with her pretty eyes on Richard Henry. But she sticks like wax to her own opinion and won't believe in the 'Grey Fisher'. Of course love-making is frozen out of them now."

"A good sign she can cleave to him," I said. "That shows the girl loves him in sober honesty and for himself alone."

Fanny told me something else.

"He's living almost like a child," she said. "He's careful to avoid anything doubtful, or offering a pinch of danger, and it would puzzle anyone less than his Maker to know how death's going to catch him, or when, or where. He don't fear his end for a moment but takes mortal care not to court it."

Time passed over Bullstone and then something happened that showed May was wrong when she said that love-making had frozen out of the lovers, because Richard Henry suddenly announced that he wanted to be married before he was took off and the family found itself divided before such a doubtful idea. Joshua and May thought it was fairly reasonable: they didn't see any cause why he should not have his final flutter in Nancy's arms if he felt like it; but his mother held it highly improper for Richard Henry to think upon a wife with death at his door any moment now. She spoke to me about it one evening when she was in Packhorse Bridge and drank a dish of tea at Owl Pen on her way home.

"It's the vicar's fault," she said. "At my wishes he went for a talk with his Reverence, and I wish I hadn't sent him now, because, instead of helping my son to face eternity in a Christian spirit, Mr. Walpole declared our phantom bird was only the skeleton in our cupboard and all nonsense. He even dared to say if Richard Henry defied the 'Fisher' and married, that might help to open our eyes! And now my son clamours to do it; which shows that, though he looks after his own safety close enough, he don't spare a thought for my peace of mind when I have to face up to his widow."

I could see that the thought of Nancy, with very likely a grandchild to follow, was troubling Fanny a good deal just then.

"We can't read the pattern of it, I grant you," I said to her, "but don't you let it vex you, my dear woman, because where there's doubt, there's hope. These things are in Higher Hands, be it as it will, and your son would never have got to want a wife just now if the idea had not been put in his head for some good reason. So you will be wise to pleasure him. And what does the girl think about it herself? May tells me you can't deny that Nancy is a far more trustable maiden than you expected to find her."

"She's well-mannered, but obstinate," explained Fanny. "She comes to tea most Sundays now and her love for the man looks to be genuine enough, because, though she knows as I told her miserable father, that Richard Henry will be penniless if he marries her, yet she's prepared to go through with it. She won't take the 'Grey Fisher' seriously; but she goes so far as to say she'd sooner be my son's widow than the wife of any other man!"

"A beautiful sentiment, if you ask me," I said, and praised Nancy for it.

"Once done, then the future will open out, Fanny," I continued. "An inner voice tells me that if you pleasure them, it may bring you a fine reward and help to make you forget what you have suffered."

"They are all for it but me," she admitted. "Joshua says that if I let Richard Henry drop into his grave a bachelor, then I'll feel a lot of remorse to add to my other afflictions, when he's gone, and May has took a strong liking to Nancy. Even

149

that poor wretch her father, who came over to see me again not long since, dwelt on their obstinate affection for each other and says he admires it and feels that Providence can't overlook such a fine attitude. He said it was a lifelong habit with him to trust Providence, and he pulled his moustache and patted his knee and once dared to pat mine till I put him in his place, and told him to keep his paws off. Then he went so far as to say that he would plan a proper wedding feast for them, though he could ill afford it."

After holding out for a month without anything happening, Fanny suddenly crumpled up and gave in, so everybody was very pleased; and the very next day after his mother yielded, Richard Henry went to Ashburton to buy a wedding ring and be measured for a new suit of clothes, and the following Sunday they were called and the wedding fixed for after Christmas if nothing fearful rose up to stop it.

May told me that her mother was taking the preparations with great courage but finding the whole business unreal. She had a tiresome feeling that, once the bridegroom donned his wedding garments, he would fall dead as he stood at the altar rails, if not sooner. Meantime she compounded with Tobias Bloom and let him pay for the wedding breakfast and make all the arrangements; but she ordained for the feast to be held at Bullstone Farm as a more fitting scene for it than the 'Cat and Fiddle'.

All of which duly happened and the pair of them drove away afterwards for Dartmouth, where their honeymoon was to be spent, God willing; but the day was by no means finished after the guests were all gone but myself, and it was then my turn to lift the veil and make all clear.

In a manner of speaking you may say that I sacrificed a tidy lot of my lifelong friendship with Fanny that evening and, while bringing an end to her master trouble, heaped not a few lesser vexations upon Richard Henry's mother. But the balance ran much in her favour, or so I always thought.

Before I went off and the eventful day was done I faced up to Joshua and May and their mother and got pretty much what I expected from the women, but better than I hoped from the man.

"Talk on, Cherry, if you must," said Fanny. "Now there's only the final crash to come. But talk on, talk on if you want to."

That gave me a good opening so I launched forth upon a difficult job of work.

"You don't need to wait for any more crashes, dear Fanny," I said, "because I'm going to bring a most joyful one upon you before I go home. It's my duty and a most painful duty in one respect, but a very happy and glorious duty in another. I've got a sad confession to begin with, and if I lose your friendship in consequence so much the worse for me; but you must take the motives into your consideration in your usual large-minded manner, because by our motives we shall be judged hereafter."

She was interested but puzzled.

"What the mischief are you aiming at?" she asked. "What have your motives got to do with my misfortunes?"

"I'm sure never was a kinder well-wisher to mother than you always have been," declared May handsomely.

"And shall so continue if you are willing to let me," I promised, "but my friendship has got a wondrous quality of its own, May: it's not just everyday good willing. I look forward and weigh the days yet to dawn and note the shape of things to come before they do come. And people should always trust me well enough to forgive my lines of action."

I was paving my way you see to the jolt I had got to give them; but Fanny had gone through such a lot of various emotions since the morning that she wasn't feeling very interested.

"Well, get on with it, Cherry," she said, "we all know you're a marvel of cleverness and have a lot to your credit in many quarters; but none of your famous wisdom was equal to stopping Richard Henry's marriage, nor altering what hangs over him."

"I'm coming to that this instant moment, Fanny," I answered. "There's a far-reaching story you need to hear and all depends as to how you take it."

"If it's another sad story, I don't want to listen," she replied.

151

"It's a complicated story with the motives good and a triumphant ending," I told her. "It's a tale that ends in happiness for you, in fact very likely the happiest event in your difficult life."

That softened her for a minute and, with all their eyes fixed upon me, I got on with it as she had bidden me to do.

"A good bit ago," I began, "your eldest came to see me, knowing my fame and well aware that I was a sworn friend to his family and highly thought upon by you, dear Fanny. But he didn't come alone. He fetched Nancy along with him that I might come acquaint with her and form my own opinion of the girl. Needless to say I felt from the first I was on your side, because many a time I have seen how your judgment of human character is unequalled and often been guided by your reading of a doubtful nature."

That was a lie, of course, because nobody yet ever influenced me, or interfered with my judgment as to other people, least of all Fanny. But my words pleased her and she believed them.

"I found, however," I went on, "that for once I didn't see quite eye to eye with you. I heard what Richard Henry had to say and marked the few sentences Nancy let drop, and I saw in her a very genuine love for him and a decent, maidenly attitude to the situation along with good, native common-sense. I couldn't but feel that here was a case where two young people might combine to make a very happy married life for the pair of them. The girl was just suited to bring out the fine qualities of the young man, and he, with a mother like you behind him, would furnish such a husband as any young woman might well be proud of. I saw them fitting into the home life here under your guidance, with your son pulling his weight and helping Joshua with the conduct and prosperity of the farm, and I also saw Nancy a well-mannered, industrious and clever help-mate to May and you, with nice, hopeful grandchildren around you."

I took breath then and gave Fanny time to see the picture. Then I went on again, feeling myself at my peak of cleverness.

"But against such a cheerful sight was your present hard and fast opinions, Fanny, and, before all else, I naturally respected them. I warned Richard Henry it was unlikely I

152

could see any issue to suit both his mother and himself, and after that I had speech with you and found you would not relent under any persuasions whatever, yet was positive for once you were mistook. So I stood on the side of the boy and girl against you. You might almost say I was terrified to find myself so, though never terrified before and never like to be again. Then my mind moved in one of those flashes I get on great occasions and I was quickened to take a hand—not against you, God forbid, but for your future happiness. The way promised to look dark and devious and you were going to suffer, which thought made me suffer too; but light would follow the darkness and hope was the guiding star that led me on."

"What you might have thought to do was all useless when my son saw the 'Grey Fisher'," said Fanny, "so why dwell on the subject any more now? Since you had nought to do with it, why do you want to talk as if you had?"

I was not sorry that she helped me to come to the point.

"I'm glad you said that, because it goes to the root of the matter," I replied. "I had everything to do with it, Fanny. I took an awful risk and showed your blessed boy his line of action. He was a free agent, you understand, and under no compulsion to play the part he did play; but when I pointed out the good results if all went well, he jumped at it and was ready to face the music, and full of clever thoughts how to do it."

Fanny frowned a bit at that. "You plotted against me and now you're trying to cover it up and whitewash yourself," she said, which was only too true.

"Not against you, my love, but for your betterment," I explained. "The task that was set for us was to get you in a frame of mind when you would go back on your fierce determinations against Richard Henry's marriage, and I found a way to do it! Yes, for there came to my aid the famous tradition of your family and, by an act of Providence, I saw that the Bullstone curse could be turned for once into a blessing and the 'Grey Fisher' bring life and not death."

They all stared, and who shall blame them?

"What the mischief may you hap to be talking about?"

burst out Joshua, stirred for once from his usual silence into speech by my mysterious words.

"I'd go so far," he dared to add, "I'd go so far as to say you must have drunk a glass too much of Toby Bloom's black port at our wedding feast, Miss Crymes, if you'll excuse me for saying so."

"Most natural of you, Joshua," I answered, "but give heed for two minutes longer and you'll see I was never more sober than at this moment, my dear man. The family bird foretold your father's death, as we know too well, and if it was to appear again, it would surely aim at Richard Henry; but the thing for you to grasp now is this : it didn't appear! You thought it had, and your mother thought it had, and Mike Duffy would have sworn it had, and another man also ; but Richard Henry only pretended it had, well knowing all the time it had not. And when I laid my scheme before the lovers, I want to make clear that Nancy Bloom thought of you, Fanny, and only you. She doubted most properly whether you should be submitted to such a shock, and I granted that was the fly in the amber, though for my part I was of the opinion your constitution would stand the strain, dear Fanny, which it has done. Richard Henry was also sure you'd be equal to the passing jar. He took to the device and highly approved and said the minute all was laid bare and the point gained, then you would find yourself much too rejoiced to waste any time fretting about details. In a word he hungered to get to work."

"Where was the 'Grey Fisher' coming from, Cherry?" asked May.

"In this manner," I explained. "Among the odds and ends I have at Owl Pen are still a good few creatures my father shot in his day and afterwards stuffed to decorate the house-place. He set store by them though my mother always hated them, and after he died she put them all away in our lumber-store down in the garden. She wouldn't burn them, but never wanted to see any of them again. And, since she went herself, I've often thought to put a match to them, but something held my hand, and now I know why. Among the things was a heron that father shot and preserved to the best of his power ; but he

154

couldn't stuff dead things so as to make them look like live ones and his heron had that about it to make you feel shivery and out of heart. And when I showed it to Richard Henry, he said that must surely be the living likeness of the 'Grey Fisher' —a right heron and yet something about it far ways different from herons in general. The details were left to him and his deep affection for you made him as quick as lightning and helped him to do everything dead right. He took the bird by night, waited for just the proper morning, with fog about and poor light, to display it by Nicky Pool, knowing that you'd see it when you looked out of your bedroom window, Fanny. And he planned for Duffy to see it also; then, when the fog hid all, he took it away and buried it and came in the house and carried on as if he was doomed. He tells me he played his part to perfection, but I shall always feel how Providence pulled the strings and saw the end from the beginning as only Providence knows how to do. You stood up to it nobly and your son carried on with great craft and hid what he was feeling. But he and Nancy longed to relieve your anxiety and they will be thankful to God now to think you are happy again, as I hope and pray you find yourself. In a word all is well with him and he may live and flourish for half a century yet if not more."

I put my handkerchief to my eyes then and shed a few genuine tears, for I was quite as much overcome for the moment as any of them. The truth of what I had done, set out stark, did look pretty grim.

"He may live and flourish for half a century yet," said Fanny, who broke the silence when I had done, "but I'll never forgive him, nor yet you, Charity Crymes, so long as I live myself."

"But he's saved, Mother: Richard Henry's saved!" cried May. "He's saved to make it up to you, which will be his first thought now. You must forgive him because he was in love, and Cherry because of her good motives."

It was after that. I couldn't help feeling how their anti-climax was working upon them. These people had all been living, not in a fool's paradise, but in a proper misery over the eldest son of the house and now, love him as they did, the sudden, violent change of everything, though

155

a source of joy to banish their woe, left them struck off their balance and bewildered, mazed and dazed and a bit flat and even shamefaced that their excitement and chatter and mixed emotions at the doom of Richard Henry had all come to nothing. So they got a queer feeling that the salt of their lives had changed to sugar, but they couldn't hide the loss of the salt, nor even much enjoy the sugar till they got used to it.

Fanny never forgave me ; but May did, and Joshua was so overjoyed to think his brother would reign at Bullstone after all that he forgave me too. Of course they all forgave the wedded pair after they came home again. That's fifty years ago now and Richard Henry proved a good father and an average husband, though never a farmer. Bullstone was his, but Joshua always the backbone of it.

X

VARIOUS circumstances contributed to a remarkable tale, which I still like to reflect upon, when no less than three facts, all as different from each other as possible, ran together into a most formidable affair.

First was the memorial ordained for the late Sir Norman Voysey of Clyst St. Mark, and long since set up in our church, where of old he was wont to worship and read the lessons at Morning Prayer. His widow, Lady Ann, had stood surety for the new stained-glass window and also for a pair of notable candlesticks to stand upon the Holy Table. And Lady Ann, as the money came out of her pocket, had chosen the subject for the new window, which some applauded while others did not. Sir Norman was always a keen supporter of our village and a fine man in his day and a great loss. He happed to be a sportsman all his life and unfortunately rode to hounds on his seventy-fifth birthday, to mark the event; but he caught cold in the east wind on Fur Tor and died of it a fortnight later, much to the people's regret. So Lady Ann decided his window should represent the mighty hunter of Scripture, namely Nimrod, and ordered for him to be engaged in slaying a lion. The vicar of those days told her ladyship that something a thought less savage and more helpful to religion might better meet the case; but Lady Ann was a strong character and famous for her loveliness in her young days. She stuck to Nimrod and there was none in her circle of admirers, nor yet her children, who could make her change her mind, or troubled to try. So a very brilliant masterpiece was added to the little church, and to this day it keeps the school-children quiet upon Sundays, when they sit and gaze upwards at the hero thrusting his spear into the raging lion. As for the pair of candlesticks, they also made a great addition and adornment, standing four feet tall and solid silver through and through—proper, sacred furniture that must have cost a fortune.

That is the first ancient fact to be recorded, while nothing could have looked more utterly different and of no importance whatever to anybody than the next fact, which was the coming of a lodger to Mrs. Maine on Merripit Hill. He was a quiet, little elderly man, said to be a widower and a foreigner from London, but very agreeable and well-mannered to all who took any notice of him. His name was Arthur Pumbleby and he said he had come to breathe the Dartmoor air for a few months, because his tubes wanted strengthening. A most unnoticeable man was Mr. Pumbleby and gave no trouble; while Widow Maine reported him very clean and orderly and punctual with his weekly rent, which was all that mattered about him to her. He visited the 'Hearty Welcome' most nights for an hour or two and would sing a song now and again when pressed to do so. I never saw the man myself, yet this shadowy creature was caught up in the affair and became you might say the cornerstone of it! Mrs. Maine told me what she knew about him when he came into the forefront of the news; but she could advance nothing for or against the man. He liked an under-cooked egg to his breakfast and was always early to rise. He had a bald head, a round back, rather bowed legs and a clean-shaved genial face, with silly, trustful blue eyes looking out of it. Once, in Widow Maine's memory, a man had called to see him —the only visitor he was ever known to receive. The man had stopped but ten minutes and then driven off in a dog-cart with another man. Mr. Pumbleby never mentioned the incident to his landlady after they were gone and she didn't hear anything they said, because they stood out in her vegetable patch when they said it.

The third and last of the three contrary facts related to Avisa Bolt, daughter of Albert Bolt who worked at the granite quarries. She was a plain, quiet girl, of no account, but on very good terms with herself notwithstanding, and, after all, it is only the account which you owe to yourself which really matters. She was engaged to marry Saul Todd, a night watchman who served at Packhorse Bridge and lived there with his parents. It happened that I knew the Todds very well and had taken something of a fancy to Saul, because he befriended me and my donkey more than once after he rose to become a guardian of the law and, from a nice little boy, grew into a goodhearted and well-meaning young man. He was tall, powerful, slow-moving, and hopeful of advancement some day; but he was simple-minded and little likely to reach any great heights in his office. He thought a lot of me and, knowing me from his cradlehood, always called me 'Aunt Cherry'. I knew Avisa Bolt also, and, of course, she was aware of my fame, like everybody else, so when a time came that the girl happened to find herself suffering from a raging faceache she hastened to me to medicine it. That was round about midway in my own career and I still used my mother's charms and simples for many human ills, applying them with the addition of my own deeper knowledge. I found Avisa suffered from a wisdom tooth, and late wisdom teeth, when striving to rise up and break the flesh over them, are often a lot more trouble than they are worth. Any skilled tooth-drawer will tell you that, though they are the last to come, they are often the first to go. So, while it was pushing up, her tooth gave Avisa a fearful time and she came to me. First I hurt her worse than ever and lanced the gum over the tooth, which caused her to bleed buckets; and then, knowing she would want something more for the half-crown she was going to pay me, I prescribed an ancient remedy which was little likely to do any real good, but couldn't do harm and would please her in any case.

So there it stood: those three divers events, all as different as chalk from cheese and utterly removed each from the others, yet all blowing up like a thunderstorm to combine in one remarkable affair.

For the minute, then, you've got the adornments in church, Arthur Pumbleby lodging along with Widow Maine, and Avisa Bolt and her aching wisdom tooth; and it was the silly charm I gave her against any more toothache that started the ball rolling.

"You will need an item easy for you to get," I said, "because Mr. Churchward is a friend of your father and no doubt a friend to yourself also, and he won't raise raise any objection. Indeed he has pleasured other of my customers before today and they have got advantage by it."

Weston Churchward was the parish sexton in those days— a kindly man well thought upon and among my own friends,

159

who would serve those I sent him when in his power to do so.

"What you want for your charm is a dead man's tooth, my dear—the certain thing to cure a toothache if handled with faith," I told Avisa. "But you must gather it yourself, wrap it tight in a morsel of flannel and wear it next your skin on a bit of thread between your breasts. Then you'll be little likely to feel another pang."

She nodded and showed interest.

"As to getting the tooth, that's easy as you say," she said, "because down in the shed, where Mr. Churchward keeps his tools, there's a box in which he stores the relics that he digs out, and what I want will be there for certain."

"Exactly so, Avisa," I answered, "Churchward collects the fragments that oft turn up from the unmarked graves of long-forgotten folk, and when there's enough to call a whole skeleton, he'll bury 'em again on Chrisomer's Hill—that part of the yard where still-born babes and unknown strangers and the other doubtful ones go in, so that the Almighty can deal with them as He thinks best when the time shall come. But there's more to it for you than that. You've got to take a tooth with your own hand, and you must needs to get it at a full moon after midnight. And you will doubtless find yourself brave enough to follow that commandment without flinching, else all's lost and the charm useless."

"It would take more than old bones to fright me," she said with great confidence, and I knew she had the faith that moves mountains, let alone a tooth from a dead man's jaw-bone.

That night Avisa asked her father when it was going to be full moon, and he found the moon in *Old Moore's Almanac*, and told Avisa there was a full moon offering in five days' time.

"You'd best to see Churchward," he said to her, "and tell him your requirements."

Which Avisa did do, and the sexton was very understanding and told her there was that in his bone-box to meet the case exactly.

"Upon the top of the fragments I'll lay a jaw-bone set with sound teeth yet," said Churchward, "and you can have the

160

key of the tool-shed and lock it up when you've taken what you need and give the key back to me next morning."

Some maidens might have feared the task and little liked to travel down among the dead all alone at noon of night, but not so Albert Bolt's daughter. She believed in ghosts of course, and in mostly everything else that the folk believed in of olden times, because, before the Board Schools, it was no shame for the young to put faith in their parents' wisdom; and Avisa also trusted in the Lord and felt terrible certain that no hurt could overtake a harmless, well-conducted young woman engaged in the innocent job of curing her toothache. Then came the appointed night, and the moment church clock had told twelve, off she went with never a pinch of fear, or shadow of doubt. Before, when I suggested it might be a clever thought to tell Saul Todd, so that he could take occasion to be round that way on his beat and in reach of her, she refused to do so. She had told him nothing and didn't mean to till next day. That was where I entered into the affair, for I saw Saul, told him what Avisa was up to and thought that it would be wise for him to keep watch out of her sight and see all went well with her, but never tell her afterwards.

"She's fearless," he said, "and there's nothing could possibly overtake her; but if you say so, Aunt Cherry, I'll make a note to be around that way."

So Avisa sailed off down the high road on her odd errand through a still and peaceful fashion of night. Though a full moon shone, it was invisible owing to a veil of thin clouds drawn over the sky; but you could see the moon's place through them and there was a dim, silvery vapour spread upon the earth. The girl carried a candle-end and a box of matches with her, and a time came when I heard from her own lips of the adventures that followed after she entered into the churchyard.

Turning off from among the graves of the bettermost she passed to the back side of the holy building where sexton's tool-shed stood nigh the vestry door. And, coming light-footed over the grass, none could have heard her, of course; but suddenly she stopped short, for there was the sound of talking in the tool-house and Avisa had just fetched out the key to open the door when she heard menfolk murmuring inside and marked the door stood ajar. In another moment she would have walked on top of those that might be there, but she heard them just in time. She felt no fear, only a great curiosity to know who on earth but herself could find their business there at such an hour. Yet, in the great silence, voices were clearly to be heard, so she crept a thought closer and listened. Any other girl would most likely have cleared out and fled for her own safety's sake before a hazard so strange; but, feeling sure that it was human speech and no ghosts chattering over their own earthly fragments in the bone-box, Avisa held on close enough to listen. She soon discovered there were a brace of stark scoundrels there, talking quietly together; and then she got her first pretty sharp shock, for one of the speakers was well known to her. The voice belonged to a local man, an estate carpenter by the name of Tom Luscombe, who worked at Oakshotts Manor, but lived in Packhorse Bridge parish. He was a middle-aged man, who didn't bear a particular good name and was thought to be a poacher and a thief in a small way. But he had never been in serious trouble, though now, as Avisa listened with growing amazement, it looked to her as if the carpenter was heading for his own destruction.

"We'll bide till clock tells one," summed up Luscombe, just as Avisa gave heed to them, and lifting his voice a trifle to do so. "Then we'll set about it, and I lay you never had an easier job, because there's going to be no shadow of a clue for anybody to go by—only the candlesticks gone and nothing to show where to."

A voice unknown to Avisa replied: an old voice but clear enough.

"They're a thought heavy for my powers, but when you've sawn them up small, I can take one bag to the hiding-place and you the two others. There they'll lie safe enough till hue and cry's over and the excitement died down. They'll suspect me, but my alibi's sound, and nobody's going to think you had any hand in it."

They talked a bit longer and Avisa took it all in. The candlesticks were going to be broken up into small pieces and hid in a secret spot for a while; then when the coast was clear,

162

and the hunt for them given over, they would be conveyed to Plymouth to some rogues' roost there and melted down and the silver sold for the profit of the thieves. So the listener heard tell how a great crime was just going to be committed by Luscombe and some unknown limb of Satan, and fearful sacrilege done upon the famous Voysey candlesticks. Then the evil-doers would share the booty—one half to the unknown man who had planned this wickedness and the other half to Tom Luscombe and the accomplices at Plymouth. But what the girl did not know was that the ringleader of the affair was Widow Maine's lodger, Mr. Arthur Pumbleby. Now, however, she let her indignation master her common-sense and a minute later Avisa, full of rage and brave as need be, burst in upon them and was facing the rascals, much to their astonishment. Of course a pinch of caution would have warned against any such rash action as that and shown her rightful duty was to creep away and run to get the law on her side and catch the criminals before they caught her; but, as she confessed afterwards, she never stopped to consider what she was going to do about it when she confronted two angry men singlehanded, nor yet what they were going to do about it when she appeared. To such heights did the silly creature rise in her wrath that she just bounced in upon them, faced them and asked them what they were up to and how they dared to be in such a place at such an hour.

"I'm come to work a charm for my toothache," she said, "all honest and in order; but for what wickedness are you here, Tom Luscombe?"

The carpenter was a good deal vexed for such an unexpected thing as this to happen, but Pumbleby returned a soft answer. He introduced himself, told Avisa to fear nothing and explained to her how he and his companion were just taking the night air and having a quiet chat. He showed great interest about Avisa's toothache and offered to help her find her charm, but then she answered that she had heard their villainies and they weren't going to steal the candlesticks if she could prevent it. That altered their plans a good bit, of course, and soon they were properly savage with the girl, especially Luscombe, because he stood to face destruction and disgrace

163

after this, whatever happened. But, being a capable sort of man, he saw his only salvation now depended on the candle-sticks. If they disappeared, he'd be called to disappear too, and rely on Pumbleby for his share of the spoil; so he bluffed and told his companion that Avisa didn't matter a damn, but after they had got the candlesticks, they must clear off the Moor with them that very night while the going was good. And Pumbleby saw the point of that.

"The only other course would be to kill her," he said gently, "but I've never had blood on my hands, and never so intend. It's a case of patience for you, my girl, because you will have a good many long hours to regret your foolish conduct before they find you."

Then they bound her hand and foot with the ropes used at funerals, and made her fast so that no effort on her part could free her; but, though she didn't try to fight, knowing herself powerless before them, just as they had tied her up and were going to gag her, she suddenly yelled out 'Murder!' at the very top of her voice. But only once, for then the gag was drove in pretty near far enough to choke her; and a moment after-wards the godless pair put home the tool-shed door and went off to the vestry. That was the last Avisa saw of them and she knew that all remaining for her to do was to exercise what patience she might command, as Mr. Pumbleby had advised. Dumb and powerless was she, and so remained for many a long hour, while the church-breakers, armed with their bags and two hack-saws, went upon their way and got to the altar where stood the loot. As the world would soon know who were the thieves, it must be needful for both to vanish and escape the quest that would swiftly follow upon rescue of Avisa.

Sufficient moonlight streamed through the glass window, where Nimrod was killing his lion, to help them with their task, and when I heard the details afterwards I wished it had been possible for the hero to descend from his place aloft and slay that brace of rascals instead of the lion. But the scamps didn't know the watching Lord was looking after His own house that night in any case; and now I can take up the story and tell where Saul Todd came into it during his night's work.

Round about half after one o'clock, it must have been, when I was wakened from my sleep by a loud summons on the door of Owl Pen, so up I rose and gazing out found there was enough light from the overcast moon for me to see that Saul Todd stood below. He was full of news and greatly excited, and his first thought had been to rush up and let me learn all the wondrous things he'd done before another morning published his cleverness to the parish, so I rayed myself and went down house to hear what had overtook him.

"Begin at the beginning," I said, "and don't let your tongue trip over your speech, but talk slow."

This he did and travelled so that I could follow him.

"I ordained as you counselled me, Aunt Cherry, to make a beat around by the church tonight with my eyes and ears alert for any possible mischance," he began, "and it stood about half after midnight when I went on my way. All still and orderly and nought moving but a stray cat here and there, and the moon same as it has been all the night—full but overset by thin clouds. I advanced towards the church and, so sure as I'm a living man, when I was two hundred yards away from it, there came a cry through the air. A faint cry, but a human cry and a mighty ugly cry at that, because it yelled out 'Murder' and no less! That's a fearful word at any time to a night-watchman's ear, but when suddenly screeched out in the dead of night, from the midst of a village all lost in slumber, same as Packhorse Bridge, it brought me up sharp in my tracks with the suspicion of dirty work. I girt myself for action and pre-pared to attack at any cost, but, just for one instant moment, I bided still that I might hear the cry again and mark where it came from. Because I can tell you it's none too easy, when the silence of night is suddenly broken, to judge where a sound may arise from."

"Tell me what you did. It don't matter a button what you thought," I said.

"I waited in vain to hear anything more," he continued. 'Just that one beastly word reached me, but it was not repeated nor yet any other signal of woe that there must be trouble brewing; but I reckoned that the cry had come from the neighbourhood of the churchyard, or else the trees beyond it,

165

and went in that direction at a good gait with my ears open, I warn you, and my eyes open also, against any sight or sign or sound of evil."

It was almost heartbreaking to hear the young man, or think any human tongue could creep so slow. Another five minutes he took to relate how he had got to the churchyard in due course, and how he'd seen a fox sitting on the churchyard wall and wondered what might have brought the creature to such an unusual spot. Then he had cruised about and at last made a remarkable discovery and found the vestry door wide open. After that he went on a morsel faster, to what followed.

"Well, needless to say, Aunt Cherry, when I found the vestry door wide to the night, I felt it could only have happened by human hands and that ten to one them who had opened the door might be busy in the church and about some nefarious occupation."

So spoke Saul and related how he had entered and proceeded silently and cautiously through the door that opened from the empty vestry into the church. And there, sure enough, were Luscombe and Arthur Pumbleby—too busy to mark or hear him. Under the semi-darkness they were engaged in sawing up the silver candlesticks for their easier conveyance.

"Not another second did I delay," went on Todd. "I gripped my truncheon, blazed on my bull's-eye lantern, burst upon 'em and roared out like the Trump of Doom. I couldn't hold both, but it was Devil take the hindmost for 'em and the hindmost was a stranger man not known to me for the moment. But the one that fled I had seen and knew. Tom Luscombe that was, and his number's up now. But the chap I have captured is a lot more interesting than Luscombe—an amazing character and famous for years, and a proper stir will be made when 'tis known I have took him singlehanded."

"What have you done with him?" I asked.

"I concentrated upon the felon from the moment my hand fastened on his collar, Aunt Cherry," he answered. "I marched him straight out into the night and took him to the lock-up. There he'll be till they come and fetch him to Plymouth tomorrow. He's been lurking in our midst and calling himself

'Arthur Pumbleby' and abiding with Mrs. Maine till his plans were ripe. 'Tis clear he found Luscombe just the manner of man he wanted to help him, and made friends according, and tonight they pounced on the church candlesticks, little guessing there was one sent by God's good will to pounce upon them instead! Pumbleby took his downfall calmly and came quiet. He's a far famous church-lifter and been in prison scores of times already for that crime, but he confessed he had counted upon a handsome haul when he saw our silver candlesticks and was a lot disappointed at his failure and greatly interested to hear how I got wind of his plot. But I bandied no words as to that."

It came out afterwards that Pumbleby's lifelong occupation, when free to practise it, was breaking into churches. His real name was Badger and he had made a great name at his job of work, and spent years of his life in gaol and was well known to the forces of the law. He turned out to be on ticket-of-leave when taking the air at Packhorse Bridge, and the man who had called upon him once was an officer from Moreton to see if the address he had given the authorities was genuine. Then, quite by chance while he was enjoying his freedom, he had visited our church from force of habit, heard all about the candlesticks, much admired them, and set about a robbery that looked easy and promised a big reward. He had heard Tom Luscombe's opinions in the bar of the 'Hearty Welcome' and found in him a trustworthy accomplice. But the sequel was five years' imprisonment for the professional and two for Luscombe, his amateur assistant.

Saul gloried in his triumph and wondered what advancement might be in store for him and when his promotion was like to come, so seeing dawn quicken upon the eastern edge of the Moor, and thinking of another person rather than this vainglorious lad, I gave him something else to consider.

"If you were too busy to lock up the vestry when you took Pumbleby away, perhaps it would be a clever thing to run back and do so," I suggested, "because Luscombe may have watched you when you marched off with his friend and popped back and stole the candlesticks after all. And there's yet another little point you have overlooked, my dear: what was

167

it set you on the right track and took you down to the burying ground just at the right moment?"

"The voice, Aunt Cherry," he replied, "the voice and that fatal word 'Murder'."

"Exactly so," I said. "Granted that anybody in trouble may yell 'Murder', even though they are not being murdered; yet, when a guardian of the law hears the word bawled out in the middle of the night from a lone churchyard, it might be proper for him to look into the matter, especially when he knows his sweetheart is on that identical spot at the time. But maybe it don't matter to you whether Avisa Bolt is alive or dead, now you are such a grand fellow."

Then the well-meaning idiot perceived what he had clean forgot in his desire to shine before the nation. His jaw dropped and he rose up with a long face and prepared to fly.

"By God," he said, "if she hadn't slipped my memory!"

Then he was gone and I heard no more details until the next afternoon. From Avisa herself I learned them and felt glad to see she was looking much as usual. She told me how Saul had hunted the graveyard and bawled her name, then thrust into Churchward's tool-shed at last and found her gagged and bound and pretty near unconscious. He had loosed her with thanksgivings and thought to cheer her up with his triumphant performance; and then he'd seen her to her home, where her father was still sleeping, having gone to bed as usual round about ten o'clock, long before Avisa left the house on her errand. Albert Bolt found himself much astonished to hear his daughter's adventures; but she gave me to understand it was no case of all being well that ended well. In fact Avisa experienced a sharp change of outlook upon Saul Todd.

"When he told me that," she said to me, "I got the shock of my life, Miss Crymes, for it showed the man didn't know one single, darned thing about true love. That's the limit and I've done with him for ever more."

I reminded her that he had only just enough brain power to do one thing at a time; but it was all in vain.

"If he don't know enough to put first things first, then God help him," said Avisa; and she never passed so much as the time of day with the night-watchman again.

But he got his good marks notwithstanding, and the Voysey family sent him a five-pound note and had the silver candlesticks mended and ordered that they should always be looked after a lot sharper in the future.

For my own part the most interesting figure in that tangled tale has always been Widow Maine's lodger—Arthur Pumbleby, so to call him. We heard that they welcomed Arthur back to prison like a lost sheep, and he showed himself quite contented to settle down in it once more. For, by all accounts, no gaol-bird ever won a higher reputation for nice ways, or gave less trouble to them set over him. He had reached to such a pitch now that it was felt he only tried to break into holy houses from force of habit, and though he was reported to have said that his failure at Packhorse Bridge would always be his bitterest disappointment, yet he was well content to be back where he had no responsibility, because freedom for him only meant just a little passing insecurity now and then before being safe under lock and key once more. I should have liked to become acquaint with the man and gathered his views on life in general.

XI

HUMAN character is often such a proper cargo of deceptions that no man can add up his neighbour with any certainty of getting the sum right. What looks clear, with no sign offering to contradict it, may only be a disguise to hide the inner truth, and many of us don't even know we are wearing a disguise, and so deceive ourselves as well as our fellow creatures by acting a part far different from reality. But if we can go so far as to hoodwink our own selves, then small wonder we diddle our neighbours too. Of course, when people are up against a woman such as me, that don't happen, because it is a commonplace for me to know more about other people than they do themselves, and in the case of Alfred French and Job Jordan, though they startled the village in their time, their inner natures were never beyond me and my hidden hand served to drag out the quality of Job, while as for Alfred he ran true to his own instincts and only amazed such as never perceived what those instincts happened to be. The pair worked side by side as head man and horseman at Laughter Hole Farm—a tenement nigh to Owl Pen and called after Laughter Tor, which rose behind it with the land sloping down to East Dart running through the vale beneath. An ancient pine wood clustered southerly of the farm and, when the world was younger than now, a heronry flourished in the high tops of the trees.

Farmer Redmayne owned the homestead and its acres had been increased by the energy of his forbears. But now the race ran low, for there was none left of the direct line to follow Michael Redmayne when he dropped. With a woman the race was going to peter out and at best could only persist if Clarice Redmayne, Michael's daughter, wedded some man ready and willing to carry on the farm. More than that Michael also desired to happen : he hoped that when Clarice fell in love, a possible husband for her might be ready and willing to call himself 'Redmayne' and raise up sons that should preserve the

170

old name. Jordan had worked twenty years at Laughter Hole when the head man died, and he expected to take Martin Gee's place; but that did not happen. He obtained no preferment, for his master chose another—a man he had met by chance at cattle market—took a fancy to and engaged. He was Alfred French from the South Hams and brought with him a measure of lightheartedness and cheerfulness mostly lacking at Laughter Hole. In truth Redmayne was not one given to merriment and had no thought of engaging French to disturb the monotonous home life he lived with Clarice and an elderly dairymaid and Job Jordan. Michael was far from gloomy by nature, but just jog-trot, uninterested in social life, wrapped up in his farm and regarded as a sound but somewhat dull and flat person by his friends. He felt glad to secure French, on the strength of an excellent character, and reckoned him to be better for leadership than his faithful but commonplace horseman, Job Jordan. Clarice, who was twenty-five years old when the new head man came to Laughter Hole, resembled her father in mind and he loved her well. She was stolid, industrious and not given to pleasure. She knew the ambition that her parent had for her and regarded it as reasonable; but no man had awakened her emotions as yet. I knew her mother, who died young, and I was friendly with Clarice, for she and her father happed to be my nearest neighbours, and it fell out, soon after the arrival of Alfred French, that Redmayne, when meeting with me, returned to a subject which he had often discussed before.

"How's your new chap, Michael," I inquired, "and what does he think of Dartmoor?"

"I wanted to see you," he answered, "because betwixt you and me and the post, Cherry, there was more reasons than one that I chose him."

"I guessed as much for that matter," I replied. "I know very well what's working at the back of your mind: you want to see if your new head man finds himself likely to make a son-in-law some fine day and satisfy all your requirements."

"That's about the size of it," he admitted. "It's a bit of a venture, but worth trying. He has sense as well as good looks, I may tell you."

171

"Does he get on clever with Job?"

"Everybody gets on all right with Job."

"I thought that, when you didn't advance him, your horse-man might leave you."

"Jordan won't leave me. He knows what he is to me—my right hand and most faithful friend also. There's never been any feeling about it; but he's promised to keep an eye on French, because he will have many more chances to do so than I shall. It's what Clarice thinks, or don't think, of my new head man that matters."

"Give her plenty of time and don't seek to influence her," I warned him. "You must remember that Clarice is a good bit of a catch. All her future husband has got to do is to change his name, marry a fine woman and carry on your family. A tolerable tempting prospect that is; but you can trust her not to fall in love without she finds something more than just a handsome man and a clever tongue. Most likely some of his gifts will be wasted on her, because many a man in love has found that just what he most prided himself upon made no appeal to the woman, but she liked him for something quite different he may not even have known was in him."

"He is handsome in her opinion, for she's told me so; but she hasn't revealed no more interest in him than she might in a new agricultural machine so far," explained Michael.

"Nature will take its course," I said. "You can ask Job his views behind the scenes, but not Clarice. Jordan is always fair and sensible in my experience and comes to his fellow creatures with an open mind."

"Sensible and loyal both," declared the farmer. "Job's the sort apt to be overlooked because he's a silent and shadowy fashion of man, not always bawling and pushing himself into the forefront and talking about his great powers rather than taking his coat off and showing them. He's never asked for a rise in his life since he came here, though he's got a tidy few rises all the same and he is good for another half-crown after next Christmas. But the new chap stands on a higher plane than Jordan—you might even say on a higher plane han me myself. He's seen more of life and is better educated than us and he's got that in him which might well attract a maid like

172

Clarice. He's a few years older than Job—thirty-five—but years older in general knowledge, and lighterhearted too. He knows a lot more concerning females than Jordan does."

"He's a pleasant object to the eye," I agreed, "and he'll be feeling his way no doubt."

It was a few weeks after that I came to meet Alfred French myself for the first time. He appeared at Owl Pen with a message from Michael, who wanted to borrow some mole-traps that I had by me, and he came in and shook hands and told me who he was and made friends in a cheerful fashion and praised my fame.

"If ever I'm in a fix, I shall come to you, Miss Crymes, to get me out of it," he said, with an attractive grin. He was six foot tall, well set up, clean-shaved with a fair complexion and blue eyes. There was a great independence about his manner and his outlook. He gave me the impression of a clever and well-behaved but watchful chap and likely to know which side his bread was buttered. He proved not unkindly by nature, although little really interested in anybody outside himself. He was very breezy in his conversation and liked talking. But such as like talking often tell you much more about themselves than they think they are telling. From time to time after that visit I met French and made him trust me. In fact we reached a stage when he opened out a bit and gave me a glimpse into his nature and opinions.

"I'm always glad to have a tell with you," he said once, "because you're a woman of the world and never shocked at anything you see or hear. You find there's a comical side to being alive, which so many never do find. To me anybody properly shocked is a comical sight in itself."

He got to the stage presently when he would talk about his employer; but he knew I was an old friend of the Redmaynes, both father and daughter, and took care to pick his words. He admired Michael and thought him a trustable type of employer for any man.

"We suit each other down to the ground," said Alfred. "We're both workers and both put his farm first. But he's no great lover of a joke. If there's a joke in the air, the master may be dimly conscious it's there, but he don't see it. And a lot of

173

subjects—all quite innocent in truth—make him vexed rather than amused, so he loses their funny side in consequence."

"Some of your ideas about fun certainly would not please him," I said, "any more than they would please any other respectable person. What may make the bar loafers at the 'Hearty Welcome' laugh won't raise your stock at Laughter Hole and you ought to know that by now."

"I'm careful. I don't skate on thin ice with Mr. Redmayne, still less with Miss."

"I should hope not," I replied and changed the subject. "And what's your opinion of the horseman?" I asked.

"He's as his God made him. In a manner of speaking I'm sorry for Jordan."

"Why?" I inquired, and then he gave me a double surprise.

"Because the poor beggar's in love with Clarice Redmayne and thinks nobody's found it out but himself. I know a lot about love—been up to my neck in it scores of times—and I can read Job like a book. He's such a humble worm that he would reckon it high treason for the likes of him to look as high as Clarice. But that's what's been biting Jordan for a month of Sundays, I reckon, and now he's blunted the edge of it and just goes on getting a sort of lefthanded comfort from thinking about her."

"There's a kind of queer folk who do grow into the way of loving ghosts, and I've known such," I said. "How did you find out something neither she nor her father ever guessed? They both think a lot of Job, but certainly never picture him as the sort of man to marry Clarice."

"They are a stupid pair, between you and me, and none knows that better than you, Miss Crymes," he said boldly. "And I'll also bet you know what the master wants to happen, and what may happen, and what I'm beginning to think will happen. And, liking Jordan well enough, I'm sorry for his sake, but the oyster ought to have opened his shell a bit sooner."

"Too late now, you'd say?" I asked him.

"Much too late. Of course it's never too late for a woman to change her mind; but now the case is altered, because Mr.

174

Redmayne finds me all he could wish and wants me to get on with it."

I knew this was true, for Michael had declared himself to me as mightily pleased with French and hopeful that it was going to run smoothly between him and Clarice.

"What about the young woman herself?" I asked, and he laughed.

"Virgin soil," he said. "Virgin soil, Miss Crymes. She's never been in love yet and most like never will be. Her sort seldom knows what love means; but if you're clever enough, you can make them think they do."

"You're rather a cold-blooded devil to talk like that, Alfred," I told him.

"I may be, but I'm honest. I'd keep the bargain. I'd treat her well and respect her, and change my name to 'Redmayne', and serve Laughter Hole handsomely; because somewhat more could be got out of the place than has been yet."

"You take it for granted you can win her if you want her?"

"Why not? She couldn't do better. She's got no ideas on the subject except to please her father and do her duty. I wish there was more money with her because I've never had any money to name. Still, the old man's been a saver all his life it seems, and he's well-to-do in a small way."

"What would such as you make of big money?" I wondered.

"Given big money, plus a wife and children," he answered, "I'd think first of them and spend money on educating the kids and making my partner happy and contented."

As a set off to this talk with the newcomer, I had another with the horseman some few days afterwards when passing under the lands of Laughter Hole, where Jordan was plough- ing. I sat on my donkey, venturing afield to Ashburton by way of Dartmeet and the hour was early; but time meant nothing to Job. He rose with the sun and to plough all alone with two horses was always his favourite fashion of hard work. So I knew he'd be in a good humour and stopped a minute. Early spring had come with the days growing longer. I called him to the road and asked him to tighten my harness, because I was taking panniers for a bit of shopping.

"How's 'Clarice'?" I asked, meaning one of the plough-horses—a fine grey mare called after his master's daughter. But he missed my meaning, and that was the first time I saw for myself what French had told me was true. Job didn't seem so content with the spring morning. A certain anxiety always marked his expression, but there was a careworn look in his eyes I did not remember to have seen before. When I named Clarice, I had clearly struck an echo. He didn't answer very quickly for it was his habit to weigh the most trivial question before replying; yet he showed there was only one Clarice in his mind for the moment when he responded.

"She's had a cold upon her chest, but is getting the better of it, Cherry," he said, "and, when to Plymouth last week, French fetched her a bunch of foreign grapes, which pleased her."

"That was kind of him, Job."

"So the master thought."

"You find him good company and pleasant to work with by now I hope?"

It took him a full half minute before he spoke, and then he praised Alfred.

"He's what you might call a very clever chap. Alf can both read and write and he's a lot more than just a man of the soil. A very good farmer, else Mr. Redmayne wouldn't have put him top; but all of us here are well content for him to be head. There's school larning in Alf. He throws a light on things that I never so much as heard tell about till he's named 'em."

"A proper addition to Laughter Hole then?"

"An addition without a doubt."

"What do the women think of him at Laughter Hole?"

Again Job delayed. A cautious expression came into his big grey eyes and he looked round about him as though he might be overheard. But there were only my donkey and the two plough-horses and myself to listen. At last he spoke.

"He said a rude thing to the dairymaid, and she's against him, and I don't blame her for it. It was hushed up after and never came to the master's ears, else French would have been chastened, because Mr. Redmayne won't stand for anything coarse. But Alf was very regretful after and confessed to me that, from his standpoint, such a thing was only a joke and not worthy of a second thought."

"Clarice wouldn't have liked it."

"My God! A woman with a mind so pure as new fallen snow like her!"

"Better forgot, Job. Be sure he won't slip again," I promised. Then Jordan continued to consider the head man.

"To say it kindly," he confessed, "Alf may be thought to suffer from two weak spots, though I never presumed to point them out, he being my superior."

"Like your good sense to keep shut about them," I said.

"Yes, that's right, but I can tell you how he strikes me. Firstly he's a lot too fond of the girls—a fault in a man who is planning to court one of 'em, or so I think. And secondly he's death on money. He says it's money makes the world go round and is the only thing worth living for in his opinion, which is a shameful idea and contrary to Christianity."

So I went on my way never expecting any action from me was likely to be called upon as to Clarice and her father and the two labouring men, French and Jordan, yet feeling well disposed to them all. I held no opinion as to what might happen, and it was well I did not, because Fate presently planned a most fantastic situation of affairs. For the time being they all drifted along and most folk thought a day would soon dawn when we should hear that his head man had offered for the farmer's daughter and been accepted by her. But they took their time, and meanwhile I got to know a little more than most about Alfred at Laughter Hole. He was the only one there that kept much about himself up his sleeve, though not from me. I fancy he thought we were birds of a feather and he liked a word with me now and again and allowed himself to go pretty far. I'd pretend to laugh at his wild opinions and lewd tales, though they did not entertain me in reality; but if you want to learn the truth about a man, you need to pretend a friendly sympathy with his ideas, even though you hate them, because that hides from him what you may be really thinking and loosens his tongue as to himself. French was quick-witted and lightminded. He told me that he was sorry for Job, because he knew the poor devil loved Clarice but hadn't got a dog's chance in that quarter, as he meant to marry her himself. He reckoned, though not a first prize for anybody, she meant the farm some day, and might be considered a fair bargain. He also showed me what Jordan had already discovered; that he cared more about money than any other thing, and he summed up his intentions in a few words to me not a week before he set about to put them into action.

"Now it's time I got a move on, Miss Crymes," he said, with his jackdaw eyes twinkling. "My old man's growing restive and giving me a hint or two. I've always spoke with great admiration about Clarice, and now he's confessed that nothing would suit him better than to have me for his son-in-law—of course assuming that the woman approved. And as Clarice don't know anything more about love than a caterpillar, but wouldn't cross her dad's wishes for the world, it's up to me to start upon her."

Which he did do, because the next thing I heard came from Michael Redmayne, who imparted to me in great good humour that things were moving at last and to good purpose.

"You knew my intentions from the first, Cherry," he told me, "and now I'm glad to find them on the way to bear fruit. Alf wanted a word in season and I have spoke it. Though full of admiration for my girl, he never made no advancement, and that surprised me for he's not a man to be feared of the maidens. So I let it be understood I shouldn't frown upon him if he tried his luck."

"And is he doing so, Mike?" I inquired.

"Yes," he said. "Clarice is waking up to his fine nature and hearing things, no doubt, she never thought upon before. When he comes to declare himself, he'll tell her, of course, she's the only woman on earth he ever staked his heart upon, as we all do, God forgive us; and then Clarice will be in a man's arms for the first time in her life, so far as I know." So spoke Redmayne and I judged he was right.

"She's never been in love yet," I said. "For she couldn't have hid it from me if she had been. She's too open and honest, like yourself, Mike. But you'll soon see how the cat jumps now, for if she is going to love him, then you'll be first to learn of it."

"I can't think of any chap more like to wake her up," he assured me. "She ain't like one of them neuter bee sort of women—only wishful to be let alone and get on with her work. In my opinion she's much on the pattern of her mother, who made a very fine wife, though never much one for the private antics of the matrimonial state."

From that time forward I saw little of the parties concerned except for Job Jordan, and I marked, at a chance meeting with him, that he had bated of his earlier admiration for French. Little guessing at the violent operations so soon to overtake himself, the horseman was concerned with other people and above all anxious about the destiny of one. I asked him how things were faring in a general way at the farm and praised the fine June weather.

"No great news for the minute, Job?" I asked, and he shook his head.

"Only a question of time now, I'm fearing, because he's got her, hard and fast."

"What do you fear? You praised him not so long ago."

"I know a bit more than I did then," answered Job. "To those that don't matter Alf will speak open, and of course I don't signify to anybody, so being much given to chatter, he's let me have an ugly sight of his inner man."

"Rather a gay bird perhaps," I granted, "but if he's straight and stands to work, what more would you expect?"

"It's not what I expect. It's the girl," he explained. "She's only waiting now for him to ask, and then she'll take him ; but I'll go so far as to say it will be a misfortunate thing for her if she does."

"You can't put in your oar, however," I suggested.

"Oh no. I know my place ; but all the same it's borne in upon me that French was never meant for the woman's happiness. My hope was that he'd let a bit of his true self appear for her to catch sight of. That might have made her think twice. But he's been too crafty to make any slip like

179

that. He knows her fine nature now and watches his step according."

"He'll hope to waken her love if he can," I said.

"Not honest to goodness love," declared Job.

"But backed up by her love for her father, because she knows he wants it to happen."

"Once it did happen I doubt I could stop there," he answered. "I couldn't bide at Laughter Hole if I saw the woman married and suffering."

He continued to reveal his own affection for Clarice in this simple fashion.

"In a measure it puzzles me to feel so cast down for her," he confessed. "My use is to take a tolerable guarded view of life and reckon one thing often balances out another and nothing matters a deuce of a lot in any case. But this is different. I wouldn't like for Clarice to be up against the sort of misery that's beyond all power of salvation."

I admired his simple faith in Michael's daughter and felt little doubt that he would have made a better husband for her than Alfred; but I feel very little sympathy with the humble and meek as a rule and did not see an object of much interest in the horseman just then.

The next one that came to me with another chapter of the tale was Clarice herself. She would drop in now and again with the little things that served to fill her mind, but now was full of the biggest thing that had ever occupied it and must be telling me. French had offered for her and she had taken him and was full of happiness and excitement. She sat beside me in my garden and prattled along in her gentle, rather pleading sort of voice like a brooklet running, while I smoked my pipe and knitted and listened. Though never one to sparkle, that morning her adventures had put an edge to her speech.

"I'll tell you from the beginning, Cherry," she started. "I've told father every bit, and Job every bit, and now I'll tell it again to you, because I love to go over every minute of it. In fact you may say there's two stories to tell; but the big one is about me and Alfred French."

"You've took him, my dear. I hear it in your voice and see it in your face," I said.

But she wasn't going to be robbed of the details.

"We started for a stroll after supper last night and something told me the time had come," began she. "Once or twice before, when he's asked me to go out of an evening, I've felt the appointed hour was going to strike, only to find myself mistaken; but last night it did strike. We went at his wish up to Laughter Tor—to hear churn owl. The bird's arrived home for his usual summer visit, and Alfred likes his noise. And we met Jordan just as we started, returning from the village, where he'd been to the forge all day helping blacksmith with a job for father. Job had got a letter by the morning post—a most uncommon thing to happen to him—and, as we went off, I asked him what it was about and hoped it might be good news; and he said he would tell me when he opened it, which he had not yet done. Then Alf and I went up the hill and heard the queer bird churning his song. Then I catched sight of a glow-worm, like a little green head of fire in the grass, and French said that was a lucky token and we sat down on a mossy stone and the moon rose over the heath, so red as a blood orange. Then Alf came to business. 'I can't put off talking to you no longer, Clarice,' he said, 'for if I was to delay another hour, I'd miss my market most likely, you being the good value you are to any man lucky enough to win you.' He went on to say he couldn't bide at Laughter Hole, or breathe the same air with me any longer, if I didn't marry him and take him for keeps. He declared that he wasn't worthy to tie my shoe-string, but nevertheless he loved me body and soul. He finds himself repeating all my opinions over and over again like an echo! He said, 'Your name is music as sweet as the blackbird on the bough.'"

"Made a pretty job of it sure enough, my dear," I said.

"Oh yes, indeed he did, Cherry," she continued, "and next he put his arm round me and blessed his luck and swore that such a marvel of good fortune was beyond his poor deserving."

I thought that was most likely the first true word she'd heard from Alf, but didn't put it into words.

"And then you found yourself to be loving him back with all your heart, no doubt," I suggested.

"With the churn owl bawling all the while!" laughed

181

Clarice. "And then he gave me his first kiss, Cherry—the only time any man ever kissed me but father. After that I called his attention to the lovely moonshine, grown silver bright by now, and he said there wasn't going to be any moonshine about our courting if he knew it, but he was going to worship me under sun and moon both. 'And if any human can be worthy of such a darling wonder as you, Clarice,' he said, 'then I'll prove to be that man!'" She laughed again but hadn't nearly done.

"After a lot more talk," she continued, "the church clock told ten and we was both amazed to see how the time had sped, so we rose up and went home, to find father and Job Jordan in deep talk together. I guessed that father already knew what had happened to me and was most likely telling Job the changes that would soon follow after my marriage took place; but I was quite wrong there. Father was full of excitement and interest over Job himself, because there was his letter open on the table between them and it had brought amazing news."

"Fancy that!" I said. "But surely nothing could overshadow what you and Alf had brought back with you?"

"It did, Cherry! Both Alfred and me forgot even ourselves for a moment or two when we heard. 'Let me tell 'em, Jordan,' said father, as we came in. 'Wonders never cease,' he went on. 'Here's old Job come by two thousand pounds! Two thousand along of his father's brother dying in Exeter where he kept a baker's shop. And all because Job did the man good service in years past. He worked for his uncle as a boy for two years, but never heard anything about him afterwards and thought the baker was dead years and years ago; yet only last month the old chap passed away and left this big money to his nephew!'"

I told Clarice how properly pleased I was to hear such great news. "Nobody ever deserved a slice of good luck better than your horseman," I declared. "And how did Job stand up to it?"

"Curiously," she answered. "When he spoke, he never even named the money. 'Now for your news,' he said, 'because I reckon that's a bigger thing than what's overtook me.' Of course it was in truth, though for the moment such a huge sum

182

of money as that properly dazzled both father and Alfred. We hadn't brought back a surprise exactly, because father and Job knew it was going to happen any minute now; but nobody on earth ever imagined what had happened to Job."

"A most interesting thing, sure enough. And when Jordan turned his attention to it, what did he say?" I asked again.

"Mighty little," she declared. "In fact you felt somehow that he was no more excited than if he'd been left a five-pound note! Father would open a bottle of sherry wine, to drink good luck to all three of us, and we drank Job's health and he nodded to us and drank ours and just swallowed down his drink and then went off to bed. It was Alf and father who made merry, and Alf dwelt on his wonderful fortune, though I couldn't help feeling all the time that, for him, Job's two thousand pounds was the high-water mark of the evening, not me. That seemed rather a queer thing to feel and I asked him this morning why another man's money interested him so much, and he said that money was dust in the balance and always would be weighed against love. 'We well know what we are going to be to each other,' he said, 'but we don't know what his two thousand quid are going to be to Job.' I do believe that Alf is more excited about Job's come-by-chance than Job is himself!"

"He would be, but that's nothing to fret you, my dear," I answered. "You'll find that, by his nature, French is a lot drawn to money, well knowing his own wants to be such that money could always supply them; whereas just now, Job don't feel to need what money could buy."

"Father's feared he'll flit for certain," said Clarice, "and Alf's figured it out and says that Job will get five per centum and at least a hundred pounds a year without doing a stroke of work for it. So he agrees with father that Jordan will give notice, because nobody in his senses is going to do horseman's work on a farm if he has got such money behind him as that. So father's in two moods—cast down about his losing Job, yet joyous at me winning Alfred."

That was what Clarice told me, and when we parted I occupied my thoughts by taking a bird's-eye view of the situation. If you are built like I am, you do not need to go to the play-house to see a story told, but can watch men and women acting stories all round you gratis and for nothing. One event I did not as yet see before I took the stage myself, and for the minute only French looked very interesting. Both he and Jordan found a tidy tang of bitterness in their lives now; but I soon saw the head man's easy triumph with Clarice looked nought to him against Job's two thousand pounds. He wasn't proud of his own luck, but only busy envying the other man's. In fact each had got what the other one most wanted, and that was a very fine situation for such as me to watch unfold.

The first manifestation I had came from the horseman. Job looked in one night with a petition that he was fathering from the village begging the Hunt to pay better money to those who were losing their chickens by the foxes; and when I had signed my name to it, because foxes multiplied a lot faster than hounds could catch them, then, in answer to my question if the wedding was in sight, Jordan spoke.

"As to the date, it's held over till after our oats are saved," he said. "Mr. Redmayne's wishful to keep Clarice at his elbow for a bit longer, because he knows she won't be as of old when she's wed. Of course she don't mind, and Alf don't look to be in any hurry neither. He's a man with spacious ideas, and some of 'em beastly; but he don't mind confessing to me. We had a tidy turn of speech out on the land not long since, where we were working and had knocked off for our midday meal. And he began by chaffing me about my money. He said I was a lucky sweep to be what he called a 'capitalist', and have a bit of the ready to burn, and be in reach of adventures that can only come to them with plenty of cash. And he wondered what a dead-alive chap like me was going to do about it. He said, so far as he could see, I didn't care a brass farthing for the stuff; and then I had a bright thought myself and told him that he didn't look to care about his luck no better than I felt to care for mine. Though he carries on all right with Clarice and her father, there's a darned lot in his life that shows he's far short of all they think he is, and I'm so anxious for her as ever I was."

"Brooding on her married future when the gilt's off the

gingerbread and Alf firm in the saddle at Laughter Hole?" I asked.

"Yes. They tell me there's one or two other girls in the village who have been opening their mouths since his tokening was known. I can't rest easy myself—far from it—though God knows I ain't one to breed trouble for other people. But the simplest way for me looks to be I should clear out, though on her account I'd bide if I could be of any service to her. In that case trouble would be a pleasure."

"Time may be on her side come presently," I suggested; and then he said a thing that threw more light for me than any word yet spoken.

"Comparing our luck in one of his coarse speeches," he went on, "Alf told me the difference between his good fortune and mine was the difference between bread-and-butter pudding and a cherry tart."

"Clarice being the bread-and-butter pudding, Job?"

"That was his shameful meaning. But he was sorry the next minute and granted that he didn't ought to have said such a thing to me of all people. 'For two pins, Alf,' I said to him, 'I'd smash your face in for that.'"

"He's greatly interested, no doubt, to hear what you decree to do with your money?" I asked, by way of changing the subject.

"He was, and so was the master, and I've told 'em, seeing it natural they should wish to know. In fact Mr. Redmayne went so far as to hope my fortune wasn't going to take me away from Laughter Hole; and I answered that as to that, it still looked an open question, while as for the money, I had left it in the lawyer's hands—him that wrote and told me about it. He's putting it out to goody for me, and vested it in the hands of the Government, where it is safe from danger."

"What did they think of that, Job?" I asked.

"The master thought well of it, but French said I ought to get far better returns. He also wondered whether the lawyer's an honest man and straight and trustable; but I told him he was judging others by what he'd very like do himself and that he had no right to think the lawyer was a thief."

I laughed to hear that.

"It's a common mistake among the crooked to take it for granted everybody else must be crooked too," I told him.

"Love and money are Alf's favourite subjects," went on Jordan. "If you was to ask him what's the best thing in the world, he would say so instantly. Hard cash, first and last and always. That's what he thinks. 'Would you put money higher than love for a fine maid?' I asked him once, and he said that, given enough money, you could buy most any fine maid worth buying, because a golden key opens every lock. I showed amazement to hear such stuff even from him. 'Do you in sober earnest hold the affections and trust of Clarice a lesser thing than hard cash?' I asked him, and he pointed out how it looked to him. 'I certainly do,' he answered, 'because ready money can turn into all I'm ever like to want. Between you and me, Job, and without any disrespect to her, there's a lot finer than Clarice going begging, and though Laughter Hole is all right in its small way, you've got to face the filthy climate up here and a thousand drawbacks for such as me. In fact the farm is barely good enough to balance against what I'm paying for it. Redmayne may last another ten years as like as not, and ten years is a tolerable good slice of my time. I'm very fond of my future wife and I shall jog along with her all right; but one day I shall sell this place and get off this blasted wilderness. So, when you ask whether two thousand golden pounds could compare with my future outlook, you can see there's no comparison whatever.' That," concluded Jordan, "is what he had the barefaced wickedness to say to me, and then, having heard more than enough, I parted from him."

Of course I could read a great deal deeper between the lines of this conversation than could Job, and I now felt myself getting a full picture of the situation. The centrepiece of the affair was no longer Alfred, but the horseman. I saw tolerable clear as to French, but remained in doubt of Jordan. A pretty stiff challenge might face him, but seeing no reward could be hoped on his account if he accepted it, yet there looked to be no harm in setting the deed before him. A few days later I asked him to come and talk some night along with me about a point of view. This he consented to do, and I began by praising him.

"It was a masterly stroke on your part," I said, "to lay bare Alf's character to him, and I only wish you had probed a thought deeper yet. Most like you have no urge to go any deeper, but to do so might open out a line of action well worth your consideration to think upon. For my part I'd much like to know what French would do in a certain situation. Supposing it had been possible for him to choose between two thousand pounds and freedom, or marriage with Clarice and Laughter Hole, which would he have taken?"

"No need to ask that," he answered. "What I should like to know is what he would have done with the two thousand pounds if it was his."

"A good question," I agreed, "and be sure to ask it. The answer may put some ideas in your mind, Job."

And I was very much in the right, for within another week Jordan took my hint, which led instanter to a remarkable outcome far greater than I expected. He told me about it himself for, in the course of his next exchanges with Alfred, that happed which cried for my aid, because the seed I sowed in Job's mind quickly ripened for harvest and called me to put the curb upon him for his own sake.

"I asked him flat out what he'd do with my fortune," Job told me, "and he made no bones about it. He said he would chuck his native land altogether if such money was ever in his pocket and take up virgin land, which would be a lot more likely to suit him than a virgin lass, in South Africa, or Australia. That's what Alf would do, and he wondered why the mischief I didn't do so myself. 'Seeing that you think such a devil of a lot of Clarice,' he said, 'the strange thing is that you can bide here now that all hope is dead.' But I told him hope wasn't dead, because it never lived. 'There never was no hope,' I said, 'and I never was so foolish as to imagine any such thing; but you can sometimes do another person a good turn, though it may be beyond their power to offer payment.'"

That showed me like a flash of lightning how his mind was working.

"A very fine Christian idea, Job," I assured him.

"So Alf thought," went on Jordan. "He grinned all over

187

his face and applauded me. He said that, if I felt that way, no doubt I'd be minded to give Clarice a grand wedding present and he prayed for me to let it be cash, because there was no better safeguard to marriage than a bit in the bank; and after that something drove me to come to closer quarters with the man. A thought clamoured to be spoke and, almost before I'd turned it over properly, the words popped out of my mouth. 'No,' I said, 'I won't give Clarice no present; but I'd very much like her wedding with you broke off, if it could be, Alf.' 'The hell you would!' he answered me. 'And what have I done against you?' 'Nothing,' I replied. 'But it's what you aim to do against her. No need to get hot. I don't mean no harm whatever to you and couldn't harm you if I wanted to. But you have been very open with me and made it clear you don't care two straws about the woman herself and will sell her farm some day and take her off the Moor, which is her native home, so soon as you get the chance to do it. That shows you was never made to shine as her husband. And you never would shine as a husband unless you picked a female strong enough to master you, which you are a lot too downy to do. And because Clarice Redmayne is going to be a darned unhappy woman after six months of you, that's why I'd put a spoke in your wheel if I could, Alf.' Then it was his turn, and he pretended to be in a furious rage," went on Job. "He told me that I was a damned, insolent, interfering fool, and as soon as he commanded at the farm, I'd be the first he'd fire. 'And if you tell any of this trash to Redmayne, I'll have you up for libel,' he said. But I kept calm. 'I don't want to influence anybody against you,' I assured him. 'Folk can form their own opinions as to you. I only say I won't give Clarice no wedding gift; but you needn't fancy I'd waste my wind speaking a word to her against you, because she wouldn't believe an angel if the creature flew down from Heaven and told her the fatal truth about you. And no more would Michael Redmayne believe it. But I feel so terrible wishful for the woman to live in peace and safety, that I'd make it a matter of money to get you out of her path. And since you put cash higher than her, it's no impertinence to tell you so.' "

My heart properly warmed to Job on hearing this.

188

"And what had he to say to that, you valiant chap?" I asked.

"He calmed down immediate," explained Jordan. "I don't see through people very quick, but owing to my feelings for Clarice, I couldn't fail to see through him just then. He looked at me with joyful astonishment in his eyes, as if he'd found a full purse and nobody in sight to claim it. 'Now you're talking!' he said, and then went on to tell that, if I felt disposed for a business deal, he might be quite willing to consider it."

On hearing this much, I told Job that any transactions with Alfred were like to be tricky, and full of dangers for all concerned and a dead loss for him in any case. But he was full of ardour about his idea and said that to save Clarice from marrying French would be good value for money in his opinion. At first I greatly doubted if he could honestly think so, or whether an ignorant and humble working man like him could rise to loving a girl in such a heroical fashion as all that. I judged he still hoped at heart to get the woman for himself in the long run if he paid enough for her. So I warned him against any such dream.

"It would be quite all right for Alfred to take a spot of your money on condition that he bolted afterwards and vanished off the scene of action," I said ; "but you mustn't take for granted it's going to be equally all right for you, Job. You must face how such a disgrace will look to Clarice."

"Strange to say Alf pointed that out also," he answered. "Alf said that the utter beastliness of what would happen if we came to terms would naturally make Clarice hate him worse than hell fire ; but he explained that because she would naturally hate him to the best of her powers, it didn't follow that she was going to fall on my neck. I replied that I well knew she was not for me, but would be willing to endure her anger also when she heard it was my money got Alf away from her. And that cleared the air for him. 'As to that,' he suggested, 'if you're set on this fine caper and don't want any reward, then there's no reason why you should have any blame either. The truth need never come to her ears at all. Then she can concentrate on hating me and there won't be no risk of Redmayne sacking you. You can be as much horrified as all

189

the rest of them when I shoot the moon some fine night and are seen no more, for there's nobody to tell them about our piece of business if you don't.' "

"And what was your answer, Job?" I inquired.

"I said silence all round was the right word once he was bought off her. 'Good lad!' he said. 'Then it's a deal!' "

"You haven't gone so far as that, surely?" I asked. "If you have done, I lay he named a pretty tough price."

Then came out the shocking truth, though it was I who felt shocked, not Jordan.

"We didn't waste time haggling after that. The bargain was struck in two minutes," he answered. "Alf named his price and I agreed to pay it. He explained that less than my two thousand wouldn't make it worth his while to give up what he'd got already; but by good chance two thousand pounds was just about the figure to give him the start he wanted and, as I appeared to feel Clarice's escape from him was worth all the money, then our bargain looked to be fair enough. That seemed to me quite reasonable and only helped to show the wickedness of the man. It's all going to be put in the lawyer's hands and signed and sealed so there shall be no double dealings."

He declared himself as well satisfied and the better for confiding in me about it, and I knew it useless to blame him, or tell him he was a lunatic, or be cross with him. But it changed my opinions about Job himself and showed me a fine fashion of love outside my experience till then. I offered to approach French and use all my powers to get the scamp to bate his price; but Jordan begged me to do no such thing and take no step that would keep Alf a day longer at Laughter Hole than need be.

"I've no wish to go back on it," he declared most earnestly. "It may look bad business to some, but it's a good bargain to me."

For once in a way I found myself without my usual flow of invention. The interest was now shifted off both men to the woman and I considered what course of action a girl with her modest wits was likely to take and what her feelings were going to be when this happened. That would depend upon how much she learned about the facts. If the truth was hid from her, then

190

her rage would fall on Alf himself and nobody else; but if she found what Job had done, then he was going to catch it also, with no choice but to leave Laughter Hole, and get out of her sight. In truth, if he didn't give notice, he'd surely get it. Or it might fall out differently. Should she hear the truth, then Clarice might have enough brain power to feel that, if French was the sort to put big money before his affection for her, then she'd be better in the long run without him. It was possible also that Michael Redmayne would see it and help her to see it too.

Things soon moved and I was not called to wait long, for after another three weeks, and just as I was going to see Job again, the crash came like a bolt from the blue, as they say. Alfred French didn't appear to his breakfast one fine morning —the day after pay-day—and inquiry showed that he hadn't pressed his bed that night. He was gone like the dew off the fleece, and left nought save a short letter stuck on his bedroom mantelshelf addressed to Michael Redmayne. In that he bade Laughter Hole 'good-bye' and said he hoped to be spared the sight of Dartmoor for ever more. He tossed a bone to Clarice and told her not to worry about him because he had long since seen they weren't suited to double harness but hadn't the heart to tell her so. And that was all.

The poor girl acted like a woman stunned and couldn't grasp what had happened to her for quite a time, while her father wasted his energy in a lot of senseless anger. He came to me full of fury to know how he must set about bringing French to book and making him pay for his wickedness; but I could only say that no way existed to do so.

"He's done nothing you can fasten upon, Mike," I explained. "You can't lock him up, and you can't sue him for breach of promise before you find him, and how are you going to do that?"

It took the farmer a week or two before he calmed down, and Clarice, shaken to her roots by such treatment, behaved as if she'd done something wicked herself. But, after the man was gone beyond reach, a good deal about him came to the ears of the wronged parties that, for false charity, had been hidden from them until now. Then Michael began to see that, since

French had proved himself no better than a wolf in sheep's clothing, it was a good thing that he had showed his real nature before marriage and not kept it hid till after. And Clarice, once over the shame of being jilted, pulled herself together bravely enough and in six weeks was sorrier for her father's disappointment than for herself. She couldn't suffer as some finer characters might have done, not being built to love in a very grand manner at her best; but she was truly troubled to have failed her parent and quenched his hopes.

"Him being so wishful for grandchildren," she told me, "makes it a bit of a blow; but I try to cheer him up by telling him that, with a father like Alfred, they might have been imps of Satan and better unborn. But now poor Dad won't have anything to dance on his knee—imps or otherwise."

"Think nothing of it: you've got your life before you yet and Alf wasn't the only pebble on the beach in any case," I told her.

After that I took the business into my own hands and found myself well equal to carrying it through—with Job Jordan in the front of the picture, though only Providence and myself yet knew it. I didn't strike while the iron was hot, but decided on a roundabout plan of action more in line with my usual practice. The horseman kept his mouth close shut after the explosion, of course, and trusted me to do the like; but before I played my hand, it was needful for him to follow my directions in one particular. He needed to hurt his master now and so concentrate attention on himself, the last thing he was in the habit of doing. I knew he wouldn't like that, and he didn't.

"You must yield your opinions to mine, Job," I told him privately. "You must be prepared to do exactly as I bid you and trust me with the future, else I can't do all for you that lies well in my power to do. Agree to obey me and everything looks to point favourable. Though you have not laid down your life for Clarice, which wasn't called for, yet you have laid down all else you'd got in the world worth talking about, and the next thing you need to do is to trust me a bit further yet."

"I've trusted you, as you know," he answered, "and will so continue if there's aught more to be done for her that I can accomplish. I see no more to it myself, but grant your powers to look ahead."

Then I told him what must be done and why.

"All for her welfare is our motto, so first you take a strong step, though you may not understand it," I said, and then told him he must give in his notice and let it be clearly understood he ordained to quit Laughter Hole at the end of his month.

"No need to pull a long face," I assured him. "You can leave Redmayne and his daughter to do that. But, though a pain and grief to them, it's only all done for their good. It calls for great faith to do it, I grant you that; and lots of our most vital actions in life call for faith to do them. So I bid you announce you are going. Then, seeing they still believe in your big money, though they will both feel terrible sorry, they won't be surprised. The master will wring his hands and Clarice will take it hard for his sake; while all you need is to tell yourself that you are only sowing bread upon the waters which is going to return to you."

He confessed that he couldn't see top nor tail in what I was aiming at, yet admitted it might be a sensible thing to do if I said so.

"Not for any present good to her that I can see," he said, "but, with me out of the way, the road will be clear for master to start fresh with two new men—head man and horseman. Then, perchance one of them——"

"No, Job," I interrupted sharply. "You need not to expect anything like that again. Clarice has had her dose of love-making with the unknown, and I promise, if only to put a bit of starch into your faith, that you can wipe out any fear of that from your mind. I don't intend anything of that sort to happen and I wouldn't suffer it. But go on trusting me to the end. I'm not one to gamble with other people's fortunes, for if I was, I shouldn't stand where I do stand."

So Job rose to the trial and put his faith and trust in me. He give notice, which was the last straw on Michael's back, for he didn't know what lay behind this unexpected blow, and Job had to listen to his master's lamentations and reproofs, while bitterer still for his ears was to hear Clarice declare that she was properly sorry also, and much distressed for her father's sake that he was going to lose his right hand and his dearest friend.

"Not that we think any worse of you, Job," she told him, "because it's fitting you shouldn't hide your talents in a napkin any longer with us at Laughter Hole."

Then came my last great stroke, which had been all along to let out Jordan's performance where it was going to tell to the utmost, just when Redmayne smarted under his approaching loss; and I had to choose whether he or his daughter should be the first to hear it. Then things rushed to their climax, as they often will when Providence gets tired of our dawdling, and I decided for Clarice. I met her one morning on her way to the village and bade her drop in upon me early the following day as I had an interesting and wondrous spot of news. Something convinced me that what I had to tell would move her a lot, though even I didn't guess at the violent response she made to it. She came, just as I had finished my breakfast, and heard the whole story. There was no need to put any adornments on to it, nor draw any conclusions from it, for the bare bones of Job's great sacrifice were best told naked without any trimmings.

I first declared how vexed I felt to know that their horseman was leaving the farm, being fond of him myself, and then I told her of his sacrifices and threw light for Clarice on all Job had done and above all his high motives for doing it. I talked on a light note and said it was a very heroical way to show what he felt for her and a credit to his fine nature; and the effect upon the woman was instantaneous: I never knew her face to put on such a lot of lively expressions.

"Just his native modesty, Clarice," I explained, "to hide his feelings from you."

"There's times when modesty is proper madness!" she cried, "and this was one of 'em. And, but for your sense, he'd have turned his back on his salvation and his affections never been known and the proper answer to 'em never been heard."

"That's what I saw facing Jordan, my dear," I answered, "but it's going to be a proper shock to him to find I've squeaked for he believed I was sworn to secrecy."

194

"Thank God you did squeak then, and now you can leave the man to me, Cherry. This is my job," she told me.

"When you think what he did and what he lost by doing it," I began; but she cut me short.

"Leave him to me," she said again. "I'll handle Job, since he looks to be unable to handle me."

"Many a man in love has been helped on his way by an understanding woman who knew how to take time by the forelock," I told her. "We are more apt to recognise the passing hour than they are."

"There's one thing I will know anyway," she answered, "and I must have it from his own lips and no others. His deeds show it must be so; but I can only be dead sure it's true from himself. He's taking the market-cart to Moreton presently, so I'll travel in it. I'll go right away back now and don my hat and jacket and say I'm going with him."

I applauded this idea.

"A most clever thought and well worthy of you," I said. "Go gay, Clarice; go smart and be cheerful and lighthearted, as you have good reason to be. Put on your hat with the red fuchsias in it, that always looks as if it was trimmed with shrimps and suits you so well."

So off she went full of determination.

"This will be the making of father," she promised, "and the making of Job, too, if the wonders you tell are true; but if you've got it all wrong, my dear, then I'm going to look a bigger fool than I do already."

"Stand no more nonsense from him," I warned her. "When he hears you know what he's done, it's likely he'll never forgive me for telling you, but that don't matter a button."

Nobody can do more than surmise exactly how it went between them that forenoon, and how her father took it when they got home again; but all agreed afterwards that I was their good angel and Michael Redmayne found a bit of useful money on the quiet, to pay me for my endeavours. Clarice related something of her ride to Moreton, though not all. She came to see me next day and was full of joyous triumph.

"When I slapped out with it, Cherry," she began, "he

195

started by nearly running the cart into the water-table and upsetting the pair of us. Then he pulled up as if he was shot and looked as if he was condemned to sudden death. 'You done this for your own mad reasons, no doubt, Job,' I said to him, 'and though some women might want to scratch your eyes out for it, and most like I should myself if I'd heard of it sooner; I don't feel that way now, quite the contrary in fact. There's only one more word to be spoke on the subject and, though silent as the grave you may still choose to be, I demand an answer.' It was long in coming, however. He only stroked the horse's neck gently with his whip and paltered and put it off as if time was eternity. 'So long as I'm forgiven before I quit, 'tis no odds about anything else,' he got out at last. 'Forgiven or not forgiven,' I said; 'why did you fling away your fortune only to save me from Alfred French? What made you do it, Job? I will know the answer to that.' 'Because I felt wishful for your future to go suent,' was all he could say and he said it in a voice as if he was confessing a crime. 'And what the mischief did my future matter to you?' I snapped at him, and he looked down at me where I sat on his left side and told me afterwards there was tears in my eyes when I looked up at him. 'I done it,' he said at last, 'because I should have felt no more peace afterwards if you found yourself an unhappy woman.' I was on tricky ground now yet dashed on. 'But that's love, you idiot!' I cried out, as if it was the discovery of my lifetime, and he heaved a sigh and said, 'Think nothing more of it—nothing of it at all, Clarice.' 'Never did I dream a level-headed man like you could have risen to any such thing,' I answered just to fill time; but all to no purpose. He rambled on that he'd be out of my sight once for all in a week and tolerable contented if I had forgiven him. That happened going to Moreton and we dropped the subject until coming home again. Then I took charge of the situation once for all."

"High time you did," I said.

"Yes. I told him I had no mind for him to leave Laughter Hole, but chose he should stop there for father's sake. 'And for mine also,' I said. 'If you're cruel put about for my comfort and contentment, Job,' I continued, 'then you'd best to carry on with the good work, my dear man, and bide close to me, where you can keep your sad eyes upon me by night so well as day."

"A very clever touch on your part," I told her. "That brought him to his senses no doubt."

"He was cornered and run to earth at last," she assured me. "The rest is our own affair; but you needn't to fear he'll be angered with you, Cherry, when next you pass the time of day with him. He'll only say, 'Thank God for all His wonders', same as he's saying to everybody."

Be it as it will, they wed three months later, and Michael Redmayne danced a grandson on his knee in due course.

XII

TODAY you'll find folk fear less for their future than they were taught to do of old. Then it was driven into our heads that there were two famous places where we go to spend eternity; but nobody would know which their souls were bound for until they got there and found out. We were warned of the long odds as to where most of the human race might be counted upon to arrive; but now all is changed and the outlook a lot brightened for us. In my early days the Bad Place was counted an ugly fact, and every child learnt about it, just as he learned his letters and figures; but now are come pious and learned people to discover there is no such region as Hell hotting up for us beyond the grave, and the Pit of Darkness lies here on earth and nowhere else. Hell belongs to us only so long as we were alive, and in truth death is the only sure and certain way to keep out of it! When I was young belief in hell-fire kept millions of people straight, and fear of it acted like a curb to those with the natural bent to do evil; but now, it looks more difficult for our pastors and masters to steer human nature on the narrow path, and I have lived to see the laws softened down and a great deal of kindly thought shown even to the most shameful of evil-doers; and if that's going to work out in improvement of behaviour all round, so much the better. For then your feelings, before the tale I now set out to tell, may take a new colour.

The scene of this outlandish bit of work was itself in a way fantastic for, where men pit themselves against Nature, the peaceful face of the earth is apt to change and its orderly countenance grow scored and torn and fouled by battle. Lasting wounds appear as the fight goes on, and we leave sure and bitter signs of our victory when we win it, but if Nature conquers, then her purpose is to hide the destruction and heal the carnage and draw over all again her ancient mantle.

Ruddy Lake, the region was called—a great peat bed two

miles north of Packhorse Bridge, where folk fought for their fuel on the face of the Moor and yearly tore away tons and tons of the stuff to keep their home fires burning.

Here was its birthplace in Ruddy Lake, a chaos of old peat-ties sprawling their broken acres upon the heart of the Moor. The slabs of the new-cut stuff are laid out to dry, or piled against each other, like a pixy lodge of little tents planted together. Round about the old rubbish and litter is crusted with grey lichen, where the ties gape in a huge confusion, some tracks ruined and deserted, others freshly worked and ranging from ebony, black and chocolate to yellow, where they run in low cliffs above the quagmires and pools from which they lift. With peat knife and peat iron the cutters rend off the living skin of the heather and sedge and whortle, then dig out the rich soil beneath in wet slabs to be exposed and dried before the sledges come to drag it down into civilisation below. Gay flowers light up the bogs in high summer and the plovers peeve and the heath larks sing overhead ; but, come winter, all the land may be frozen hard, or hidden under snow. It was mid-autumn and the peat harvest in course of saving when these things happened under a blanket of cumbersome fog, sent by the will of Providence to shield them from every eye but my own.

The tale proper begins with a man called Solomon Yeo, who had Packhorse Bridge terrified for long years, like a man-eating tiger terrifies an Indian village. He was by nature cruel, and the cruel are often cowardly, which he was not. But when you get cruelty combined with fearless courage, then you most times catch a tartar. Yeo was one who knew a thousand ways to torment and torture his fellow creatures, and practised them all. Usury stood for his favourite weapon and he made his money take toll and, by extortion, furnish him with his chiefest pleasure and profit. He had strength of character and a quick brain, and such was his iron will-power that once folk got in his grip, they curled up like frightened wood-lice and were thankful if he'd only pass them by without setting his foot upon them. A little, spare man he was, not above five feet and an inch or two high ; but with a pinch of Satan in his black eyes and a flint-stone for his heart.

199

His father had once farmed Twin Trees, and he owned the steading now and rented it to Grace Morley, the widow of the last tenant; but it was only a small part of his possessions and, along with his schemes to trade on the troubles of other people, he made his money breed not only a big sum of cash, but gathered in a lot of house property also. In fact it was common belief that Yeo owned half the village and hungered yet for land and houses. And when unlucky men reached a point where they could pay the rent on his mortgages no more, then he would foreclose like the stroke of doom.

He hated me for one thing and another, though we were never called to clash in the open. None caught Yeo in a right-down crooked deed any more than in a decent one. To the windy side of the law he kept and employed a lawyer at Moreton, who worked with him and was under his thumb, same as lot of other people. He flourished, you might say, on a weakness of human nature, for if we know there's a man at hand ever ready to lend, then we find ourselves with a growing inclination to borrow. Not that Solomon ever appeared to drive a very hard bargain on the face of it. He was too clever for that, and when silly fools—out to get married or what not —would seek advances, they always left him under the impression they had got the best of the deal. It was only when their interest hung fire and hard circumstances made them beg for time, or mercy, that they found where they stood. And now he had reached to such power that he quite over-crowed Pack-horse Bridge and woke nought but fear and hate against himself and all his ways.

That is how things stood and it was then that I got a flood of light at present hid from everybody but Solomon Yeo himself and one other. He had but a single relative, a nephew, who lived with him in a new house of brick and stone that the moneylender built. Yeo never married, but he took his nephew, when the boy was left a destitute orphan, and trained him for a clerk to keep his books and do his will. David Yeo was the young man's name and he had long sunk under his uncle's dominion and now become little more than a machine. He was gentle by nature, but with no prospects outside his uncle, and so he bided on his chains and hoped that some day he might win out and get repaid for his servitude when the elder dropped. But now, all of a sudden, David's turn came and he found to his alarm that his master had got a sharp and unexpected use for him. To me he brought his quandary and much astonished was I to get a call one night, for though we'd pass the time of day when we met, I never thought to see David upon a private matter, well knowing that if his uncle had heard he was wishful to consult me, he would have forbidden it. However, young Yeo soon let me learn that he was come in strict secrecy.

"You'll understand this is a matter of confidence, Miss Crymes, and between ourselves alone," he began, and I assured him he could rest easy in his mind about that. Then a very interesting thing happened, for when he found my quality, he opened out to an amazing extent, unburdened his soul of many things and ended by telling me a great deal more than he had set out to do. I found that he had but one close friend in the world, a loving but stupid girl, and so it proved of great satisfaction to him to pour his confidences into the ear of a cleverer person than himself. He had been properly educated because his uncle saw to that, and he spoke clearly as to what at present filled his mind. Before we parted he gave me a respectful word of praise and wished we had been better acquaint sooner.

"I haven't talked so plainly as this in all my life," he said at the finish ; and in truth he did speak very plain indeed, while, as I listened, I perceived what pleasure it gave him to unlock his thoughts in the company of such a far-seeing spirit as myself.

"Smoke your pipe," I said, after he arrived, "and tell me as much as you please and know it's safe to do so. With one like your uncle, difficulties arise no doubt. . . ." David laughed. He had a lefthanded sense of humour which made him laugh at his own position, though not sufficient will-power to try and mend it.

"Uncle Sol says you are the only one in the parish he hasn't bested," began the young man. "He hates you, but he knows you for a pretty tough customer and he'd like to score off you if he could."

"I can well believe he's got no use for me any more than I have for him," I answered.

"He's got a use for everything," explained David, "and now I'm sorry to find he's got a use for me. Everybody is a future meal hanging in his larder, and he'll keep 'em on the hooks till their turn comes."

"An ugly picture sure enough," I said. "You know his strength and his weakness better than most of us, no doubt."

"He's only got one weakness and that's in his voice," declared young Yeo. "His voice is gentle, but, though mild and never lifted, few ever heard a friendly note in it. He can cut to the bone with words when he's minded to, and he never smiles till he hears a man groaning, or sees a woman in tears."

"And now he's got a use for you which don't chime with your own wishes, David," I suggested, calling him by his Christian name and showing my friendly interest.

"Two nights ago he opened out on me," explained the young fellow, "and you can judge the figure I cut to hear him. My uncle started this way. 'Touching Widow Morley,' he began, 'I've got a move planned in that quarter, and you can help me to kill two birds with one stone.' 'Always ready to lend a hand, Uncle,' I said, and he went on : 'It's like this then : you're twenty-six and wife-old now, and through you I can save money. So I've cast my eyes around and found what I wanted at Twin Trees. Grace Morley has gone down the hill this longful time, and I've lent her money and paid her debts and even suffered passing loss by her ; but now my patience has given out, because she's got nothing left to borrow on except her daughter, Eve. The girl has character and a lot more sense than her mother. She looks life in the face and happens to be a very fine woman. I could do with her about my house and I should not be called upon to pay her money if she was married to you, like I pay Jane Mason at present. Eve would be my housekeeper, but as your wife would work gratis and stand in the same position as you do yourself. She knows what poverty is and wouldn't waste my money like Jane does. And Jane's past work anyway now and can go on the parish. So all fits together very well and, in exchange for Eve married to you, I'll put Grace Morley on her feet again and sack the pair of

202

zanies she employs at Twin Trees and get some labour for her and let her be carefree, as far as a fool like her ever can be.'"

"So that's what you are called to face?" I asked David.

"That's it in a nutshell," he replied. "Uncle's so used to things going as he plans them that he talked as if the matter was finished. His next words will show you. I reminded him that a good few others besides myself must be taken into account, and then he spoke in his gentle voice. 'Others?' he asked. 'Who do you think I am? What others matter? The Widow will thank God for her luck and the only others are the girl and you; and I don't see either of you doubting your luck either.'

"Well," continued young Yeo, "I've long learned his line of approach and ceased to waste many sighs for those he gets into his claws. His first pleasure is always the misery of somebody else, and to see me right down distressed would have been meat and drink to him; but this was outrageous and indecent and striking at the roots of my whole life. So I started to kick good and hard, and I began by telling the old devil something he didn't yet know concerning myself—something I had hidden because I reckoned he would oppose it. Now he had given me my chance, however; but I went to work very crafty. 'Marriage is a pretty big order, Uncle Sol,' I said, 'though as a matter of fact a wife has crossed my mind a good bit of late. But it looked to me only my own affair though I never overlooked that your affection for me would make it your affair too. You are very wise about Jane Mason retiring, because the time has come for you to have better cooking than hers and also a stronger, smarter woman for your housewife, so, thinking of you quite as much as myself, I can't help feeling there is just the right woman to suit us both; but she's not Eve Morley. Jane Mason's niece, Barbara Mason, is the one for both of us: she that helps Jane every week and does your sewing and darning and cooks to perfection. She's the right and proper one—made for the job—and we would unite in our efforts to pleasure you and add to your comfort and convenience in every sort of way.'"

"It's whispered round about that you and Barbara are

pretty close friends, David. And what did Mr. Yeo answer to that?" I asked.

"In a voice as soft as cream and with words as bitter as gall. 'To hell with Barbara Mason, and now you can shut your mouth and listen to me.' That's what he said," replied David. "And he added that there was no need to waste any more mouth-speech on the subject. 'I ordain for this to happen and it will happen,' he said; 'you might so well marry a guinea-pig as Barbara Mason and I hate the sight of her in any case. Eve Morley's different. She don't cringe and has got tolerable sane ideas for a woman. She'll jump at the chance to help her mother and feather her own nest both. So you can get on with your part. I shall tell the widow my intentions and let her understand that she can bide at Twin Trees if you marry Eve inside six months.' That's Uncle Sol's programme for me, Miss Crymes."

He grinned a wry sort of grin; then he fell silent and seemed to stare in his imagination at the future planned for him.

"I've stuck to him all these years," he said, "because he must drop soon or late, and it would be foolish to quarrel with my future prospects; but he can't defy reason and order and common sense, and I've told him so."

I saw how the iron had entered into David's feeble soul and could not in honesty very much admire him, which he saw and tried to put up an excuse.

"I showed a spark of courage then," he went on, "though the old man did his best to put it out. I told him you cannot forge other people's lives to your own pattern that way and he wasn't God Almighty. 'There's little you don't know, Uncle Sol,' I said, 'but woman are a branch of learning you never troubled to study and I've heard you tell, time and again, that all a female shall ever do for you is to lay you out when you're dead. There's such a thing as true love,' I assured him, 'and you can't banish love out of the hearts of ordinary men.'"

"What had he to say to that great fact?" I asked.

"My voice had risen a bit, for I was growing pretty hot; so first he told me not to bellow at him, because he wouldn't stand bluster from anybody. 'Use your maggot's brain,' he said. 'There's only one on this earth that you have to reckon

204

with and that's me. So show your sense and gratitude, and turn to it and set the ball rolling. And now go to bed.' "

"Ordered you to bed !" I exclaimed.

"And I went. He'll often cut me short when he's sick of the sight of me and wants to be alone. Like ice running down your back his voice can be, yet so gentle that you often don't feel the lash till you find yourself bleeding. But I had a bit more to say that night before I left him. 'One thing you'd best learn before we part tonight, Uncle Sol,' I said, 'because it puts a stopper to your wishes once for all. Maybe you haven't heard of Rodney Hull? He was warrener at Wistman's Wood while Mr. Fortesque rented the warrens, but now he works for Duchy and lodges at Twin Trees with Mrs. Morley. And Hull is tokened to Eve Morley. She promised him a fortnight ago.' 'You can leave the man to me,' he answered calmly. 'Your part is to carry on with the woman. I'll talk to her mother tomorrow. Go to bed now.' So with that I cleared out of his sight."

David ceased. He'd thrown a tidy spot of light on his uncle and himself. But for the moment it seemed that there was no case, because if Eve Morley honestly loved where she had promised to wed, then that was the end of it. I knew something of her, though not enough to be certain how she would act. No doubt old Yeo felt Eve was going to be on his side and didn't doubt the issue.

Silence fell for a while between me and David ; then I broke it and turned to him.

"What manner of chap is this Rodney Hull?" I inquired.

"He's a wrestler—quite well known in sporting circles at Plymouth—and the harmless, amiable sort that strong men often are," answered David. "Good-tempered by all accounts ; but what sort of a line he would take if he found somebody courting his sweetheart, I wouldn't care to find out."

He left me soon after that and I told him I would bear the matter in mind.

"Most likely," I said, "Eve Morley will cut the knot herself ; but I can't know about that till I find out whether she's the sort to sacrifice herself for her mother's sake. Probably not if she's in love."

"My uncle will put her in a cleft stick," declared David.

"You can break a cleft stick like any other stick if you've got the strength to do so," I told him.

I didn't know Grace Morley's girl but hit on an easy way to do so and judge of her character. The whortleberry harvest was just in full swing at this time and women and children would daily stream away to the Moor with their baskets to pick the berries and earn a bit of money ; so, knowing Eve did well at it and worked pretty regular while the glut lasted, I journeyed up to the berry grounds with the rest one morning and took my basket and contrived I should find myself in talking distance of the young woman.

She was a sturdy piece, well set up, but without any airs and graces to attract the average man. Common sense looked to be her best suit. She showed pleasure to find me scrape acquaintance with her and woke to sharp interest when I related what had made me do so and heard how David Yeo was among my customers for the minute. Then she blossomed out and added to my knowledge.

"Old Sol has put it all before mother," she said, "and finding it possible for her to stop at Twin Trees if I marry Yeo's nephew, it's natural for mother to feel it was an answer to her prayers when David's uncle came along to show how things might be. He granted his slack-twisted nephew is no prize-packet in himself ; but said, if I'll wed him, then mother's safe and my fortune's made. He also said, 'It don't matter a damn if Eve suits David, but her future is safe if she suits me.' "

The girl stopped to laugh and I laughed too.

"Let's hear a bit more of what he said to your mother, my dear, and what Mrs. Morley said to him," I suggested.

"Of course mother could but grant it was a grand idea. ' 'Tis beyond dreaming,' mother said, and he agreed it was. 'But I never dream,' he told her. 'All's in reach and you only need to say so.' Then he added, as if it was barely worth naming, that he'd heard I was tokened to a rabbit-catcher, or some such rubbish, but judged me a tidy lot too sensible to let a day labourer spoil my chances now. Then he concluded

206

how he was going to bid his nephew set about me and wished mother good morning and went off on his piebald pony."

Eve laughed again while I praised her amusement.

"Thank your stars you've got the wit to find his impertinence amuse you," I said. "No doubt it all sounds the working of Providence to Mrs. Morley."

"She sees somebody's got to go down, but don't think it should be her."

"You've all thought upon it, no doubt."

"Oh yes, we are all turning it over good and hard. Where that old miser goes, he always leaves a trail of slime, like a shell-snail. ' 'Tis amazing the ideas that get into that little monster's head,' I told mother. But she didn't see anything monstrous in his plans. 'I never heard him bode anything so hopeful as this before,' said mother, and after that went on to tell how her woes would all fall off her like autumn leaves when such a thing happened."

I stopped Eve there because I could see she was looking at her basket.

"Get to work," I said. "I see where the knot lies, among you, but I don't yet see why it should be beyond power of loosing."

"I do, and so does the chap that wants to marry me," said Eve. Then I had an idea.

"You are aiming at Rodney Hull, of course—David told me about him and says he's a very fine fellow. But young Yeo's on your side too and it looks as if his uncle wasn't going to get his way for once."

"It does, until you think of my mother," admitted she.

"A bold challenge even for a mind like mine," I told her, "and you can bring your Rodney to see me one evening if you care to ; but only if he's willing."

"Very kind, I'm sure, Miss Crymes. He's like me—well intending, but far quicker in the uptake than me," she explained. "He's marked how a lot of people at Packhorse Bridge go under the dominion of Mr. Yeo, and he's wondered what there is in the little creature to make folk use crooked words against him and hate his shadow. But I tell Rodney how some of the leastest of insects carry the worst sting."

207

Then, when I'd eaten my meal and drunk of a water-sweet brook, I went my way home.

Eve did as I directed, and on a night two days afterwards she brought Rodney Hull to visit me. He was a fit mate for her —just the powerful build for a wrestler. He looked a fair, clean-shaved man with blue eyes and a hard mouth. Justice seemed to be his standby and he didn't lack for ambition. It was clear that the Duchy thought well of him and they had sent him to this region so he might master it and learn all there was to know about the people and the conditions. Then the Duchy were going to appoint him as one of the four moor-men, or wardens, who administered the Forest of Dartmoor.

"Once I'm a warden, I'll draw better money and be situate to wed," he told me, "because I've got education and can read and write and keep accounts and stand to work."

His attitude to the situation was one of grim amusement.

"What use would that old weasel's nephew be to Eve?" he asked me. "Dave Yeo's harmless, no doubt, but do you see Eve putting that weakling before the likes of me?"

The girl answered for herself.

"He's a shadow to Rodney," she said, "and I ain't built to wed a shadow, Miss Crymes."

"Like the little hornet's damned cheek is what I say," added Rodney.

"There's a double edge to all he does," I explained.

"He's like a snake seemingly," said Rodney. "Leave him alone and he won't hurt you. And the instant moment he heard Eve happened to be tokened to me should have been the end of the matter."

"We see that clear enough," agreed Eve, "but my mother can't. She has no quarrel with Rodney for falling in love with me, but declares now that his love ought to make him give me up because David would be a much finer husband for me than Rodney. Which is foolery, and mother knows it but pretends different."

"Your mother trembles to be turned out of her lifelong home, Eve, and who shall blame her for that?" I asked.

"Not me," declared Hull. "With reasonable demands and the will to give and take, you can get round most posers

208

between sensible people; but there's no compromise with this obstinate little idiot. What he wants is contrary to justice and decent behaviour and common sense. Till now I've respected and thought well of Eve's mother, but now I see how self conquers all else and Twin Trees is her ruling passion. That's why we are troubling you, because Eve hopes you have the cleverness to see a peaceful way—where we see none."

"We must burrow into things and find if any weak spot offers," I told him. "What would you say to Solomon Yeo if you got the chance to be heard?"

"I'd say to him same as I can say to you and have said to Mrs. Morley," he replied. "Just this. I'm a poor man, or I'd cut this coil with the needful cash and free Twin Trees for Mrs. Morley's future; but that's beyond my power, so what I will do is to make her home safe with Eve and me when we join up, and I'll see her life shall be as comfortable as lies in my power. Security is always worth paying for, but she'll have that for nothing with us."

"Mother makes it so painful that Rodney's looking out for a change of lodgement already," sighed Eve. "She goes on at him as an honest man to set me free, but of course Rodney swears by God he won't cry off his match with me until I bid him do so. And why should I break my heart for rubbish like that?"

"Have you heard anything from David Yeo yet?" I asked, and the man answered:

"There's another mad side to it. Young Yeo don't want Eve any more than she wants him. If he had the pluck of a louse he'd put down his foot and cry shame on the old man for his folly. But nobody seems equal to standing up to the little pest, so it looks as though I must seek him out and browbeat him for once in his beastly life."

"Don't be in any hurry to do that," I advised. "Bring patience to the job and see if you can't both unite to show him he must throw up the sponge and behave himself."

Then I asked Eve a question.

"Do you know Barbara Mason, the girl David was counting to marry?"

"Yes," she said. "Quite well, but Barbara's no use. I've had a talk with David since I saw you, Miss Crymes, and he was very funny about it and sees what a comical side it has got for everybody but his uncle. He told me that the only way he sees to win out is to bolt with Barbara, or else for me to bolt with Rodney; but of course Rodney ain't built to bolt from anybody and he's got his future to think upon. I tell him to be patient and keep a pinch of mercy for mother and see what line Mr. Yeo takes next when he understands there is nothing doing."

"And if he haven't found that out before we meet, he's going to do so afterwards," declared young Hull.

They left me then and, when they had gone, I turned over the situation and came to the conclusion that it could only end in what they call a stalemate. Strange to say David Yeo himself named something that would cut the knot when next he came to see me a week later. Of course he spoke in jest and I blamed him sharply for doing so, because the matter was nothing to breed laughter.

"As I see it," he said, "somebody's got to bell the cat once for all. With Uncle Sol gone to his reward, everybody else would be as happy as a king, and if you can tell me how to polish off the old devil without getting strung up for it myself, then something worth doing might be done."

"A very improper and wicked thing to suggest, as well you know," I said.

He laughed his silly laugh.

"Then you won't lend a hand and earn your money?" he asked. "Yet just consider how this storm in a tea-cup would calm down if you could. I'd be the big noise then and everybody on their knees to me before you could look round. But perhaps you've hit on something already? What about a pinch of henbane in his liquor?"

"Murder's no subject for joking in any case," I said, "and you ought to know better than to name the word. You're the sort might pay somebody else to risk his skin, but you'd take mighty good care not to jeopard your own. Have you talked to Eve Morley as your uncle ordered you?"

"Oh yes. We've had a good laugh over it—in which Hull joined. He's going to have a tell with Uncle Sol."

"Be sure, with two men that know their own minds so well, something definite should arise," I said, "but you want brains for this business, and patience and reasoning powers. The Duchy's man has got a good brain and should be able to show your uncle he's made a big mistake."

David considered this.

"I'd much like to watch the meeting between them," he declared. "I can't imagine Hull, or anybody else, persuading Uncle Sol he's made a big mistake. I've told the old man that Eve herself laughed about it ; but he only answered that I was a fool to let her laugh. He reckons the thought of seeing her mother in the street had better be rubbed into Eve and then she will laugh no more."

"Hull has told Eve and her mother the answer to that," I pointed out. "He stands high with his employers and counts to be a warden with a warden's money and have his mother-in-law to live with them when Eve and he are wed."

David shook his head.

"Nobody has seen the old fox bested yet," he said, "and, whether or no, I don't fancy a chap like Hull will do the trick ; but I'd like to see the battle all the same. Uncle Sol loves to show his power and welcomes the chance to use it. To one like him Rodney's no more than a labouring man—not even that : just a green boy ; and did anybody ever see him going down before a green boy ?"

I could only tell young Yeo to wait and watch.

"Since we all know you can't put your foot down, David, then we'll see what happens when Hull puts down his," I said. "Most likely you won't enter into the argument at all. It's they must have it out, and Rodney's got Eve behind him, which ought to clinch it ; but you never can be sure, when sparks are flying, what will catch alight before the fire is quenched."

You may say Nature was on the side of Providence upon the Sunday when this matter came to its climax, and when you consider the parties chosen for the task, you marvel to think of the secret wisdom that chose them. It looked or once as if Providence could command the elements to its purpose, for the day dawned heavily fog-ridden and miles of dense white mist rolled over the uplands that Sabbath morn; but those concerned were all Moor bred and the mist held no terrors for them. Three acted out the tale and their desires took all three into the midst of the fog where they were destined to meet.

Rodney Hull ascended to Ruddy Lake that morning for his own reasons alone and little counting to meet anybody else up there. He loved work as the mainspring of life and never could see why he should knock off labour every seventh day and rob himself of his favourite occupation because it was Sunday. He had mastered all to be learned in these central regions of Dartmoor and counted soon to be appointed guardian of that Quarter; but upon Sundays he liked to toil with his hands as well as his head, and this being the season of peat-cutting, turned to Ruddy Lake for a pastime on the holy day and travelled up to the ties with iron and knife to lay out a tidy load of slabs to dry for Twin Trees peat-stack against the time when winter came again. To pleasure Mrs. Morley this was done, and often Eve would go with him and watch him work or do some wool-gathering, or wander in the cuttings and mayhap pick a nosegay of fairy bog-bean and other wild blossoms, to take home when they went back for Sunday dinner. That day, however, he went alone because rain offered and the fog was wet. Rodney's practice was well known and, among others familiar with it, there happed to be Solomon Yeo, for David had told his uncle all about Hull. So Sol, caring no more than Rodney for weather, chose this sulky morn to tackle the newcomer and let him learn he was going contrary to the elder's wishes. He saddled his piebald pony himself and rode forth upon this business just when most of the neighbours were going to church, or chapel, and none knew or cared whither he might be bound.

Lastly I myself went to Ruddy Lake that forenoon, being wishful to see Hull alone and put before him a certain plan of adventure that looked pretty good to me, though only for lack of a better. I felt by now that he would have to cut the knot and win out by direct action; but direct action is apt to be disorderly and there was a doubt if what I had in mind might be safe. The question turned on whether Duchy would suffer

Rodney to do it, for if such a deed angered his employers, it would lose him his fine prospects. I wanted the young man's opinion and, judging Eve would not join him on such a fog-laden day, went aloft to get him to myself.

Mist deadens sound as well as muffles sight, and the Moor was parlous still with not a bird calling, no kine bellowing, no sheep-bell jangling as I went along all unconsciously to take my place with the two men now closing in upon each other. Hull had been at work an hour or more before Sol arrived and it was old Yeo who overtook me on my way a quarter of a mile before we reached the peat workings. Suddenly I heard a horse trotting behind me as I approached my goal and knew that it was no wild pony by the iron clink of its shoes, so I squatted down behind a big boulder, like a hare in her form, and watched to learn who it might be if he came near enough for me to find out. Then Sol Yeo's little, sparkey,[1] yellow and white nag went by within a few yards and I knew, of course, where to he was bound. My first thought inclined me to leave them to it and go home; but I changed my mind as to that, for something told me how Solomon, tired by now of inaction and thinking to find Hull alone, was here for an understanding and much might depend for me upon knowing how things went. The weather granted me power to creep close to them without being seen, and I obeyed my inner voice and followed the pony. The next thing was that his rider, reaching the peat works, drew up to listen till he heard Rodney at work and could guide his mount where to find him. So he stood still for half a minute, and when he stopped, I stopped. But though there came no sound of a peat iron, we heard Hull whistling to himself at work, so Yeo picked a way through the mire and water of the workings and I came secretly after.

There followed a gap of five minutes when those two men clashed, so the opening of their exchanges I was not near enough to hear with my own ears; but at a later time I was able to fill the gap, and can record without any doubt the whole story. Each event is set down in its just order and the humans responsible all play their proper part and no more.

Rodney, whistling and cheerful, as hard work always made

[1] Sparkey = Piebald.

him, was toiling away in the fog. He counted to cut a hundred scads before he gave over; but then, suddenly through the murk, he marked the colours of the pony loom out and there was Sol sitting on top of it close to him. So he dropped his tool, stopped his whistling, grinned and addressed the visitor in friendly tones. Sight of the little horseman's ugly face well pleased him.

"Good morning, sir!" he said.

"You'll be the Duchy's man they tell about—Hull by name," replied Sol without returning Rodney's greeting, "and I want a tell with you for two minutes."

"And welcome," answered the other, then turned down the sleeves of his shirt and strode over to the pony's side.

"Welcome or not is no matter," said Yeo. "You're a new-comer, I understand, lodging at my farm, Twin Trees, for the moment, and they tell me you've got a fancy you'd like to wed Widow Morley's daughter, Eve. But it happens she was marked down for another man long before ever she set eyes on you and I'm wishful for her future to be as I've planned it. So least said soonest mended, and I've taken the trouble to give you this hint in person."

Such a sharp attack banished the younger's amiable approach and he stared blankly at Solomon while the elder spoke on.

"You'll understand after today that woman's not for you, so you had best to clear out of Twin Trees and find accommodation some place else."

"And who ordains she's not for me if she wills to join me?" asked Rodney, keeping as calm as the rider himself.

"I do, and my name's Solomon Yeo, so you'll act wiser to listen and not ask fool questions. You have known this girl but a month or two at most so no harm's done, and I'll throw a bit of light on your darkness and tell you that I'm a man who never asks anything for nothing. They'll tell you my will runs in Packhorse Bridge and round about without much question, and those who obey my commands find they get good returns for doing so."

"What's that to me? I'm not under your commands."

"In this matter and from this moment you are. Better keep

214

a still tongue in your head and not make an enemy of one who can be a powerful friend. When you drop this moonshine about Eve Morley, I'll take you off the Duchy's hands and mend their measly wages and put you first at Twin Trees after I've sacked the fools working there now. You can be head man there and earn two pounds a week."

Which was big money in those days; but Hull felt no temptation. He only found himself concerned with the other's contempt for justice and that angered him.

"And if I refuse to drop my intended at your orders, what then?" he asked.

"Then I shall bring you to heel as I've brought many another fool and make you sorry for the day you were born, you hulking idiot," answered Solomon in his quietest, coldest voice. Rodney reddened at this insult, but held in. They were got to this point while I had crept nearer, though not near enough to be seen. They felt too interested in each other now to trouble as to what the fog might hide around about, and so I stood behind a pile of waste peat peeping over the top of it, close enough to hear every word and dimly mark their movements also. Hull answered the other's threats in a most contemptuous tone and, although he did not know it, any show of contempt was always poison to Yeo and enraged him most.

"Why do the people run from you as if they was coneys with a weasel after them, I wonder?" he asked, and Sol's voice quickened at the sneer.

"I'll tell you," he said. "They run to do my bidding because there's that in me they fear, and with good reason; and if you want to know what it is, you mighty soon shall. But I'll give you another chance yet, because I only use my strength against them that dare to challenge it—not for clod-poles and trash like you. I'll break you into dust if you oppose me, so think twice and let sleeping dogs lie. That's the wisest thing to do for a man of your quality."

Hull spat on the ground and thrust forward his head.

"Begone, you crooked imp, and get back to hell where you belong!" he roared out. "Who the devil are you to bully your betters and devour widow's houses and darken the face of the

215

land like a plague ? I've heard tell about your dirty manner of life ; but it will take more than the like of you to break me, and that you'll darned soon find when I'm made warden of this Quarter !"

They were close to each other now and within arm's length, but Sol did not answer for a moment. He seldom allowed himself the luxury of rage and was master of his temper as of everything else about him ; but he dearly loved to let himself go now and again and enjoyed, in some rare flash of passion, to bring unexpected woe upon an enemy—just as another man might enjoy an extra glass of strong liquor once in a way, and when he did let his wrath loose it would take shape in violent action rather than words. Once spurred to it, he'd use the tool nearest to hand and smite like a thunder-stone fallen from the blue. Feared he never was of anything, no more than a game-cock, and now his answer to Rodney's scorn took shape, for, swift as a fork of lightning, he lifted his heavy riding whip, struck with all his strength and split the side of Hull's face from his forehead to his chin.

"There, you dog !" he hissed out, gloating on the blood that leapt to find who knocked so unkindly, "that'll larn you your manners ! You come to me tonight with your tail between your legs, or you'll find yourself an outcast man on the rubbish-heap in a week."

He glared for one moment, then shook up his pony to go, while Hull fell back and put his hand to his face, fearing, as he told me afterwards, to feel his eye rolling down his face 'like a poached egg'. But his sight had escaped : he could see clear enough and it was all over in twenty seconds now. He took one great stride forward, and set his hands on Yeo's collar before the pony started to gallop. He didn't stop to think : it was vengeance and the old Adam boiled over in him then. For a fatal moment he lost himself, hauled Yeo out of his saddle on to the earth, then struck him one awful blow with the edge of his hand upon the niddick bone behind the ears, like a warrener kills rabbits. And that was how Solomon Yeo went to his Maker. A terrible swift end he had and no hangman's rope ever acted quicker.

It was the first and last time I ever faced stark murder, but my thinking parts worked to perfection, for I was in my prime when this happened and now I emerged upon Rodney out of the fog, where he stood looking down at his work and coming back to his senses.

"You !" he said. "Sent for a witness !"

"Sent for a lot more than that," I answered. "Sent for you to put yourself in my hands and do as I order you ; sent for the salvation of a lot of better people than yourself. For this you was born most like and fashioned by God Almighty to do His dirty work !"

He took a red cotton pocket handkerchief from his breeches pocket and held it to his bleeding cheek, but only stared at me and didn't speak till I put him a question.

"Is he dead, Rodney ?" I asked.

"I've killed him all right."

"Then don't waste no time while the fog holds over us. Dig his grave and finish off what you've begun."

"Others can do that," he answered. "I must give myself up. I must get down to the police-station so soon as I can. He's stone dead and I'm glad I've killed him, but I must pay for it." There was no remorse in his voice, only his blind sense of justice coming to life again.

"Time for that when you see as clear as I see," I answered. "The future's hid as yet, but the present is calling for his burial. Dig his grave this instant moment, and no more talk till he's underground."

This stern order nerved him.

"Fight for my own neck, you'd say ?" he asked.

"For more than that, for better than that," I told him. "Dig—dig his grave—not in the peat-ties, where any spade might find him tomorrow, but here—here in the path, where a score of feet will tramp over him in a few hours' time and never guess there's a dead man under their feet."

I was thankful he wasted no word in arguments once I overpowered him. Then he set about obeying me, though a bit dazed in his mind. The ope-way into the cuttings was ankle-deep in sludge and mire, all flattened by the little sledges brought to carry away the fuel when dry and ready to be handled, so Hull saw my scheme to baffle those who might soon be questing here for a vanished man. He tied up his bleeding face and then began to dig a hole in the open road.

"Three feet is deep enough to hide him till the day of doom," I said, "and this peat eats lime like a dog eats bones, so there won't be enough left to swear by very long."

He worked hard and only stopped to mop his face now and again, while I thought hard and planned his future and my own.

"We can't tell what he may have said to his nephew before he set out this morning," I told Rodney, "and very like he said nothing, for he wasn't given to publish his intentions. More likely than not he told no man where he was riding today, in which case there will be none to know but us that he came here at all. I'll look after the pony, and what you have got to do is to look after yourself. Your smashed face must needs be explained, and the story stuck to. It's an ugly wound and most likely wants to be sewn up, so don't go back to Twin Trees but go down by way of Wistman's Wood to Two Bridges. Then get a lift there, or else travel up to Prince's Town on foot and seek the doctor. Then you can feed and rest and get home."

He agreed to this. "And when they ax how I came by it, I'll tell that the handle of my iron broke and the blade caught my jowl," he said. "It will be known in any case that I was at Ruddy Lake and that such a thing was possible to happen to any man. I often smash a tool owing to my strength."

With that he broke his iron and dropped the pieces beside where he had been at work. He was quite calm now and intent to save his life if it could be done, and while he dug the grave I explained to him that the disappearance of Solomon Yeo would alter their outlook upon life for a lot of humble people.

Then the piebald pony gave a neigh, where he stood close by—just to remind us he was there.

"He's my job," I explained to Rodney. "When all's done here, you'll leave your broken peat iron and your bloody handkerchief to be found and prove your words true, but there must be no sign left of Yeo nor yet his pony. I'll ride it clean away, and leave it nigh the upper waters of Teign—so far off as I can count to travel back myself on foot. Somebody will

218

pick him up soon or late, and everybody knows him. He'll be wearing his bridle and saddle and none the worse."

When all was ready, Hull got his dead man into the hole dug for him and I searched most carefully around for any clue to show he had been there. But nothing did I find save his whip and cap, and they went to ground along with him. Then we filled up and trampled down hard to make the muddy pathway look as usual, and dragged one of the little 'truck-a-muck' sledges up and down over it once or twice to leave their tracks upon the sodden mess of the road. After that I impressed upon Rodney that he had done well, but must watch his every future word and action close and careful. He helped me on to the piebald and we left that fog-foundered place of slaughter and each went our own way.

"Remember, for your life and maybe for mine also," I said, "that we must hold sleepless watch over our tongues and our words and even our thoughts also, while his disappearance is filling the people's minds. And not only when hue and cry dies down, but afterwards, when his life comes to light and his deeds are known. Only I and you in all this world need ever know what happened to Solomon Yeo and, if Providence is on our side, then there's no reason why the truth should escape."

All happened to us as I planned it and for my part, being anxious to keep out of the story for ever, after I had ridden afar and left the pony to himself, I set out to get home while the fog held. It thinned towards evening and I lay low and rested till night fell, then steered back to the high Moreton road and at last got home to Owl Pen, starving and footsore as never before or since. Once off I slumbered till the next noon, then arose refreshed and alert for any news that might reach me, and when it came I took it, like everybody else, with blank wonder as to what could have befallen Yeo.

First came David Yeo, to say his old man was missing with no trace yet discovered either of him or his pony.

"All I know is that he turned out after breakfast yesterday and saddled and trotted off into the mist," he told me. "Uncle said not a word as to his intentions, but he didn't return nor send me any message where he had gone. There's small likelihood the fog would have made him lose his bearings."

219

"Surely not if he was fit and well," I said; "but the mystery is what should have drawn him out at all on a Sunday."

"Your mind gets out of hand before such a queer thing," confessed David, "but of course we must hope for the best and trust to hear before very long."

"You are friends again, I suppose, and he sees it's impossible for you to do what he wants?" I asked.

"Far from it. He's still death on having his own way."

"Have a care to make your own position clear to him," I warned, "because, if he thought you were not doing your best to win Eve and serve him, he'd very likely cast you off altogether."

"He's hinted at just that, Miss Crymes," said David, "but he knows well enough the first step will be to get her free of Hull. I expect his next blow will be struck in that quarter. You never know with a crafty toad like him what's up his sleeve.

"Hull stands all right with Duchy," he went on, "and his masters won't quarrel with him because he declines to please Uncle Sol. The old rip is so used to getting his own way that he can't believe yet he's going to be bawked for once. He asked me not long since why I didn't make a bolt for it with Eve and disappear and then come back again man and wife. He offered to pay me well for the job! 'But, if the girl refuses to bolt with me, how can I make her?' I asked him, and all he said was 'Kidnap the bitch!' But we aren't as savage as all that still."

"No," I agreed. "You can't do such things now—not even on Dartmoor; but if Rodney was to suggest running away with her, she might well agree, and then the tables would be turned."

But I didn't tell David it was the very course I had intended to put before Hull on that fatal morning!

Another who came up to see me was Eve herself from Twin Trees. She had not heard anything about Solomon, and did not yet know that he was missing, but she told me of her sweetheart's accident and let me gather how he had followed out our plans in every particular.

"His peat knife broke in his hand," she said, "and he's given himself a proper awful gash down his face. But when he found what he'd done, he went straight away to Prince's Town, and a doctor has stitched and plastered him, and now he's a cruel sight, poor chap, but makes little of it, for thankfulness he didn't lose his eye."

I was shocked to hear of Rodney's ill-fortune, but made no mention of Yeo. Then, towards evening when I went into the village, I found how everybody knew now he was missing, and that his piebald had been seen running with a herd of wild ponies miles away from where I left him nigh Steeperton Tor. Next day they caught him and fetched him home none the worse.

Then began a pretty stiff hunt for the lost man, and plenty who shared in it felt that to find his dead body would well repay their trouble; but nought rewarded the search parties. None knew what had taken him into the high moors that morning, and time stretched out to weeks without a ray of light until there waxed a pretty general hope that his fellow creatures had seen their last of Solomon Yeo. David soon stirred himself and journeyed to Moreton to see about business and learn how the future stood; but the attorney was as thankful as everybody else and only trusted that sure legal evidence might presently appear to prove death. He didn't pretend any false regrets, but said nothing better for the world at large could happen than that Solomon was gone out of it. No will existed and, as next of kin, David found himself destined to taste power for the first time in his life; while as to Rodney Hull, I secretly marked how the sight of cheerful faces and the chatter of hopeful tongues around him went a long way to lighten his burden.

" 'Tis a case," I told him, when next he came to see me, "where vengeance and justice marched together hand in hand."

That was my honest opinion at the time and I've stuck to it all my life since. He told me in after days how the scar on his face was the sole thing that ever brought his Sunday's work to mind; and it is certain that a fortnight after Yeo was in his secret grave Hull walked over him with no more concern than anybody else. More than half a century has slipped away since that happened; new peat-ties are opened elsewhere and Ruddy Lake long since deserted.

All efforts to get to the bottom of Yeo's disappearance failed, so his nephew reigned in his stead and the lawyer helped gladly enough to strengthen David's legal powers as far as that might be done. He acted with abundant Christian good will, though length of time was called to pass before Solomon's death could be lawfully assumed. But he cancelled debts, and showed his humanity for not a few folk beyond their utmost hopes. He also lost not a needful day before he married Barbara Mason and told me how he never enjoyed a peaceful or secure moment until the deed was done.

"I went in terror he might be all alive somewhere waiting to burst out upon me," said David, "and shivered to think what would become of me and my friends if he did!"

As for Hull, he got his wardenship and married Eve, while Widow Morley bided all her life at Twin Trees in peace if not plenty. But all are gone now. With Rodney and myself the secret remained while he lived, for he was always under my orders never to tell even his wife.

"The only danger," I warned him, "is that you might dream about it and let truth loose in the dead of night for Eve to face you with come morning."

But he feared nothing as to that.

"I never dreamed a dream in all my life," he assured me, "and ain't very likely to start such capers now."

XIII

WHEN you come to sort them out, you will find that most of the tales I have been telling are only love stories, with Nature setting her master-trap for men and women alike, and brewing gall or honey as the case may hap. I never fell into love myself; but I've seen the trap set and sprung, sometimes helping to save the unconscious victims from taking the fatal step and sometimes urging them to take it. A looker-on with vision like to mine sees far deeper most times than the players can, all blinded as they are by the fire and fury of the game. A woman usually knows much more about a man than he will ever learn about her, because his favourite subject is always himself and we are better listeners and far quicker learners also than they are. We gather a lot they like to tell us, but would not dream to tell one another, and so we get truer pictures of them than they are apt to have even of themselves, let alone of us.

The murder of Solomon Yeo enlarged my mind quite a lot and, in the long run, actually was herald to some of my finest opinions. When first I thought of his hereafter at the time he went to it, there came a pinch of regret that hell was lost to us, for where find a more suitable fireside for that blistered and poisonous devil? But presently my mind rose to greater heights. In a world like this, so close-packed with doubtful ones, it looks to me now that, in common justice, the Everlasting Mercy might well fashion some sort of a cage, or limbo, or half-way house, where the bulk of human souls could be herded together and work their passage, if not too late, for that Happy Land still counted to be the prime feature of Eternity. And that was the kingpin and properest idea ever I came by in all my life.

My hand has not lost its cunning so far, nor my brains their contrivance. I am busy still in a small way on behalf of folk brought face to face with mishaps beyond their power to mend, or let and hindered by questions calling for a deeper mind than any in Packhorse Bridge, save at Owl Pen. They pay me as they can and do not lack for gratefulness.

Today has come the dark news how that magnificent female, Queen Victoria, is dead and gone at last to her royal rewards. Her Majesty and myself were much of a muchness. We both left our mark on our generation and advanced the welfare of the common people.

Which is all that needs to be set down before I bring my feats of penmanship to a close, for while many adventures are still stored in my memory, I grow too weary to tell them. Aged am I and tired and shrunk in my muscles and distrustful of my breathing parts and clouded sight. I fear harsh weather and the elements and I dursn't ride on my donkey any longer. I'm given to sleeping as sound as a dormouse in the daylight hours and mighty fond of my bed come nightfall. You might say that my bed is the truest friend that's left to me now; yet still I rise up and carry on and like to be alive; still I count upon another bud-break and the Spring song of the storm-thrush just once again.

THE END